CORNISH CONUNDRUM

CORNISH CONUNDRUM

A MORT SINCLAIR & PRISCILLA BOOTH MYSTERY

Gene Stratton

Authors Choice Press

San Jose New York Lincoln Shanghai

Cornish Conundrum
A Mort Sinclair & Priscilla Booth Mystery

Authors Choice Press
an imprint of iUniverse.com, Inc.

For information address:
iUniverse.com, Inc.
620 North 48th Street, Suite 201
Lincoln, NE 68504-3467
www.iuniverse.com

ISBN: 0-595-13205-7

Printed in the United States of America

For Stan and Gwen Lee of St. Cleer, Cornwall, whose friendship provided a traveling education of Cornwall which made this book possible,

And for Colin and Dorothy Dexter of Oxford, who gave the incentive
and furnished good advice, as well as good companionship.

Who is Sylvia? What is she
That all our swains commend her?

The Two Gentlemen of Verona, William Shakespeare

Cast Of Characters

GILES BACON—Writer living in the upstairs flat of Sylvia's house in Treleggan, Cornwall.

PRISCILLA BOOTH—American homicide detective on leave in Cornwall after attending her cousin Sylvia's funeral.

FRANK CAWTHORNE—Sylvia's wealthy, socially prominent physician husband living in London.

SYLVIA (FITZPEN) CAWTHORNE—Priscilla's cousin; Dr. Cawthorne's wife; gone but hardly forgotten.

CHARLES FITZPEN—A solicitor in Treleggan, cousin to Sylvia and Priscilla; once married to Gwen.

ELSPETH (REDVERS) FITZPEN—Charles's wife; once married to Tony.

JOANNA GIFFORD—Curvaceous scriptwriter for the television company.

MAGNUS MANDEVILLE—Producer of a television historical drama being filmed at Penstead Manor in Cornwall.

GEOFFREY PENHALIGON—The overworked CID detective inspector in charge of the murder investigation.

WINIFRED REDRUTH—Gwen's mother, owner of the pub *The Case Is Altered.*

MORT SINCLAIR—Priscilla's Scots-born criminologist friend living in Oxford.

ROBIN STEELE—Television actor famous for his historical roles.

GWEN (REDRUTH) TRELAWNEY—Winifred's daughter, Tony's wife.

TONY TRELAWNEY—Owner with wife Gwen of a Treleggan gift shop.

Author's Note On Spelling and Words

Wanting to give more verisimilitude to this English-style detective novel, I have used British spelling and a few particularly British words and expressions. Since British spelling is used in many books imported from England to the United States, it will be familiar to many Americans. For specal British words, many can be understood in general from the context. For readers who might want a more precise meaning, a Glossary is given in the back of this book.

CHAPTER *ONE*

The blood-red Ford Sierra pulled over with a screeching halt in a lay-by on the A390 in Cornwall. The driver thrust her door open and jumped out, her long flame-coloured hair whirling across her face like the strands of a silk scarf before receding to her shoulders. She charged around the back and presented herself stiffly on the other side. Cobalt-blue eyes blazed impatiently as she watched her somewhat older companion push against the left side door, raise his knees while lowering his head to clear the opening, and ease out of his seat.

Standing beside her he wore a half-suppressed grin, as if he were trying hard not to see humour in the situation. He opened his mouth to speak, stopped before the first word could come out, then hurriedly scooted around the front to take over as driver. Priscilla Booth had already changed to the passenger seat on the left and was adjusting her seat belt.

They continued in silence for some five minutes, then she said, "But I still don't think I was driving terribly fast."

"You are too used to driving like a police officer," Mortimer Sinclair responded in a softly didactic voice, "only here you have no authority. The speed limit's sixty miles an hour, and you were exceeding ninety."

Priscilla waited another minute or two before replying. After some trial and error with the radio, they had found a good station, and now the light-hearted strains of Vivaldi's *Four Seasons* had a soothing effect on them. She smiled and said, though still with a trace of petulance in her voice, "Wouldn't you expect them to have reciprocity for a fellow police officer?" She knew what his answer would be and she knew he was right. And she also knew that the British were tough on driving offences. Maybe it was better for him to drive anyway. After all, it was his rental car and he was far more accustomed to driving on the left side of the road. And she couldn't change the habits of eight years. Worry-free fast driving was one of the perks of being a police officer, wasn't it? The pay wasn't that good.

Besides, it was difficult to keep her eye out for the road to Treleggan while driving with her foot all the way depressed on the accelerator. Mort had been the navigator while she was driving, but she couldn't expect him to recognise the small turnoff, for he'd never been there. At least she knew what to look for.

*   *   *   *   *   *

Irresistibly her thoughts drew her backwards and her eyes became glazed. There was the get-together in London following the funeral of her cousin Sylvia. Frank Cawthorne had obviously not expected Priscilla to fly all the way from America to attend his wife's funeral, and the look in his eyes said he wasn't happy about her sudden appearance. But his words were gracious enough, and he insisted she come to his Chelsea town house with the others for post-funeral food and drink.

To think, she had actually met Robin Steele there, and he had been a good friend of Sylvia's. He held Priscilla's hand in his as he looked into her eyes and said in his velvety sincere voice that she was by far the loveliest woman present. As she looked back into his eyes, she saw Lord Byron, the Earl of Essex, and Count d'Orsay all rolled up in one, all parts she had seen him play. She was no longer Priscilla Booth, police detective sergeant in the Bay City homicide section, but rather, for a moment, she was Caroline Lamb about to be seduced by the most scandalous poet in England. She was Queen Elizabeth I being wooed by her young, overly ambitious courtier. At one and the same time she was Lady Blessington, Mary Queen of Scots, and the Duchess of Windsor.

"Mort," she said suddenly, "are you watching for the Treleggan sign?"

"I thought you were navigating now."

"Yes, but it's so small. Tichy as people in Cornwall say. And the road seems even smaller. We should both be looking."

It had been three years since she had last seen the house, the house she was now to own. Own, that is, provided she live in it for thirty continuous days. What kind of weird provision in a will was that anyway? Why on earth had Sylvia insisted on such a ridiculous condition? Why had she even left the house to her in the first place? They were only second cousins, close once when they shared a room during their years at Bennington. Though they corresponded after graduation, they had seen each other again only that one time three years ago when Priscilla spent two weeks at Sylvia's holiday house in Treleggan.

She thought of Sylvia's death again. Poor Sylvia! Dead at thirty, only a year older than Priscilla. Charles Fitzpen, another distant cousin and a villager, attended the funeral, and he gave Priscilla some of the details. Sylvia frequently took walks on the cliffs overlooking the bay, sometimes with a companion, sometimes, as on this occasion, alone. Her body was found at the foot of the cliffs, badly bruised and bloodied by the sharp rocks, her face hardly recognisable. There was no suspicion of foul play, nor of suicide. It happened at the most dangerous part of the path where it came within inches of the precipitous edge, and Sylvia was not the first person who had lost her footing there.

Sylvia's husband had the body cremated, as he said she would have wanted. Otherwise Frank Cawthorne had not been talkative. At first Priscilla attributed his reticence to continuing shock, but from remarks dropped by others after the funeral she began wondering just how close Frank and Sylvia had really been.

The day after the funeral Mort came up from Oxford to spend a few hours with her, and she tried to talk him into accompanying her on a week's quickie tour of Europe.

"I would not have thought you'd have time for that," he said.

"I can't afford not to" she responded. "Having spent most of my spring vacation money to fly over, I might as well see something while I'm here. But do come with me."

He wanted to, but had already committed himself to fly to New York for a talk with his publisher. He gave her instead some names of friends to look up in various countries. And she did enjoy herself, Mort's friends in particular helping her make good use of her time, though it would have been nicer had Mort gone along, too.

Returning for her last few days in London before having to go back to work in the States, she phoned Sylvia's solicitor, as he had asked her to do. No one could have been more surprised than Priscilla when the solicitor told her about the house Sylvia had left her and the condition. It was in a codicil, he said, made just two weeks before Sylvia died. Sylvia had seemed very anxious to make the change leaving the Treleggan house to her cousin instead of her husband.

After some agonised thinking, Priscilla telephoned Captain Bumpus in Bay City and with the greatest difficulty obtained permission to take another month of leave, this time without pay. She knew she was jeopardising her chances of being selected for lieutenant—was that small house worth it?

Of course, she would take advantage of the occasion also to do some genealogical research. After all, her grandmother had come from Treleggan before going to New England and marrying Priscilla's grandfather. Grannie, whom she had known only as a child, had left many relations in that small fishing village on the Cornish coast, including, of course, the brother who eventually became Sylvia's grandfather. Priscilla's Cornish lines were the weak part of her genealogical efforts, but she was positive that a little on-site research would be most productive. Surely there would be someone there in Treleggan among her various distant relatives who could help her expand the Fitzpen line. She liked the sound of the name and its earlier form—FitzPen—it smacked of nobility and might even lead to royalty. She'd like a royal line. After all, didn't every amateur genealogist have a royal line or two?

Was the house haunted? Wasn't that a common theme in stories, the provision that one had to live in a house, not necessarily thirty days, but overnight, and then all sorts of weird things happened in the middle of the night? She was glad Mort Sinclair was with her. It was so fortunate his having moved to Oxford to research his new book, thus being able to take time off if he wanted. He hemmed and hawed, of course, but this was far more important than just going on some tour. They met by prearrangement in Reading, she taking the train and he driving. Good old reliable Mort.

Not that they had known each other a long time. Mort was a brainy type, versed among other disciplines in history, law, genealogy, genetics, international affairs, political science, police training techniques, and what not? They had been first together on Fogge Island when she was in charge of a murder investigation and brought him in as a genealogical consultant because she sensed a peculiar pattern in the killings. Then some months later she flew to Salt Lake City to attend a conference where he was a lecturer, and they happened to solve another murder. Later they spent a wonderful time together in Canada. There were telephone calls and letters afterwards and that was it, other than the few hours he spent with her in London the day of the funeral. But, no, it was not the quantity of their time together—it was the quality. They really did know each other well.

But should they go on this way, long separations and intense reunions? She had fallen in love with him—she was sure this time—and she was almost certain that he was in love with her, though she knew the age difference bothered him. Was marriage the goal they were heading toward? There was no impediment, she being divorced and Mort a widower. But there was stubbornness. She was not about to leave her job as the first woman promoted to sergeant on the Bay City police force and the leading candidate for the next lieutenant vacancy, and Mort was not about to move to Bay City and become Mr. Sergeant Booth. They would not even be together now except for that strange will.

Out of the corner of her eye she sneaked a glance at him. "You'll have to stay at the house, of course," she said. "My being there and you in a hotel just wouldn't do."

Mort laughed. "And what will all those proper village folk say about these brash outlanders who openly flaunt their immoral ways?"

"I'll tell them you're my fiancé—to use the modern term. Really, Mort, being cloistered in the Bodleian Library doesn't teach you much about the modern world. I know these people; I spent two weeks with them—don't laugh, they were very intensive weeks. I found the people in Treleggan astonishingly frank and open-minded about sexual matters. We'll be the height of respectability if I just tell them you're my fiancé—instead of some stranger I picked up for the occasion." After a short hesitation she said, "I should tell you sometime about that weird hotel where I stayed in Fowey."

"*O tempora! O mores!*"

"Speaking of tempura reminds me. I don't think there's a Japanese restaurant in the village, but there's an awesome East Indian place. Samosas, onion bhajis, poppadoms, and a vindaloo curry that will make your mouth feel as if it had been sprayed with a flame-thrower. Hmm! Yum!"

"Sounds wonderful. Let's eat there tonight."

"You're on, love."

That meant that he was not going to give her a fight about staying at the house. Terrific! And one night would lead to thirty. With that strange provision in the will he would not have let her stay alone, but he might have insisted—at least long enough to give her discomfort—that she find some local woman for a companion.

According to Charles Fitzpen, Sylvia had almost always stayed in the house alone, Frank Cawthorne being too busy with his Harley Street practice. In fact, Charles revealed that Sylvia bought the house in the first place as a remedy for boredom. Her husband never seemed to have time for her. She was lonely and she moped.

"Why don't you take some of that money you received from your parents," said the doctor, "and invest it in something that will keep you busy?" Sylvia asked "What?" Her husband replied, "Well, buy a house in that village you like so much. Even better, buy one with two flats and let one out while keeping the other as a holiday home for us."

That was what Sylvia had done. It kept her busy. During the winter in London she handled correspondence and deposits from people who wanted anything from one to four weeks in the upper flat in summer, and during the summer she lived in the lower flat and managed her property, arranged for the services of a cleaning woman, paid the bills, and received new tenants. It was profitable, for summer rentals in Cornwall were not cheap.

Besides having the lower flat in summer, during the rest of the year she could take a holiday whenever she wished. Sometimes Frank would join her, but not often. He seemed to be married to his work. She took up painting, read a lot, and went in for gourmet cooking, often inviting this or that person for dinner. She had been born in a place several villages away from Treleggan, but her parents had taken her there to visit relatives when she was young, so she knew and loved the place.

"Everyone liked her," Charles told Priscilla. "Elspeth and I thought the world of her."

How well Priscilla remembered her vivacious cousin! Four years of sharing a room at the university in Vermont had let them know each other well. They ate together, studied together, went out on double dates together, and became a clique of two in playing little jokes together. They invented their own secret language with code words for everything and everybody and could talk disrespectfully in front of others with no one understanding what they were saying. They had little hiding places where they would leave notes for each other, and everyone else in the dorm would be mystified as to how one could go and the other come and know everything that had happened in her absence. And how Sylvia would take dares—it seemed nothing ever daunted her.

*   *   *   *   *   *

"Do you think we have passed it?" said Mort. "We'll be in Truro soon."

"It's this side of Truro. If we come to a big stone bridge we've gone too far."

However, the turn-off to Treleggan was just beyond the next bend and Mort braked violently to avoid missing it. The road was barely broad enough for the width of their car, and the hedgerows on both sides—sometimes eight or ten feet high—loomed like castle walls over their heads. The winding way gave them no vision in front and the hedgerows negated looking over the sides. Here and there a pocket had been carved out of the hedge so that one car could pull over if another came from the opposite direction. That is, if they saw each other in time.

"Now this is driving!" said Priscilla. "Don't you just love these awesome hedgerows? Cornish hedgerows are different from all others, bigger and more interesting. And there's all kind of life in them, pheasants, badgers, foxes, everything."

"I just hope there will still be some life in us when we get to the end of this maze. Is it this tight all the way?"

"No," she said, laughing. "This is the wide part of the road. It gets narrower ahead."

It was mid-afternoon when they reached Treleggan, perched placidly half on the flat top of the cliffs and half sloping steeply down the side, with the main street leading as directly as it could to the small harbor filled with moored fishing boats stranded in the mud as the tide was out. The sides of the street contained tightly packed, brightly painted wood or whitewashed stone houses, each with trim front yard and low stone wall. A fairly wide cross-street divided the town in two, and Priscilla had Mort take the right, going past the pub, called *The Case Is Altered*, then continuing beyond the village green, lined with benches and of all things, Priscilla suddenly recalled, palm trees in the centre. A large car park was on the other side of the green, and after they passed it they turned left, drove one more short block, and turned right again.

"This is Haunted Lane," she said, "and my house, called The Deaconry, is down there where the road comes to a dead-end at the cow pasture. Go past the garden allotments on the left, now past my house on the right, and there's a place for two cars on the far side. Yes, this is it. That gray Volkswagen probably belongs to Giles Bacon, the writer, who's renting the upper flat. He wrote the book that the TV company is filming here."

"What book? You didn't say anything about TV filming."

"I don't know much myself. Robin Steele told me about it. Did I tell you I met him in London? Imagine meeting Robin Steele after seeing him in all those TV dramas! Oh, it's so exciting, Mort. They're making a mini-series of the book *The Urquharts of Urquhart*, and Robin Steele is playing Squire Reginald Urquhart, the head of the family."

"Sounds like a costume drama."

"It starts during the Restoration and goes up to the beginning of the reign of King James II. They did the first series last fall and it was so terrifically successful that now they're doing a second series, using Penstead Manor for most of the scenes. And they did the Duke of Monmouth invasion at Treleggan."

"But that took place at Lyme Regis in Dorset."

"But Lyme Regis doesn't look like Lyme Regis. After all, places change in three centuries. Gerald Mainwaring is playing Judge Jeffries, and they're going to do all the hangings at Penstead, so we'll probably meet him, too, our favourite villain. Oh, that leer! That reproachful look! The profile of Robin Steele and the leer of Gerald Mainwaring. Can you imagine?"

"What's that old saying about law and sausages?" said Mort.

Priscilla laughed. "You mean if you like them you shouldn't inquire too much into the making of either?"

"Yes," he said, "and that might go for TV mini-series, too."

Parking was awkward because the Volkswagen was sprawled over both places. Priscilla had no difficulty getting out from her side, but she saw that Mort, as slim as he was, was forced to squeeze himself sideways between the cars.

"I say, I'm sorry." The voice hailed them as Mort emerged dusting dirt from his clothing. "That was rather inconsiderate of me to park like that. I didn't think you were coming until tomorrow, you know."

"You must be Giles Bacon," said Priscilla. She introduced herself and Mort.

The writer was a thin man of perhaps forty years with a wispy moustache and sharp-featured face, once handsome, now waxy looking, as if he had been embalmed. The face was white except for the bright crimson nose and the start of fine red lines radiating like spider-web threads across his cheeks.

"Let me help you with your things," Bacon said.

Mort opened the boot and started taking out the suitcases. The writer took the two largest and led the way to the entrance of the lower flat on the other side of the house. Beside it was a second door that obviously led to the upstairs flat.

They entered by the kitchen and put the luggage on the floor. "You must be tired," said Bacon. "Let me go upstairs and get you a drink. Whisky or beer?"

"Ale, if you have it," said Mort.

"Me, too," said Priscilla. She looked apprehensively to Mort, knowing how fussy he was about his drinks."

With Bacon gone, Mort said, "I like the flavor of British top-fermented ales. In fact, I'm a member of the Campaign for Real Ale. CAMRA fights for the preservation of traditional ales, which have to be hand-pumped out of a wooden barrel, not pushed by gas out of a metal keg."

"But I thought you liked only all-malt beers."

He smiled. "All-malt whiskies, but I make exceptions for a good strong-flavored beer. Even though the British add sugar to get the charcteristic taste." He gave her an uncharacteristic wink.

The resemblance to her father was at times uncanny, she thought. Stubborn dogma followed by an unexpected willingness to make exceptions. She frowned and said, "Consistency is the hobgoblin of small minds, is that it?"

"A **foolish** consistency is the hobgoblin of **little** minds," he said. "It's often misquoted."

"Oh, Mort, you're such a pedantic prig!" The words burst out of her mouth spontaneously. "A lovable one," she said with laughter, "but still a prig."

The door opened and Giles Bacon came in with six half-pint cans of Devenish pale ale in his hands and three small bottles sticking out of his tweed jacket pockets. "In case you want a rather stronger beer," he said, "I've some nips of the best from St. Austell Brewery," and he displayed the six-ounce bottles of Prince's barley wine. "Eleven point seven per cent alcohol," he said, "you won't find anything much stronger. It's reputedly inflammable."

They sat at the kitchen table and by unspoken agreement started with the pale ale.

"You're very kind," said Priscilla to Bacon.

"Well, yes, I suppose I do have an ulterior motive," he replied, as he finished his glass in two gulps. "Now that you own the house, I'm rather hoping you'll let me stay on for the duration of the filming. I didn't have a written lease with Sylvia—just an understanding. Mind you, you'll be getting a proper recompense, but it's all verbal, and I'm at your mercy."

"Well, I'm sure it will be all right," Priscilla said. "I have no intention of changing any arrangement Sylvia made. After all, this whole thing has come as such a shock to me."

They killed the second round of pale ale, and Bacon opened the potent barley wine, which Mort explained was actually an exceedingly strong, malty, sweetish ale. It was a bit much for Priscilla, but she could see Mort sipping it with a connoisseur's fine appreciation. Bacon was drinking his in a single lifting of his glass.

"I hope you don't mind my asking," said Priscilla, "but I would have thought you'd be at the manor with the rest of the television company."

Bacon jumped as if her words had been a needle suddenly piercing his arm and he brought his glass down on the table with a bang. "I'd have thought so, too," he said.

"This is a fine drink," said Mort, holding his glass up to the light. "I suppose you can get it at the local pub. Is it a free house?"

"Free house?" Priscilla said.

"Not tied to any particular brewery," Mort answered.

"Yes," said Bacon, "and it makes its own real ale, too, if you're interested in that sort of thing, which I'm not. But you don't have to change the subject. I don't mind speaking about it. They've no bloody place for me at the manor. Oh, they've a place all right for everyone else, down to the grip, gaffer and best boy, but authors are not considered important enough."

Priscilla realised that Bacon had had some drinks even before they arrived. She saw Mort signaling her, and she was inclined to tell Bacon that she would have to be getting washed and such, it was getting late. She wished she could cut through all the nursing of vanity and say directly, "Well, what's wrong between you and the TV people?" but he needed no encouragement.

"You see, they asked me to be technical adviser for the second series—thought it would give them a certain cachet to have the author." He pronounced it "KAH-shay."

Priscilla, alert to hearing the differences in language, was half amused, half intrigued by the way the British pronounced French words with the accent on the penultimate syllable.

Bacon was saying, "And I thought it would give me some control over how they filmed my story—make it more authentic than the first series. But their solicitors wrote the contract and it specifies that the producer only has to listen to my advice, he doesn't have to accept it. I didn't feel right about it, but Sylvia persuaded me that it was just a formality. However, Magnus Mandeville, the producer, seemed to take a dislike to me as soon as I arrived here."

"Sylvia?" said Priscilla.

"Well, we were rather good friends in London. She knew the television people and was by way of being a go-between for us. Anyroad, they said they had no more room at the manor, and why didn't I just stay in London? I refused to accept that, so they put me in a hotel in Falmouth—can you imagine being so far away? After a few weeks Sylvia, who felt responsible for the cock-up, offered to let me have the flat here. The television company is paying for it, that's all in the contract, but they don't listen to a bloody thing I say. The boots! They have the bloody boots all wrong. Who ever heard of wearing twentieth-century boots in the seventeenth century? Isn't that an absolute horror?"

Whether by accident or deliberately, Bacon reached for the glass of barley wine that Priscilla had put down after just a taste. He made the contents disappear with two quick gulps.

"That's all right. I'll get back at them."

"How?" asked Priscilla.

"Well," he said, "for one thing, while they're paying me to sit and do nothing, I'm writing a sequel. Then just let them beg me for it! They won't get their hands on my sequel so easily."

Priscilla reflected with amusement on one of Mort's lines, the one he called Stratton's Law: Sequels stink!

For the next fifteen minutes Priscilla and Mort listened to a recitation of how historically inaccurate the television people were and of how the whole series was going to end up as a farce. At times Bacon seemed to be talking more to himself than to them, and more and more his speech became slurred and often incomprehensible. Then he said, "May I use your loo?"

"In there," said Priscilla, recalling the British terminology.

"I know," he said, wobblingly getting to his feet. "I've the same arrangement upstairs."

Bacon disappeared and was gone for what seemed a long time. When he returned, his face held a more determined look, as if he had made some important decision. He walked rapidly and without difficulty across the floor. "I must get back upstairs and let you settle in," he said in well-enunciated words.

After he departed, Mort said, "He certainly seemed anxious to get away."

"I've never seen anyone sober up so fast," said Priscilla. Now they heard him walking upstairs. "He's making an awful lot of noise. Is he mad and stomping his feet?" After a moment of reflection she said, "Oh, yes, I remember. When I was here before. The bad feature of this house is the acoustics. Everything going on upstairs can be heard downstairs."

"Let's unpack, wash up, and have some delightfully hot curry."

Priscilla agreed. "There's only one bedroom, you know."

"No, I didn't know."

"Mind?"

"I suppose not. It's not as if we're exactly strangers."

"Mort, I didn't plan it this way. I mean, I knew there was just one bedroom, but I didn't plan it like that. You know what I mean, don't you?" Her tone became more hurt. "After all, we **have** slept together before, so I don't know what difference it makes."

"Am I complaining?"

"No. No, but somehow you make me feel so darned forward. You do love me, don't you?"

He let a suitcase slide from his hand and walked over and embraced her tightly. "It's been a long time, my darling," he said as he nibbled at her ear. They kissed and stayed clung together for a timeless period.

When they relaxed their hold on each other, Mort said, "Forgive me, sweetheart, please. I know I'm dense, and I guess priggish, too. What I don't know is how to change, even though I'd like to be more the way you want me."

"I don't really want to change you, dearest, for fear that any change might destroy all those endearing things about you that I so love." She stroked his cheek and parted her lips slightly as if not sure what to say next. This was more like it, she thought, and she wondered if it would be an appropriate time to start a discussion about their future. And then the imperious tintinnabulation of the telephone jarred them apart.

"Miss Booth," a sonorous, no-nonsense voice said, "I rang several times earlier. Inspector Penhaligon of the Devon and Cornwall CID. May I drive over and see you in the morning? It's most important."

CHAPTER *TWO*

After leaving Priscilla and Mort, Giles Bacon walked upstairs to his own flat, poured himself another glass of Prince's Ale, and sat down in a lounge chair. Shifting his position and crossing his legs to make himself more comfortable, he withdrew an unevenly folded newspaper page from his jacket pocket and studied it for a long time.

The ringing of the telephone forced him to get up again. His irritation disappeared when he heard the voice of Joanna Gifford saying that she wanted to see him the next day.

"Lovely," he said. "Wouldn't you know I need to see you, too? However, my situation has changed a good bit and I'll be away tomorrow afternoon. Could we make it eight in the morning?"

She readily agreed, and he inferred with pleasure that her desire to see him was as great as his to see her. My luck keeps improving, he thought to himself.

Not what anyone would call a beautiful girl, rather plainish actually, Joanna had a shape that the loveliest girl in the world might envy. Images of Joanna, her supple body, their stimulating conversations, their physical, mental, and spiritual harmony, fought in his mind against counter images of betrayal. But Giles was more pragmatic than vengeful—perhaps in Majorca they could start with a *tabula rasa*.

They continued talking for a few minutes, then he went back to his chair with a contented look and promptly dozed. About two hours later he awoke, found his newspaper on the floor, folded the page more neatly this time, and tucked it back into his pocket. He stretched, went to the bathroom, swished some mouthwash through his teeth, and walked downstairs. Casually he strolled down Haunted Lane, crossed the car park, and approached the green, hesitating at the verge.

The direct way to *The Case Is Altered* would have been to cut across the green, but if he walked around the verge on two sides he would come to the Trelawneys' little shop and could see if the paperbacks of his books had arrived. He mentally tossed a coin and turned to his right. Just as he approached the shop, he spied Tony Trelawney coming out.

"I say, Anthony," he yelled, "do you mind waiting?" He hurried to catch up with the corpulent man who stood in front of the gift-shop nonchalantly smiling.

"Oh, ah, no, I suppose not. You're the writer. What is it, Bacon? Reminds me of Roger and Francis, but you're, er, Giles, I think."

"That's right," said Giles with an ingratiating grin on his face. "Tell me, Anthony, have my paperbacks come in yet?" There would be no royalties for him, but at least the people in the village would see his name in print and realise that he was someone of consequence.

"Ah, no, they haven't. It's really, er, too early." He stopped walking and shifted his weight ponderously from one foot to the other. "Oh, ah, would you mind calling me 'Tony'? No one except my mother ever calls me 'Anthony.'"

"Of course, if that's what you want," said Giles, thinking, You bloody well look like an Anthony, but I'll humour you if you insist. Aloud he said again, "Going to the pub, Tony?"

"Oh, ah, yes, I thought I'd see how Gwen's doing? She's helping her mother. Our assistant's looking after the shop."

Gwen! Now there was a lovely girl, too lovely for the likes of Anthony, thought Giles. Not my type though. Too much on the make all the time. Being married to Gwen would be like trying to dine on a leg of lamb in the midst of a pride of starved lions.

"I see Gwen's spending more time at the pub recently," said Giles. He reached out to place his hand on the other man's arm. "Do you think those books might come in this week?" The bloody things probably wouldn't arrive until after he left.

"What's that? Oh, your books. Well, possibly. About Gwen, well, business is slack now at the shop, but her mother's short-handed."

Yes, thought Giles, and at the pub she'll see the television people more often.

They continued along in silence until they reached the main entrance to *The Case Is Altered*. There Tony stopped and said, "Oh, I suppose you'll be going in here."

Giles blinked, glanced up at his rather bulky companion, and said, "Why, no, I'll be going along with you, Tony. To the regulars' side, of course."

"Oh, I see. Yes, of course."

*   *   *   *   *   *

The Case Is Altered, a large building sprawling out in all directions, was reputedly the oldest structure in Treleggan. Its unique part was a mammoth chimney appearing like an island in the centre of four unevenly divided rooms. Two rooms back of the chimney comprised a kitchen and dining room. In front was a single chevron-shaped bar, with one arm longer than the other, serving two drinking rooms which were divided by a partition starting from the point of the chevron. The larger room, once called the public bar, was now referred to by the villagers as the tourists' bar, and they generally avoided it. They much preferred to huddle together in the smaller, less comfortable room once reserved for the residents when the pub was also an inn, but now known among themselves as the regulars' bar.

Giles confidently followed Tony into the regulars' bar, looked around, and found the room moderately occupied for a Monday night.

Everyone greeted or nodded to Tony. Though some faces were familiar to Giles, no one said a word to him. Approaching the bar at the point where the wood partition separated the two lounges, he could look in the gigantic bar mirrors to see a good part of the adjoining tourist room, which he noted was also moderately crowded. He immediately saw Magnus Mandeville and Robin Steele as the centre of attraction at the large bar and he scowled and turned away to take a second look at the people on his own side.

Beside Giles were Charles and Elspeth Fitzpen, and next to them Tony Trelawney had stopped to talk to a short fisherman wearing an oversized large-knot wool pullover. Giles vaguely recalled there was something about the little codger he did not like.

Suddenly Giles's face reddened as he heard the fisherman say in a loud whisper, "Bloody cheek if you ask me. The whining sod oughter stay on his own side."

Tony, looking like a somewhat portly teddy bear with deep brown eyes, said in a soft-spoken voice, "Oh, ah, I wonder—er, when does an outsider become a regular?"

"The wanker oughter wait 'til he's invited," said the fisherman.

Winifred, the publican, smiled sweetly from behind the bar as she pulled a pint of best bitter for Giles, then looked over to Tony Trelawney and the fisherman and said, "Now, now, you lot. Let's mind our manners."

The fisherman twisted his face in disgust, but he kept his mouth closed. Giles knew that Winifred's word was law in *The Case Is Altered*. She had one of the friendliest, most easy-going personalities imaginable, but she ran a taut pub. He'd heard there had been some rowdy times when she bought the place many years ago, but she put an end to them. The first offence of the night provoked a warning. The second one led to the threat of expulsion for the night, and the third was accompanied by a polite but firm order to leave. Too many expulsions over a short period of time resulted in permanent exile. The yobbos soon had nowhere to go but the less comfortable *The Sword and Mace* at the edge of the village. Most of the other more decorous customers highly approved, though a minority composed mainly of tyro pub-goers who were just old enough legally to drink and who gave their custom to both public houses, chafed at Draconian restrictions on their language, manners, and ghetto-blasters while at *The Case*, but held off from giving expression to the full needs of their souls and demands of their glands until they were at *The Sword*.

Giles now glanced from Winifred to the fisherman, wondering how long the latter would respect the fiats of the former, and simultaneously he braced for a barrage of insults from the latter that in fact never came. He thought he'd been in the village long enough to be considered a regular, in spite of what any grotty fisherman might think. Equally important, he was not about to drink his beer on the more comfortable tourist side as long as it was dominated by the telly bigwigs. He could tolerate Robin Steele, who was more vain than vicious, but he did not care to expose himself to the scorn of Magnus Mandeville. The producer didn't want the writer around and he didn't hesitate to let the world know it.

Even Steele, Giles reflected, who usually cozied up to producers, directors, and cameramen, had good reason to resent Magnus, but did he? First Magnus took Joanna away from him and Robin had to console himself with Gwen Trelawney. Now it looked as if Magnus fancied Gwen. How would Robin, the self-admiring but docile peacock, take that?

Giles heard his name being voiced, but looked around and could not find the caller until he glanced in the mirror and saw Robin Steele staring glassy-eyed at him.

"You here, Giles?" said Robin.

"I think so. You sober?"

"Can't tell. I'm always the last to know."

"Joanna here?" Giles asked, regretting that he had failed to ask her if she'd be coming.

"Not on this side. She on your side?"

Involuntarily Giles took a look around him, knowing fully well that the voluptuously-bodied scriptwriter could not possibly be in the same room, for if she had entered while his back was turned, there would have been some appreciative murmur to announce her presence. "Doesn't look like it. D'you know if she's coming?" he said back to the mirror.

The handsome actor replied, "She hasn't told me her plans since we stopped sleeping together."

"Oh," said Giles. That hurt! Unlike that lot, an affair made an impression on him. He could not cavalierly dismiss the remembrance of a bed partner, and Joanna in particular meant much to him. Still looking at the mirror, Giles saw that Robin had turned away. He was just as glad.

Gwen Trelawney was pulling pints on the tourist side. An attractive woman somewhere in her late twenties, she had beautiful hair, golden all the way down to the roots, and as she moved her head, the thick tresses swished provocatively across her shoulders. She had high cheekbones and deep dimples, her lips were invitingly moist and red, and her teeth brilliantly reflected light as she laughed. The laugh itself was an earthy guttural one, a primevally erotogenic laugh that seemed to promise naked abandon, heady concupiscence, and savagely pulsating gratification.

But it was not just Gwen's physical traits alone that made her of interest to Giles as a writer. In the pub Tony's wife might appear not overly distinguishable from any other well-favoured barmaid, and indeed at times she even affected a coarseness in her speech intensifying the impression of commonness. Giles had, however, also talked to her occasionally at the gift shop and he knew her for a rather well-educated woman who could be at complete ease in the company of anyone in the village, toffs included.

A stranger might have observed a resemblance between Gwen and the older Winifred, whose own yellow hair was now faded and graying; the regulars, of course, and Giles, too, knew that Gwen was Winifred's daughter. Gwen wore a white long-staple cotton turtleneck jersey that clung to her thin frame and accentuated pert breasts tantalisingly showing through the silk-like finished fabric and proudly pointing upward.

Magnus Mandeville posed the question that others must have been asking themselves silently. "Are you wearing some type of cutaway brassiere, my dear, that gives you support but no cover?"

Gwen laughed merrily, showed her dimples, tossed her torso in an upward motion allowing her breasts to bounce up and down in graceful rhythm, and said, "That's for me to know and you to find out, isn't it, Mr. Mandeville?"

"The answer is yes, Magnus," said Robin Steele.

"Oh, do be quiet, Robin," said Gwen, still laughing. "Don't you dare give away my secrets."

"How many secrets do you have?" said Mandeville.

She put a fresh sleeve glass of keg lager in front of the producer and stopped smiling. Penetrating his eyes with hers, she said, "How many parts do you still have to fill?"

"Don't be coy," he said. "You know the casting's complete."

"Things always happen, like with Sylvia," Gwen replied, reaching up to pat her hair.

Robin Steele said, "That's right, casting's complete, Gwen. We stopped creating special parts after Sylvia died, didn't we, Magnus?"

On the other side Giles, trying to catch every word, smiled to himself. After Sylvia died…. That was when Joanna had come back to him, if only temporarily, needing him for the script changes. He had helped her write in a part for Sylvia and then he had to help her write Sylvia out again.

In the mirror Giles could see Mandeville glaring silently at Steele. Then the producer turned back to Gwen. "You come over to the manor sometime soon and perhaps we'll give you a screen test," he said, his vowels sounding very American. "I'm serious now. We always like to develop local talent."

That would put Steele in his place. Giles wondered if Mandeville had already planned for a screen test for Gwen or if it was something he improvised because Steele had provoked him. It had to be the former, of course, because most likely that was why Joanna wanted to see Giles in the morning, to write in a special part for Gwen. But what did it really signify? If Gwen started sleeping in Magnus's bed, would Joanna move back down to Robin's? Where would that leave Giles? Exactly where he was now, out in the cold. He'd be damned if he'd help them with any more changes. But at least he'd let Joanna come over in the morning, since he wanted to see her anyway on that other matter. It would give him a chance to persuade her. Who knew what might happen? Especially when she realised that Mandeville was about to cast her off.

After all, he was better looking than Mandeville, and far more intelligent than either the producer or Steele. Granted that Steele was handsome, in a vapid sort of way. Granted that they were both bigger than he, but size wasn't everything. It was money and power that attracted women to Mandeville. The lack of money is the root of all evil, he mused.

Gwen smiled at Mandeville, but addressed her next remark to Steele. "How do I compare with bitchy Sylvia, anyway, Robin? You think I'd do as good?"

"Perhaps we should let Sylvia rest in peace," said Steele, elevating his eyes to gaze into the mirror again.

Giles glanced away from the mirror and again paid attention to his own side. Tony Trelawney had moved down the bar and started to talk to him in a vague sort of way. Giles soon saw that Tony was using the mirror the same way he had been. Tony's eyes were fixed on Gwen as she joked with her customers. He bit his lower lip, wiped his tongue over it, then turned slowly, phlegmatically, away and mumbled to Giles without looking at him, "Oh, er, sorry, what did you say?"

Giles made no answer as his ears scanned through the various other conversations. Next to Tony, Elspeth Fitzpen was saying to her husband,

"They're talking about Sylvia in there. She dominates the conversation even when she's dead."

Charles Fitzpen replied, "Uh huh," and he lifted his glass to indicate to Winifred that he'd like another half pint.

Elspeth, a brunette somewhere either side of forty, was an attractive woman, except for the permanent frowns etched in her forehead. She said, "You know her cousin—your cousin—Priscilla Booth has arrived."

"How'd you know?" her husband asked. "I didn't think she was due 'til tomorrow."

"Well, there's a strange car in Sylvia's driveway. Ask him, that fellow, he lives over her." Not waiting for a response, she raised her voice. "Mr…, you down there, I forget your name."

Listening, but not looking, Giles took a moment to realise that she was talking to him. He glanced up inquiringly.

"Oh, Giles," she said, "yes, of course. Has that American woman arrived yet, Giles?"

Giles's face now assumed a pleased expression. He moved to the other side of Tony Trelawney, who willingly changed places with him, and said to Elspeth, "Oh, yes, she came in hours ago. I had a drink with her and her companion, another Yank, name of Sinclair. They seemed all right, I suppose."

"I wonder if I should go over and welcome her," said Charles.

"Oh, it's too late now," said his wife. "She's probably tired after that long drive anyway. She'll manage without you somehow."

"All right, I'll ring her in the morning then."

The short conversation had brightened Giles's evening. He felt more accepted now. He had been of some use to Elspeth, so he obviously had some right to be where he was.

Winifred had moved over to the other side of the bigger bar and was helping Gwen keep up with the large crowd, which was being augmented as more of the regulars strayed from their side to the tourist side with its glamorous attraction of television celebrities. It took Giles a minute to get someone's attention, and when he did it was Gwen who walked the length of the bar to serve him.

He said, "Another of your best, love, and have one yourself, too. While I'm in a generous mood, I'll buy for the lot of them on this side. And let's have some crisps, too. I'm hungry."

Giles turned sideways to acknowledge several mumbled thanks and continued to observe the activity around him.

Tony Trelawney was trying to catch Gwen's eye as she reached for the pump handle. He said, "Oh, ah, darling, I'll give Maggie a hand in closing. You, ah, behave while I'm gone."

Gwen, watching her husband depart, smiled sardonically, then moved her lips silently to form the words "Piss off!"

The little fisherman sidled closer to Giles and accepted his refill at the writer's cost. "I'll drink your health, mate," he said. "You're a real gent, that's what you are, a proper gent."

Giles's eyes were alert to take in every movement in the room. "Drink up and order us two more," he told the fisherman, putting some coins on the counter. "I'll be back in a second after I have a pee." He was gone much longer than a second, and on his return another full pint was resting at his place, but the glass in front of the fisherman was empty again.

Amid the multiple conversations on the regulars' side Giles could hear a single loud voice coming through from the tourist lounge, and he recognised it as belonging to Esme Polgony. Though she was normally not that prepossessing—in fact, people could pass Esme in the street without even realising anyone was there—tonight she was saying the right thing at the right time and had everyone's attention.

"Y'can talk about your Gray Lady at the manor all yer want," she was saying, "but it's the White Lady in the village that yer wanna watch out for."

"She's the one who's supposed to walk up and down Haunted Lane when it's dark," said somebody.

"Not supposed," said Esme. "She's there. I felt 'er breath a' me." She hesitated, obviously taking pleasure in knowing that they were all engrossed by her every word now. "Not long ago I was cuttin' 'cross the fields after dark and came out at 'aunted Lane. Somethin' told me not to go that way but take the long way round. But being in an 'urry I took me chances. Oh, my, I can still 'ear 'er 'owl. And then she come tearin' after me, as fast as she could run."

Giles glanced in the mirror and saw Esme getting more animated, illustrating her tale with hand and body motions.

"I couldn't scarper fast enow, and I felt 'er breathin' down me back, a cold, icy chilled breathin', the temperature a' death itself, and she was makin' weird 'issing noises, and then she reached out and pushed me in the mud. I picked meself up and yelled like bloody 'ell, and then she was gone. I just suddenly knowed she was gone, and I run 'ome and shook all night."

"You told that story before, Esme," said another person. "We thought you were going to tell something new."

"Well, these people at the manor 'aven't 'eard it, and it's just as true for the retellin'. I'm not makin' it up, yer know. I don't know about the Gray Lady, but the White Lady is real."

Others had come through from the regulars' lounge to the tourist side while Esme was talking and the room was full. Only a few remained in the smaller room, Giles Bacon, the little fisherman, Elspeth Fitzpen, and an elderly couple sitting on a bench by the wall.

Even Elspeth's husband had been drawn by Esme's intriguing tale. Having crossed over to the tourist side, Charles Fitzpen spoke up. "Of course I don't believe in ghosts, but there are things in this world that are beyond my ability to comprehend."

"Such as?" said one of the crowd. "I suppose you're going to tell us how you saw the Gray Lady."

"I didn't see her," said Charles, "but I wouldn't go in the cellar of that manor house again for all the tea in China." He could not stop now. His audience insisted on being told the whole story, even though, as with Esme, some had obviously heard it before.

Removing his glasses and holding them in his hand as a pointer, Charles said, "When I was executor for Squire Redvers's estate, I went to Penstead Manor with my clerk to make an inventory. The caretaker— you know, old Glubb—warned me about the cellar, saying I should never go down there by myself. But we didn't have a lot of time, and I didn't believe the silly stories Glubb was always telling. My clerk took the outbuildings and I went into the cellar by myself. I didn't see it, but while I was listing the wine all of a sudden I knew she, or it, or something, was there. I could feel it in every pore."

Charles stopped, smiled apologetically, turned to Gwen behind the bar and said, "Fetch my glass, will you? There's a love." He seemed to be in no hurry, obviously enjoying the wide-eyed stares and short-burst comments of his audience.

"Well, what happened?" said one impatient listener.

"Well," said Charles, lowering his voice and encircling the crowd with his eyes, "suddenly my torch was knocked out of my hand and went out and I was in complete darkness. I groped for it on the floor and something was thrown at me."

He paused again to take small sips from the glass Gwen placed in front of him. Then, wiping his lips slowly on a handkerchief, his eyes twinkling, he continued. "Finally I found the torch and managed to turn it on again only to see that the thing thrown was a sickle, as sharp and vicious looking as any I'd ever seen. And then I heard the voice, or maybe I just knew what she was saying without hearing the words. 'Bring back my lover. What have you done with my lover?' I'm not a coward, but I ran like blazes. I went outside, called my clerk, jumped into the car, and didn't stop until we were back at the office."

There was silence when Charles finished, as if his listeners had become completely mesmerised, until Magnus Mandeville said in a blustering voice, "You mean Penstead Manor, where we're filming?

Nonsense. We use the cellar for our costumes and go down there all the time. You're telling me that there are ghosts in that cellar? I thought you were a more rational man than that, Charles. I retained you as our local solicitor in the first place because you were recommended as a clear-headed chap."

"I'm not trying to frighten you, Magnus," said Charles, suddenly becoming quite serious. "I can only tell you what I thought I saw, heard, and felt with my own senses. Perhaps it was my imagination, influenced by Glubb's ghost stories. Perhaps I accidentally dropped my torch and then tripped over the sickle. Oh, you see me laughing now, Magnus, and it looks as if the whole story was just a joke, but the one thing I know for a fact is that, rational mind or not, I'll never go into that cellar again, at least not by myself."

Even the customers in the regulars' lounge had become silent so as to eavesdrop on the words coming from the other side. With a hush Elspeth Fitzpen said to Giles and the fisherman, "It's true. He told me about it when he came home that time. What he didn't mention now was that there was a big black-and-red bruise on his thigh where the handle of the sickle had hit him."

Gwen, coming over to the small bar, said, "Oh, Elspeth, you mean that mole the size of a ten-p. coin on the inside of his right thigh? That's been there for ages."

"No," said Elspeth. "We both know the mole, but this was a huge welt on the outside of his left thigh."

Giles looked first to Elspeth, then to Gwen, with something akin to astonishment on his face.

Gwen and Elspeth noticed and laughed. Elspeth said, "You didn't know I shared my husband with Gwen?"

Gwen said, "You mean I shared my husband with you. I was married to him first, you...."

Though they had started out laughing, neither was in a pleasant mood now. Elspeth said, "The only thing you have to remember, Gwen dear, is that he's my husband now, and you just keep your hands off."

Gwen started to say something back, but stopped as the outside door opened. Tony Trelawney noisily re-entered the pub, holding a money-bag in his left hand and scratching the back of his neck with his right.

Elspeth suddenly smiled again. "In case you've forgotten, Gwen, there's your husband. I gave you complete title to him. It was a fair transaction."

Giles again looked perplexed, and the fisherman whispered in his ear. "Elspeth was married to Tony but throwed him aside for Charles." He laughed, more to himself than to Giles. "Then Charles divorces Gwen and Elspeth ups and divorces Tony, and Charles marries Elspeth and Gwen marries Tony, that's how 'tis."

I see, thought Giles. Sounds like legalised wife swapping.

Tony started talking in a low voice to Gwen, and Charles came back to the regulars' side and rejoined Elspeth. Slowly more of the regulars returned to their own side, and soon the small lounge was once more characterised by a number of independent conversations.

Giles treated the little fisherman to another beer, feeling that he had bought a friend, or at least someone who could keep him informed of village undercurrents.

The fisherman was grateful and repaid his benefactor with continual conversation. "Ghosts don' scare me none. It's the smugglers yer wanna watch out for, mate. Yer see a gang o' blokes comin' down one of those dark lanes with large sacks on their backs, yer wanna go contrariwise as fast as yer feet can take yer."

"Oh, come on with you now," said Winifred, who had come back to the small lounge. "How you go on, Dinny, with those tales of yours."

"Yer say there ain't no smugglers now?"

"Not nowadays," said Winifred. "Of course, there were in the old days. Here and most of the other coast villages made their living on smuggling. Free-trading, they called it. Oh, could I tell you some stories!" Her eyes glazed upwards and a smile came to her lips.

Giles, who as a writer was captivated by local lore, readied himself for another tale, but Winifred was called away.

The fisherman said, "She don't want to say it, but weren't longer ago than the lifetimes of some—after the War—that here was where yer could buy Parker pens and American cigarettes and other things in short supply. And I could point to a good number who're still 'round that were experts in such matters, if yer know wha' I mean."

"Now, leave them be, Dinny," said Winifred, returning. "That lot are old and harmless now. With the European Union there's no need for smuggling. Doesn't pay. But he's right, they were here in the old days. Free-trading was considered an honest business, at least in Cornwall, in spite of what the English said. For all that, maybe it was a better world then."

As an Englishman Giles felt somewhat uncomfortable. He ordinarily thought of Cornwall as a bit strange, even exotic perhaps, but no more at variance from the home counties than Yorkshire was from Kent, yet every now and then since he had arrived here, words were spoken which re-emphasised to him that there was more than just a small difference, and he remembered a Cornish woman he had talked to referring to the English as *emmets*, ants, because of the numbers with which they invaded the land of Kernow each summer. "Just a little lengthening of the Tamar would solve our problems," she said, referring to the river that made the peninsula of Cornwall almost an island.

Giles, seeing Tony nudge and whisper to the fisherman, strained his ears to hear better.

With amusement in his voice, Tony was saying, "Oh, ah, I thought you couldn't stand the cheeky outsider."

Dinny put a finger up to his puckered grin, then whispered back, "Shhh, the case is altered, Tony, me boy, the bloody case is altered." He drained his glass, turned to Giles, and said in a louder voice, "Set us up again, mate?"

*   *   *   *   *   *

Both rooms at the pub seemed fully occupied when Mort entered the tourist side with Priscilla holding on to his arm. It was only with a bit of difficulty that they were able to make their way to the bar. Having had their East Indian dinner, their mouths were still aflame from the vindaloo.

"Make it a pint, Mort," said Priscilla. "A half won't do tonight."

"Two pints of your real ale," Mort said to Winifred, placing several one-pound coins on the bar. Winifred dried the bottoms of the glasses on a towel and set them in front of him. "Let's see if we can find a table in the rear where there's more room," he said to Priscilla.

They were lucky to get a just-vacated small table with two chairs. Priscilla described the pub to him, the chimney, its history as well as she knew it, and Winifred's aversion to rowdyism. "I'll have to renew acquaintance with Winifred; she looks as if my face is familiar to her, but she can't quite place me." She gave Mort a quick rundown on the few patrons she recognised. "Oh, look, there's Robin Steele at the bar with his back turned. We were almost standing beside him."

"Looks older and shorter than on TV."

"Oh, come on, Mort. Isn't he handsome?"

From the tables nearby they heard scattered conversations, and the words "Gray Lady" and "White Lady" were mentioned. Priscilla started giving Mort some background. "These are local ghosts. I think it's the White Lady in the village, because her haunting ground is supposed to be the lane where our house is. She was the wife of the village's leading Roundhead in the Civil War and the Cavaliers seized all her jewels. The Gray Lady at the manor lost her lover, who was captured by the Roundheads and hanged. So now the Gray Lady goes around frightening everybody while looking for her lover, and the White Lady spooks everyone while looking for her jewellery."

Mort glanced toward the bar and noticed Robin Steele staring at Priscilla with all the aplomb of Horatio Nelson eyeing the French and Spanish fleets at Trafalgar. Suddenly Robin strode with determination through the standing patrons to make way to their table and gallantly bow before Priscilla. "Haven't we met? Of course, we have. London. You're Sylvia's American cousin."

"Priscilla Booth," she said, "and this is my friend Dr. Mortimer Sinclair."

"I'd join you," said Robin, "but there's no chair available. It's such a pleasure to see you again." He stood over her smiling and stroking his well-trimmed, military-style moustache, seemingly speechless. Then, "I had no idea you'd be coming to Cornwall, but I'm…I'm overwhelmed that you're here."

Priscilla smiled happily. Almost purring, thought Mort.

Robin was interrupted as a much larger man came up to the table. "I might have known," he said in a loud voice, "that Robin Steele would be where the prettiest woman is. Introduce me to your friend, Robin, I don't bite. To both your friends."

Robin bowed exaggeratingly and, much subdued, made the introductions. Mort caught the change and noted that Priscilla, too, seemed shocked at how deferential the gallant hero had become in the presence of the newcomer.

Magnus Mandeville was also a rather handsome man, though his features were sharper than Robin's. His eyes were a brilliant emerald green and his chin jutted out aggressively, giving him almost a satanic appearance. His politeness seemed forced, as if he were treating them to his Sunday-best behaviour, but his general aspect suggested more that he was a man who would tolerate no opposition.

"You give me a great idea," he said to Priscilla. He stamped his foot on the floor as if he had just made an important discovery. "You must come up to the manor. Not tomorrow. I'll be in London tomorrow and Wednesday. Make it Thursday. You will come." It sounded like an order.

"I'd love to," said Priscilla. "And may Mort come, too? We'd love to see you filming some scenes."

"Of course Dr. Sinclair may come," said Magnus, smiling graciously. "I wouldn't think of not having him. You will come, too, Dr. Sinclair." Another order.

Mort relaxed and smiled. "Well, yes, I'd be happy to."

"Then it's all settled," said Magnus, starting to turn away. He flashed a look at Robin Steele. "We must get back, Robin. I'll do the driving."

After they left, Mort said, "He seems almost more American than English."

Priscilla responded, "I think he's English, but I vaguely recall Robin Steele's telling me in London that his producer occasionally affected American speech, or something like that."

There was considerable activity in the room as people moved about, their multiple conversations blending together in one continuous background susurration. Mort went to the bar to order more drinks and on his return he found a rather attractive, though frowning, woman occupying his chair, with a dark-haired man of some forty years standing beside her.

Priscilla introduced Mort to Charles and Elspeth Fitzpen. "My cousin, Treleggan's only practising solicitor."

"I'm thinking of moving my chambers to Truro," said Charles. "There's not enough demand here to support even one attorney."

"Charles has been telling everyone that for ten years," said his wife. "I'll believe it when I see it." Her tone was irritated, her eyes focused intently on Priscilla.

"Oh, don't be such a shrew," said Charles. "Come on, my love, I'll buy you one more Babycham if you're not too tired." He nodded a goodbye to Priscilla and Mort as he and Elspeth turned to walk away. They disappeared through the door leading to the other lounge.

"So that's your cousin," said Mort, sitting down again. "He seems nice enough. What's wrong with his wife?"

"I don't know her very well, but it's my guess she's just plain jealous of any woman Charles talks to. They have no children, and I suspect she gets lonely. What's a Babycham?"

He laughed. "Trademark for a carbonated perry, an alcoholic pear drink. I think it means 'baby champagne.'"

The bar was thinning out with most of the TV people having left. From the other side of the partition Priscilla and Mort could hear the slurred words of Giles Bacon as he said in a loud voice, "You're all right, Dinny, I'll tell the bloody world."

Dinny, with his voice raised even louder, said, "You're not 'alf bad yerself, mate, for a bleedin' emmet."

Another voice, that of Winifred, cut in. "All right, boys, I think that's it. Drink up. It's the last one tonight."

"Bloody 'ell!" said Dinny. "Can't be time yet."

"Yeah, what the hell!" said Giles. "It can't be bloody time yet."

"It's time for you lot," Winifred said. "Come again some other night."

*   *   *   *   *   *

Haunted Lane had no street lighting, and as Mort and Priscilla made their way back only the faint gleam of a cloud-shrouded quarter moon allowed them to see where they were stepping.

"So this is where your White Lady does her haunting?" he said in an amused tone.

"These people believe she's real, Mort. You won't find many of the villagers coming around here on a dark night like this."

"Why not? Has this White Lady ever actually hurt anyone?"

"They say she kills."

"Kills? You didn't say that in the pub."

"I don't know the full story myself. Someday we'll have one of the locals tell us about it. But in the meantime, I'm just glad you're with me." She shivered and clutched his arm tightly.

CHAPTER *THREE*

By habit more than intention Mort got up early and went into the kitchen to make coffee, but found the cupboard bare. He dressed and left the bedroom on tiptoe, looking back at Priscilla, sprawled out over both sides of the bed and clutching his pillow to her side.

Guessing that the grocer would probably be close to the centre square, he used the pub as his beacon. Thoughts of Priscilla dominated his mind, and he castigated himself for intruding on her life. She had a bad marriage and divorce, but, still in the prime of her marriageable years, she could be finding herself a worthy husband. Instead she was wasting her time on a man almost old enough to be her father, one embittered first by the death of his wife, then by a tragic love affair in Greece. Yes, he had fallen in love with her, but had no right to demand that she leave her career. God only knew how he tried not to encourage her. The best thing on earth would be for him to get out of her life.

Diagonally across from the pub was a small store with a faded painted sign reading "E. Chynoweth—Grocer." Mort selected as much basic foodstuff as he thought he could carry conveniently and brought them to the rectangular-shaped woman at the cash register. "How much for a carrier bag?" he said.

"Ten p. each," she replied, "you'll need two," and handed him two plastic bags. She counted out his change and continued speaking in a firm voice. "You're over at The Deaconry."

"I'll bet you even know my name."

A slight smile came to the corners of her lips. "You're Sinclair and she's Booth. Or are you Booth and she Sinclair?"

"You were right the first time."

She smiled more broadly. "I usually am."

Returning to the house, he soon had coffee ready, and then heard Priscilla's voice from the bedroom.

"Is that coffee I smell? How awesome to wake up and find it made! I smell bacon, too."

She came out dressed in a satiny robe just as he was getting ready to fry the eggs. "I can't believe you found all this in the house," she said. She opened the refrigerator and checked out the cupboards. "Mort, you've been out already. Why didn't you wake me?"

"You were sleeping too beautifully. Now stop talking while I prepare the eggs. Notice I have the heat on low. Always low heat for cooking any eggs except omelettes, which need a hot frying pan. The trick with fried eggs is to get the white firm and keep the yolk runny. They're just about ready, now let's eat. I can't stand cold eggs."

As they started eating they heard footsteps followed by loud banging in the upstairs flat. "Giles must be up and around," said Priscilla. "Did you hear him last night? I don't know what time it was, but he was walking back and forth and making an awful lot of noise."

"I slept like a log."

The banging stopped, but they heard footsteps coming down the stairway on the other side of the kitchen wall. There was a knock on their door. Mort started to get up, but Priscilla motioned him to stay seated. "I don't mind my eggs getting cold," she said.

He watched as Priscilla opened the door. The woman standing there was tall with beautifully set long ash-blond hair coming down past her shoulders. She might marginally have been called attractive, or she might not, for her facial features were rather vague, neither harmoniously lovely, nor obtrusively uncomely, just undemanding of attention. It was her shape that was compelling. She wore skin-tight jeans and a form-fitting maroon Jersey pullover, and the lines of her body curved in and out, up and around, sinuously smooth and precisely sculptured as if fashioned by Praxiteles, subtle in some places, boldly pronounced in others, in what had to be one of the closest-to-perfect figures Mort had ever seen. He had to stifle a low whistle, and he noticed that even Priscilla was visibly impressed.

"Hullo," said the stranger, "I'm Joanna Gifford, from the television company, and I was to meet Giles Bacon this morning, but he's not in his flat. Would you know where he is?"

"No, I haven't seen him," said Priscilla. "Mort, did you happen to see Giles when you were out?"

He swallowed a forkful hurriedly. "No, um, didn't," he said as a large piece of egg passed down his esophagus. His normal enjoyment of his food was blocked as his eyes stared in disbelief at this living Aphrodite of Cnidus outlined in the open doorway.

"You say you know he's not there?" said Priscilla.

"Why, yes, I have a key," said Joanna. She paused and smiled. "Perhaps I should explain that I'm the scriptwriter, and Giles and I had to rewrite some scenes. We work together frequently and he gave me an extra key. If you see him, tell him to ring Joanna at the manor."

"Wow!" said Mort, as the door shut. "If she had the face to go with that body, she could launch a thousand nuclear missiles."

"Oh come on, Mort, she wasn't that good. She has a face that only the Hound of the Baskervilles could love."

"Oooowoooh, oooowoooh!"

Priscilla placed her hands on her hips and tilted her chin defiantly upward. "Isn't my figure as good as hers?"

"We promised we'd always be truthful with each other?" he said with caution in his voice.

"Oh, forget it. Your eggs are getting cold. At least I'm prettier."

"No competition," said Mort, glad to be on safer ground, as he downed the remaining morsels from his plate. He poured them another cup of coffee. "What are you planning to do today?"

"Oh, I don't know," she said. "That inspector is coming. Afterwards I thought I might go to the Public Record Office in Truro and start doing some work on my Fitzpen genealogy. I'm going to find a royal line yet."

"Good luck to you. With all the generations proceeding from the legitimate and illegitimate children of medieval kings, most of us have royal lines—Charlemagne's descendants alone must number in the millions today—but the difficulty is to document it generation by generation."

"I know, Dr. Sinclair, after all, I've read your books. But I don't absolutely have to go to Truro. Perhaps after the police inspector gets here, you and I can take a walk on the cliffs."

*   *   *   *   *   *

Detective Inspector Penhaligon, thirty minutes late, apologised to Priscilla. "It seems we're somewhat understaffed, aren't we? So much to do."

A wide-shouldered handsome man perhaps just under average height, he wore a three-piece suit and bow tie and looked very efficient. Mort prided himself that though he often forgot faces, he never forgot a name. Penhaligon...Penhaligon...Inspector Penhaligon...CID. Of course, wasn't he one of the students in Mort's Cambridge lecture series last year?

On seeing Mort step out from behind Priscilla, the inspector offered an outstretched hand. "Why, Dr. Sinclair, this is an unexpected pleasure. You do remember me, don't you? I attended your lectures on the use of genealogy and genetics in forensics."

Now Mort could place him precisely. Yes, a good student, caught on fast, asked pertinent questions, cautious in voicing conclusions before he had them well thought out, serious but good natured, more solid than flamboyant. He was probably around Mort's age, certainly not ready for retirement, yet he had quite likely reached something close to the highest rank he could expect. Thinking of how rapidly younger men were being promoted in the police—Mort had met a good number of chief inspectors, superintendents, and even chief superintendents much younger than himself—he reflected that Inspector Penhaligon would probably never become a chief constable. He was of that middling variety, the real backbone of the force.

Penhaligon accepted Priscilla's offer of coffee, and the three of them sat in the small living room in front of an electric heater in the fireplace.

"It seems," Penhaligon said, taking a pad of paper and a pen from his inside jacket pocket, "that we have a nasty problem. I don't want to upset Miss Booth, but some unpleasant facts have come to our attention which must be investigated."

"Before you continue," Mort said, "in case you don't already know, Miss Booth is a police sergeant in America with years of experience in homicide."

"Oh, is she? I'm glad you told me. I can speak more professionally then, can't I? It seems we now have reason to think that Sylvia Cawthorne was murdered." Then addressing Priscilla specifically he said, "The proof is in the DNA."

Priscilla looked as if she had been punched in the stomach. "Sylvia murdered, oh no!" After a moment she glanced at Mort and then said to Penhaligon, "DNA? I've use it quite successfully in some of my cases, thanks to a quick course in genetics and DNA from a master."

Penhaligon nodded. "I took lessons, it seems, from the same master." Facing Mort he said, "Truthfully, Dr. Sinclair, even though the DNA breakthrough occurred in England, it's only since I attended your lectures that I've come to realise how important a knowledge of genetics can be to understand the intricacies of DNA."

The police detective turned back to Priscilla, "You'll understand the meaning of our finding blood near the path just a short distance from where Mrs. Cawthorne's body must have gone over the cliff. Not many years ago all we would have been able to say was that at most the blood was the same type as Mrs. Cawthorne's, a type she could have shared with thousands of others. Now thanks to DNA, we know the blood we found almost had to come from Mrs. Cawthorne. We received the results from the laboratory at Abingdon yesterday morning."

"You must have found the blood much earlier." said Mort.

"About a week ago."

"You were still investigating that long after Sylvia's death?" Priscilla said.

The inspector seemed to be appraising her expression. "Not exactly, Miss Booth. There was a coroner's inquest and it seems nothing suspicious was found. Death due to an accidental fall. But later we were notified of the blood by one of the villagers."

"I don't mind being called Sergeant Booth, Inspector," allowing her smile to linger. Then, "Even though I know I have no authority here."

Mort laughed to himself, knowing her remark to mean that if she could just train him to call her "Sergeant" he might forget about her lack of authority.

"Could you tell us who the villager was?" Priscilla asked.

A new series of ideas began racing through the convoluted pathways of Mort's brain. Sylvia murdered? That gave an entirely different meaning to their visit. Was Priscilla in any danger? Had Sylvia known she was at risk? Did it have anything to do with the house? If the murder was just being discovered now, then it was possibly premeditated, contrived by a clever person. What kind of challenge was being presented to them?

Penhaligon, who seemed to be mulling over Priscilla's question, said after a long silence, "There's nothing confidential about her identity. It was Elspeth Fitzpen, the wife of Charles Fitzpen."

"You mean Charles Fitzpen the solicitor?" Priscilla said.

"Yes, he's a relative of yours, isn't he?"

"My grandmother was a Fitzpen from this area. Charles is a cousin—a second cousin, to be precise."

"Mrs. Fitzpen came across the blood while hiking to Pendorth, that headland you can see from your window. She notified us immediately. It was a serious dereliction of duty that our man had missed it and, I assure you, he has been properly informed of the fact, though in truth we're being assigned more than we can rightly handle. The blood was about thirty yards down the path by some blackberry bushes."

Mort said, "You theorise then that Sylvia Cawthorne was attacked by someone, hit severely enough to lose a significant amount of blood, and then carried to the cliff and thrown over."

"So it seems, Dr. Sinclair. As you say, the amount of blood was significant, making a circle of some twenty centimetres in diameter. Any such wound would have been noticeable if it had occurred before she took her walk; in fact, she probably would have gone to a doctor—wouldn't she have?—and our inquiries in this regard proved negative. The most logical conclusion was that she was wounded just before she went over the cliff."

"I know it's weird," Priscilla said, "but any chance that it could have been menstrual?"

"You're right, that nothing, no matter how unlikely, should be overlooked. But Mrs. Cawthorne had a hysterectomy some years ago. Along with the blood there was also a depression the size of Mrs. Cawthorne's body in the blackberry bushes. As a matter of fact, blackberry thorns had been found in her clothing, but that was first thought to be normal for anyone walking the path. Further, some strands of Mrs. Cawthorne's pullover were found in the depression. The circumstances, it seems, are sufficient for us to ask the coroner to reconsider her verdict."

"Were there any indications," Mort began cautiously, "that Sylvia had been sexually molested?"

"There was an autopsy, yes, because the death was violent, even if believed accidental. But no evidence of rape was found."

"Is there any likelihood," said Priscilla, "that Sylvia somehow hurt herself and in a daze wandered over the cliff?"

"Likelihood, no." said the inspector. "It's a remote possibility, of course, but the absence of any trail of blood from the blackberry bushes to the cliff edge would indicate that she was carried, wouldn't it? Quite possibly her assailant put some of her clothing over the wound so as not to get himself bloody. The medical report calls special attention to a wound on her face which could have been made by the fall, but could equally well have resulted from a strong blow to the jaw."

His coffee getting cold, Penhaligon stopped to take several gulps. His dark blue eyes could be seen dancing above the rim of the cup to take studied looks at first one, then the other of his hosts. "The distinction in appearance between accident, suicide, and murder," he said, "is sometimes very small, but we must pursue the most reasonable cause, mustn't we?"

Priscilla was trembling slightly and she raised a hand to her eye to gently wipe away tears gathering in the corner. Mort put a comforting arm around her shoulder and gave her an encouraging pat. She looked at the inspector and said, "Do you have any idea who might have done it?"

"Not at this time. That's the purpose of my visit, Miss…, er, Sergeant Booth. As one policeman to another I solicit your help. Do you know of anyone who would have been sufficiently antagonistic toward Mrs. Cawthorne to want to kill her?"

Priscilla shook her head. "I'm sorry, Inspector. I hadn't seen my cousin for three years. We corresponded, but now that I think of it, she never gave me any idea who her friends and associates were. She always wrote about things she had seen, shows, fairs, a storm off Treleggan…but she never mentioned people. In fact, her letters really never said much of anything. I didn't even know she'd had a hysterectomy."

When the inspector made no response, she spoke again. "I take it you have no witnesses."

"None. We're contacting some of the people known to be regular hikers on that path. There's a housing estate for retirees a little beyond Pendorth and a lot of those people go out every day. In the meantime if you should recall anything that might be even remotely connected with this case, please contact us."

He rose and put pen and pad back in his pocket. "Or if something out of the ordinary should come to your attention…such as in this house…. We're fortunate in having someone of your experience occupying the premises."

"Of course," said Priscilla, "I'll do whatever I can to help. You'll probably want to search the house."

The inspector displayed a faint, almost apologetic, smile, "We may want to make still another search later, but we've already searched the house twice. The second time was yesterday before you arrived. We had telephone permission from Dr. Frank Cawthorne."

"Oh," said Priscilla. "Of course, I own the house, but I don't mind that you've already searched it." Her expression contradicted her words.

The inspector, who had started walking toward the door, turned to face her. "Strictly speaking, Sergeant Booth, Dr. Cawthorne as the executor of his wife's will was the person to contact for permission, was he not? He's the only person authorised by the court thus far to take possession of anything belonging to Mrs. Cawthorne."

"I'm sorry. I don't understand. You mean I don't actually own the house yet."

"Not until Dr. Cawthorne takes the necessary legal action. It seems, however, that he has no objection to your being here."

"After all, he gave me the key himself."

"There you see, you indeed have his approval, haven't you?"

"As I have been given to understand the terms of my cousin's will," Priscilla said, "I must live in the house for thirty days in order to inherit it. But now you raise the question in my mind, when does that thirty-day period begin? How can I comply with the will if I don't have legal authority in my own right to even enter on the premises?"

"That would seem to be a matter for a solicitor, Miss...Sergeant Booth." Inspector Penhaligon turned to Mort and said, "Dr. Sinclair, your friend would be well advised to consult a solicitor." He again started toward the door.

As he reached for the handle, Priscilla said, "Would you humour me on one little hypothetical matter?"

He nodded affirmatively, perhaps just a trifle startled.

"If I were stopped for speeding on one of your highways, would the police have any feeling of professional courtesy in mitigation of the offence because I'm a fellow police officer, even though of another country?"

Penhaligon smiled a little, seemingly relieved on learning what was on her mind. "I really don't know if I'm the proper person to answer that question. You might ask my super; it seems his wife was fined £50 last week for speeding on the A390."

Mort caught an amused glint in Penhaligon's eye as he disappeared through the door.

$$* \qquad * \qquad * \qquad * \qquad * \qquad *$$

In the afternoon Mort and Priscilla set out to walk to Pendorth, the headland that they had been told was two miles away. It might have been two miles in a straight line, but it was impossible to go directly from point to point, for at times they were covering more ground vertically than horizontally. Then there were impassable inlets where it was necessary to descend from the high cliff to a curving beach, walk around it, and ascend again to a point on the other side. The scenery of sea, sky, and cliff was breathtaking, the walk invigorating.

They had no difficulty in finding the place from which Sylvia must have fallen, for it had been well described to them as the point just beyond a wind-and-rain-faded sign reading, "Danger. Path Narrows." About fifty feet beyond the sign the path came to its obviously narrowest strait, caused by a sugarloaf of rock covering the entire width of the headland and barring any passage except at the precipitous edge.

They found the blackberry bushes squatting into the rocks at a short distance before the dangerous point and some thirty yards away from the path. Their intense scrutiny showed nothing of particular interest. There was no longer even any sign of bloodstains. Looking to the sea, Mort said, "That's a considerable distance for the killer to have carried her."

"Makes you think it must have been a man," she responded.

"Don't underestimate the power of adrenalin."

Priscilla looked down at the jagged rocks below and shuddered. What a horrific way to die. Was Sylvia conscious as she headed pell mell to her certain death? How those few moments must have seemed a lifetime. Of course, for Sylvia they were a lifetime. Think of this moment, thought Priscilla, as the last moment of your life. She could now imagine hearing a thud from below as the body would have come to a sudden stop. Or would it have bounced from rock to rock? Or had it been skewered on some sharp pinnacle? Poor Sylvia. Priscilla shivered again, and she began to wish that she had not come out here. After all, she was not here as a policewoman. Sylvia was her friend.

There didn't appear anything else to be seen pertinent to the case, so slowly they went back toward the village, now—forgetful of the tragedy—enjoying the wide-expanse view as they walked. As they reached the outer point of certain bends, they could see Treleggan at a seemingly close distance, gleaming whitewashed in the sun like a Greek amphitheatre with terraces and aisles. In the mole-protected harbour the tide was out again and the lines of the mud-bound fishing boats formed geometric patterns of intricate design.

"Did you see that glint of light?" asked Mort.

"What? The sun?"

"No, something reflecting the sun. It came from the direction of the village."

"Someone watching us with binoculars?"

"That's what I wondered about. Possibly. But I don't see it any more."

They continued along the path, now only half taking in the beauty of the magnificent panorama before them while they also puzzled over who might want to be watching them—and why. But gradually the scenery won over, and again, holding hands as they walked, they were left in awed contemplation of nature at its best. They were close to the beginning of the village now.

"Look, Mort," said Priscilla, tugging at his pullover. "There's someone's walking on the path away from us."

"Someone spying on us?"

"I don't think so. But I'd like to see who it is. Let's walk faster."

Now Mort, too, could make out the figure, first as an indistinct moving object, then as human, finally as female. "Joanna Gifford," he said. "No one could fail to recognise that shape even at this distance."

Within minutes they caught up with their target, who turned with a startled look as they came up behind her.

"Oh," she said, "you scared me."

"Were you just out on the cliffs?" said Mort.

Her eyes darted from one to the other and her face looked pained, as if she had been physically hurt. "No. I started walking at the beginning of the path, but changed my mind."

"Changed your mind?" repeated Priscilla, making it sound almost like an accusation.

Joanna, now trembling, was wearing a tight short skirt and high-heeled shoes, which dramatically enhanced her figure, but were hardly the clothes for cliff walking. She also carried a backpack heavily laden over her shoulder. "I…I, was looking for Giles. I went to the edge of the village to see if I could see him on the cliffs. I've looked everywhere else at the manor and in the village. I'm desperate."

Mort said, "When was he last heard from?"

"He left the pub last night with a fisherman named Dinny. I talked to Dinny, who said they separated at the car park, and he last saw Giles walking up Haunted Lane to his house." She put a hand to her forehead and nervously brushed her hair back. "I know Giles, it's just not like him."

Priscilla studied the backpack, wondering if there were binoculars in it.

Still asking questions they walked with Joanna to her car, but learned nothing more of significance. As Joanna drove off, Priscilla said, "She really seems concerned about Giles."

"Or she wants to make it appear she's concerned about him."

"No, Mort," Priscilla said, looking into his eyes. "You may be the analytical wizard, but give me due credit for my experience in dealing with people in trouble. I've seen any number of women with missing husbands or boy friends and I know for a fact that girl really cares. It's as if she fears something."

"Such as?"

Priscilla stopped, turned to look at him, all the colour drained out of her countenance, and said with an air of finality, "Such as that he's dead!"

Chapter *FOUR*

In the morning Priscilla fought with herself to stay in bed, but lost. "How can I help?" she said, as she joined Mort in the kitchen.

"Make the toast, and please don't burn it."

"Eggs again? You're going in pretty heavily for the cholesterol."

"Beer," he said, "has a lot of high density lipoproteins."

"Meaning?"

"They clean the arteries as soon as the cholesterol gets them clogged up."

"Oh, sure!" she said. "You sound more like a quack than a scientist."

"Well, I don't know if it's clinically proven. But my father's eighty-two and has two eggs every morning and four large cans of Newcastle Ale every night."

His father? The remark halted any further banter. Mort had a father? She took her own parents, both alive and healthy, for granted, but Mort was—different.

"I didn't know you had a father…, I mean, that he's still alive." She walked over to the electric cooker, which featured an open grill on top. A pan with a removable handle was inside the grill, which had a salamander in the top as its heating element. After Priscilla put the bread on the pan to toast, she turned to look at Mort with an inquiring expression on her face. "It goes to show how little we know some things about each other. Where does he live?"

"In Edinburgh, where I was born."

So he was born in Edinburgh. She knew he had come to the United States from somewhere in Scotland and later become a naturalised citizen, but it had never occurred to her that he had to come from some given place. His speech was of that world-traveler English that almost defied being placed by accent—one would find it difficult to identify him precisely as American or British. What else was there to know?

"Interesting. Tell me, Mort, what made you decide to become an American citizen?"

He smiled and said, "I was part of the brain drain. An American company offered me an irresistible salary. Not for my doctorate in history, but for my master's degree in biology. I worked for them at night while studying for a law degree during the day."

"I know you were awarded your first degree at seventeen, but why so many different degrees? Couldn't make your mind up? You're a regular jack of all trades, aren't you?"

"Oh, I suppose I like knowledge for its own sake. My father calls me a polymath, always in his best sarcastic tone. He's a retired British ambassador, you know. My mother's dead and he lives with his mistress."

"He can't really have a mistress."

"Well, he introduces her in public as his fiancée, but he's had three or four quote fiancées unquote in the past twenty years."

"Oh, Mort, you're putting me on." Priscilla walked to the cooker. "But you've got an awesome background," she said as she removed the toast from the grill.

She sat down and thought of buttering the toast, but then remembered that Mort like his buttered only after it cooled, so she would have hers the same way. She casually fingered a paperback novel on the table. Mort, with the frying pan in his hand, glanced over to see the title, Trollope's *Can You Forgive Her?* and nodded appreciatively. They had discovered long ago that one more thing they had in common was a fine appreciation of Victorian novelist Anthony Trollope as their favorite author.

Mort returned to the cooker, and another minute passed without further speech, then they heard a noise above them.

"Hear that?" she said. "Giles must have come back after all. And making as much noise as ever. I'm glad I was wrong about anything happening to him."

They could hear footsteps crossing back and forth on the floor above them, and every now and then there was a bang, as if something heavy was being deposited on the floor. Mort set the plates of sausages and eggs on the table.

Heavy footsteps were coming down the stairs.

They started buttering their toast. "He makes a lot of noise," said Mort.

There was a loud, impatient knock on the door.

"You sit there, Mort, and I'm going to let Giles know he'd better not come around here banging on our door when you're just about to eat your eggs."

She crossed the kitchen and flung the outside door open, words already formed in her mouth as she did so, but she suddenly became speechless.

"I'm astonished to find you still here, Miss Booth," said the man at the door. He was a big man, balding on top, somewhere between her and Mort in age, with an expression on his face of stifled displeasure.

"I don't know why not, Dr. Cawthorne. I told you I was coming here, and you even gave me the key."

Somehow he seemed bigger than she recalled him, his head like a massive Japanese lantern towering over her own. For just a moment she could not help but wonder how much a headhunter might prize that head as a worshipful trophy, something to set him above all his tribe.

Slowly unloosened rage came to that mammoth head, the cheeks puffing up as if attached to an air pump and the thick lips quivering as if in silent stutter. "But you said overnight." The words issued from his mouth as if they contained some terrible denunciation. "I didn't expect you'd still be here."

"I said no such thing," Priscilla answered. She glared back at him for a second, then let her face relax and assume a sweet smile. "But I'm forgetting my manners. Let me introduce you to Dr. Mortimer Sinclair."

Dr. Cawthorne looked at Mort for the first time. "Doctor?" he said.

Here we go again, thought Mort. "Doctor of Philosophy, Cambridge," he said, "and Juris Doctor in the U.S." Would two doctorates be enough for him?

The other man instantly turned away. "I don't care about your excuses, Miss Booth. There might have been some misunderstanding on your part. But as executor I have need for both flats. Now! I want you out of the house in one hour. Preferably sooner!"

Priscilla opened her mouth, but didn't know what to say. Mort slowly rose from the table and walked over to where he was within a shoe length of their caller, who outdid him some two inches in height and about three stone in weight.

"I'd appreciate your lowering your voice," Mort said slowly and softly, "and speaking more respectfully to Miss Booth." Then raising his own voice a few decibels, he added, "Or else, I'll throw you out."

The bigger man stared at him, his face reddening, then said in a slightly less loud tone, "Regardless of misunderstandings, I'm giving Miss Booth official notice to vacate these premises."

"Where is Giles Bacon?" said Mort.

"That writer?" said Cawthorne in a sneer. "How the devil do I know? Wherever he is, his belongings are in my flat. I'm having them packed and taken to a hotel in Truro at his expense."

Your wife gave him a verbal lease," said Priscilla.

"I'm a doctor, not a lawyer, but I know a verbal lease has all the legal force of a bag of wind. One hour, Miss Booth. Good day to you, Sinclair." He slammed the door behind him. A few seconds later an engine started and a car noisily sped away from the house.

Words were slow in returning to Priscilla. "Well, I like that!"

"You might," said Mort, "but I don't care for it at all. Who the hell does he think he is?"

"What are we going to do?"

"Well, for a start," Mort said, his facial muscles beginning to relax a bit, "I think we can reheat the bangers, but we'll have to throw the eggs out and fry some more." He opened the refrigerator. "Then, after we've had breakfast, I suggest we talk to a good solicitor—how about your cousin, Charles Fitzpen? In the meantime, tell me something about Sylvia."

Priscilla put the sausages in the oven while Mort prepared the new eggs.

On Sylvia, she didn't know where to start. As her mind went back to those carefree school days, she began conjuring up images of her friend and cousin. Sylvia with a tennis racket in her hand, Sylvia describing how she disabled a date-raper with a karate chop, Sylvia successfully skirmishing with the dean to defend another girl's claim to a scholarship, Sylvia in the senior yearbook as the most likely to get ahead.

"Well," Priscilla said, "her father was a British army major, and he and her mother retired to Victoria, British Columbia, until they both died not long after Sylvia returned to England from college. We corresponded frequently in the beginning. Sylvia started her own upper-crust catering business—you know, preparing fancy foods for the parties that wealthy people throw, and I think she was terribly successful at it. She was a natural since she was of the gentry class herself, though her family was not especially rich."

"What type of personality did she have?"

"Kind, fun-loving, adventuresome, although, when the situation required, she could be tough. Yet she sometimes seemed to have a feeling of insecurity. Perhaps it was because her father had been a career officer, with all the moves and changes of nannies that that implies. She was always striving for recognition and I think it motivated much of what she did at college. Don't misunderstand me, she was also very sympathetic, understanding, and generous, generous to a fault. Eventually she met a society doctor who had family, prestige, and wealth. As I say, Sylvia didn't write about individuals, even her husband, but I always assumed that she was much more happily married than I'd been."

"Was she well liked?"

"Oh, yes, decidedly." Priscilla paused. "Well, that is, by most people. A few of the girls thought she was odd—mercurial some said—but they were just jealous."

"Attractive?"

"Very. She wore glasses and suffered from night-blindness, but her face was the type that glasses made perhaps even more attractive. She was blonde, quite tall, terrific figure, well toned. Nothing physically unusual otherwise except for a birthmark on the front of her neck; she was self-conscious of it and always wore high-neck clothing or a neckerchief."

"Children?"

"None that I know of. You heard what the inspector said yesterday. I have no idea if she'd had the hysterectomy before or after her marriage, or why she had to have it in the first place. She never mentioned children in her letters." Priscilla started to say more, but hesitated.

Mort said, "And?"

"Well, she'd had an abortion at Bennington. Her fiancé died of a drug overdose when she was pregnant and she decided not to have the baby."

"What do you know about her husband?"

"Next to nothing from her letters. She mentioned him a few times during the two weeks I spent with her at Treleggan, and I sort of got an impression...."

"Yes? Go on."

"Well, it's very vague. I just sort of felt that Sylvia looked up to him; that is, she sort of felt inferior to him, but that's not exactly what I mean. It was more a mixture between respect, and, yes, fear. But I really can't explain further."

*　　*　　*　　*　　*　　*

Charles Fitzpen was dubious. "I don't want to let you down, Priscilla, but it's awkward. A matter of ethics and possible conflict of interest."

"How, Charles?" said Priscilla.

They were sitting in the kitchen and Priscilla got up to attend to the steeping tea. She was disappointed. "Please call on me," he had said in London, "for anything at all you want." How typical of people, always ready to take credit for offering help and then letting one down when it was really needed.

Mort looked on in silence.

"There was no reason to mention this before," Charles said, "but Sylvia left me a small bequest, but then, when she made the codicil, she changed her mind and took me out again." He added, "She took out some others, too."

"But you're not one of the heirs now?" said Priscilla. She placed the teapot on a tray with cream and sugar and carried it to the table.

"No, but just suppose someone contests the codicil, you and I might find ourselves on opposite sides. I know it's not likely to happen. But Frank Cawthorne lost this house by the codicil, and we can't predict what he might do. Now my bequest was only £500, but theoretically there's a conflict, don't you see?"

"You can't advise me at all?"

He looked down, put two spoons of sugar in his tea, and slowly stirred it. "Not formally. But I'll give you some informal advice. Get a good solicitor in Truro. Trevor Tremaine is tops in both probate and property law. He likes to call himself 'the fastest hired gun in the west.' But perhaps Mort had better get in touch with him for you, since under the circumstances you shouldn't leave this house. Anchor yourself in position and don't move."

"That's good advice," said Mort to Priscilla. "You have possession, don't abandon it. Stay here and I'll see Mr. Tremaine in Truro on your behalf."

"Tell him I referred you to him," said Charles. He turned from Mort. "I hope you understand my position, Priscilla." He drank his tea quickly and started to stand. "Well, I have to go to Bristol on business. I'll see you when I get back tomorrow. Oh, by the way, Elspeth asked me to invite you two to dinner Friday night, say around seven."

Priscilla looked to Mort to see that he was in agreement, then said, "Thanks, we'd be delighted." Then she added, "That is, if we're free to leave the house by then."

*   *   *   *   *   *

"While you were gone," said Priscilla, when Mort returned from Truro, "that horrible Dr. Cawthorne was back again threatening me with eviction."

"He's all bluff," said Mort. "Trevor Tremaine assured me so, and Charles is right, Tremaine is indeed the 'best in the west.'"

They sat in the living room and Mort related how Tremaine had established contact with Sylvia's attorney in London to get the pertinent details of her will and codicil. The original will, made six weeks before she died, left several £500 bequests to her maid, her cousins Charles Fitzpen and Priscilla, and her friends Tony Trelawney, Giles Bacon, and Robin Steele. She kept the maid in the codicil, but dropped the money bequests to Fitzpen, Trelawney, Bacon, Steele, and Priscilla, then added £1,000 as a new bequest to Magnus Mandeville. She also provided as something new that Priscilla would get the Treleggan house. Whatever estate remained would go to her husband.

The part about Priscilla inheriting the house included the words, "My loving cousin Priscilla Booth of the United States is to receive my house in Cornwall and all its contents whatsoever they may be without exception, provided only that she sleep thirty consecutive nights in the house starting at her earliest convenient moment, but within two months of my death at the latest." Thus Sylvia's intent was clear and Tremaine told Mort he would obtain an injunction to prevent Cawthorne from evicting Priscilla for thirty days, following which

Cawthorne could be legally required to start probate action to give Priscilla ownership.

"But why the tremendous change in Cawthorne?" Priscilla said. "Why suddenly go from being indifferent to nasty?"

"How has his situation changed?" asked Mort. "Think back, darling. At the time he gave you the key to the house, he didn't seem to mind that you'd be staying here for an indefinite period. Did he know then about Sylvia's codicil?"

"Of course, we even discussed it. He said he was glad I was the one inheriting the house because he never liked it."

"Now at that time neither he nor you thought the police viewed Sylvia's death as anything other than accidental?"

"I would suppose he learned of their suspicions only after the police rang him to get permission to search the house."

"Then all of a sudden Cawthorne is a changed man, furious, determined to get you out of the house and take possession himself, even though he must have known that legally he had little ground to stand on. But it was worth it to him to take the slight chance that you might surrender to his bluff even though by acting thusly he would be giving away the fact that something had happened to make him become very agitated."

"Run that by me again, please," said Priscilla. "Oh, look at that beautiful sailboat, Mort."

From the window they could see a large two-masted yacht gliding majestically in the bay, its white sails contrasting vividly against azure sky as it effortlessly cut through the royal purple of the sea. Mort put his arm around Priscilla's waist and bent over to rest his cheek against hers.

"That's what I love about this place," said Priscilla. "The view is never the same twice, like a kaleidoscope, always something new."

As the sailboat disappeared around the tip of Pendorth and dark clouds rapidly moved across the sky from the west to dramatically modulate the colours of all below, Mort said, "What I mean is that surely Dr.

Cawthorne is intelligent enough to realise his actions have made him look suspicious. He can expect you to tell the police how he behaved, and they will probably start paying more attention to him." He returned to his chair.

"But if he's innocent," said Priscilla, "he might not even think that he's making himself look suspicious. You could say that by acting this way he was making a display of innocence."

"Perhaps. We still have the question, why is he so interested in getting you out of the house? Is it you? Or is it just that he needs to take possession of the house himself for some unknown reason? Suppose he is the murderer, why should he want us out?"

Priscilla's eyes lit up. "Because there's something here that could incriminate him and he doesn't want us to find it."

"Exactly. But now let's take the other side. Suppose he's not guilty, then why should he want us out of the house?"

"I can't imagine why. Can you?"

"No, I can't."

"Then we're saying he must be a prime suspect."

"So we are," Mort said, laughing. "But there's something missing, some fact that we're unaware of. In the meantime, though, Inspector Penhaligon asked you to notify him of anything pertinent to his investigation. I suggest you tell him about your run-in with Cawthorne. And if that makes the police take greater interest in him, he has only himself to blame."

"It looks as if he's going to be our upstairs neighbour for a while. I suppose Giles will have to consider himself evicted."

Priscilla telephoned Penhaligon and told him about Cawthorne. As she put the phone down, it started ringing, and she picked up the receiver again.

"It's Magnus Mandeville speaking from London," she said to Mort, holding her hand over the mouthpiece. "He wants to be sure that I'll be going to the manor tomorrow. What can I tell him?"

Mort looked at her. "Do you really want to go?"

Priscilla lowered her gaze briefly, then looked up again with a smile. "Yes," she said, "it would be so interesting to see them doing the filming."

"Tell him you'll be there. I'll stay here and hold the fort until the injunction comes through."

"Thanks," she said to Mort after hanging up. "Magnus really wants me to come. He says they'll get a late start in the morning because they're shooting night scenes tonight. In any case he won't be back from London much before noon. And he says I'll be delighted with what he has to tell me."

CHAPTER *FIVE*

With Mort staying at The Deaconry to protect their possession, Priscilla left after breakfast for the manor. Though Magnus had said he did not expect to return until shortly before lunch, she was not the waiting type.

As she cruised at what was for her a gentle speed along the straight tree-and-hedgerow-lined avenue, she recalled the way from three years earlier. A patinaed stone Celtic cross in a clearing reminded her that this was the fabled land of King Geraint, King Mark, Tristram and Isolde, and King Arthur, and she felt the thrill of legend and history all about her. Perhaps next time she might walk, but it would have been too slow this morning.

There was a sudden bend in the highway and she had to turn right then make a quick left to enter the stone-lion-guarded gateway. Passing through the perimeter of trees, she came to a clearing, and there was Penstead dominating its surroundings, gnarled vines of ivy with tender new green leaves embracing the house's oyster-gray walls. She had had tea there once with Sylvia, Charles, Elspeth, and Elspeth's parents, both now dead. How long ago it seemed. How much alike the present scene was to the image in her mind, yet somehow different.

Dozens of cars, trucks, and vans were parked to one side of the main driveway. Priscilla left her Sierra in their midst to cover the remaining 100 feet on foot. As she approached the manor house, she stopped abruptly, surprised to see actors and technicians milling around so early. There was Magnus standing under a portico and staring at her. He had returned much earlier than he said. He seemed hesitant. Had her visit suddenly become unwanted? But then he smiled and came over to welcome her.

Magnus Mandeville could be gracious. Priscilla felt that the producer might have been the best actor in the company. He held out both hands to her as he approached, kissed her cheek, and pivoted around with a dramatic sweeping motion of his arm to indicate that the entire manor was at her disposal. Not even Robin Steele playing the Duke of Shrewsbury had seemed more gallant.

"I'm early," said Priscilla, "but I was so anxious to be here. I didn't expect you to start so soon."

"I let them sleep an extra hour this morning," said Magnus, "because they were all working late last night. But we're behind schedule and that costs mazoula, so we've got to keep moving. I left London myself before midnight so I could drive back to keep an eye on things this morning."

He must have driven his car like an airplane to cover that distance, thought Priscilla.

Penstead was a part Tudor, part Georgian stone house featuring two end wings which made it resemble a squat letter "H," with its back facing the sea several hundred yards downhill. The front part of the space enclosed by the "H" was extended to cover that part of the driveway that came closest to the house. This formed an open courtyard outlined by columned walls and evenly spaced porticos, two on the sides to allow access from the drive, and three in the front giving panoramic views of the estate down to the main road and beyond. On the left side of the manor was a large carriage house, now converted to a garage for cars and farm equipment.

Now that she was closer, Priscilla could see that the ivy was not as dense as it used to be. Paint was peeling from the building's wood trim and bricks were displaced from the clusters of chimneys on the roof. In spite of there being more activity than she had seen before, the exterior had a forlorn look about it.

Entering the courtyard with Magnus, she noted that the modern roadway had been covered with freshly spread gravel to help re-create the proper period. Lights, cameras, microphone booms, and large square reflectors surrounded the courtyard, all focusing on the area between the central archway and main house entrance. Priscilla recalled that the part of the house between the two wings was the oldest area, now consisting of a large banqueting hall and a good-sized kitchen.

"This" said Magnus, indicating the center of the courtyard, "is the scene where Squire Reginald Urquhart welcomes the Duke of Monmouth, thereby setting the stage for the ultimate complete ruin of his family. Duke James had just landed at Lyme Regis and his ill-fated quest for the throne was at its apogee—after that bottomsville. But here, Squire Urquhart is dreaming of restoring the family fortunes to the grandeur existing in past centuries and he is taking a daring risk in supporting the bastard son of Charles II against Charles's brother and successor. It's a poignant moment, and our mutual friend Robin—who's in the makeup caravan there—really jerks your heart out making the courageous bid that deep inside he knows is doomed to failure."

"I think it's magnificent," said Priscilla. "And you're going to be filming this scene now?"

His smile withered into a sneer as his nostrils flared, and he said, "Just as soon as our dear Robin and pretty Duke James decide to get their sweet asses out here."

Though she wanted to like Magnus, Priscilla found his way of speaking a bit disquieting. The occasional coarseness was grating and the interjection of Americanisms incongruous with the rest of his speech. But she smiled faintly and said, "How far are you along?"

"Well, this is the second series, you know. The first was filmed on the north coast and corresponded to the first four of Giles Bacon's books, and now we're filming the last three. If we went in strict accordance with the stupid way he's written it, we'd be at the end right now. But we wanted to show the viewers not only how Squire Reginald's desperate gamble failed, but also the consequences on the family, how each came to ultimate destruction. So we've added what amounts to an eighth book, and we'll probably need two to three weeks to finish."

"Did Giles write what you call the eighth book?"

"He helped our script writer work it up, though damned reluctantly. Giles is a waste of space. Seems to feel cheated that he can't be writer, producer, director, and leading man in one. You should have seen the hassle he gave us on boots."

"Boots?" Priscilla recalled Giles's complaints when she first met him."

"We had Monmouth landing at Lyme Regis with his army of eighty-two men. Giles insisted that we had to go to the expense of having period leather boots for each of them. The fact that their feet would only be seen in long shots and that only Duke James would be shown in the close shots, made no difference to him. Christ, I filmed the Battle of Waterloo with the Spanish army as my extras and only four men wore leather boots of the period; the others wore modern combat boots, but from the distance who would know? Oh, spare me that Giles!" he said, crossing his arms and hands, palms outward, in front of his face as if to ward off the devil. "I have enough other crosses to bear."

Priscilla began to wonder if her first thought had been right after all that Magnus had once been an actor.

Robin Steele emerged confidently from the caravan with a small mirror in his hand and walked toward them. He wore long shoulder-length brown hair, an avocado green coat, brocaded ivory waistcoat, and chartreuse silk pantaloons, with a leather baldric slung over his right shoulder to support a silver-hilted sword at his left side. A man wearing an olive-drab army pullover with leather shoulder and elbow patches, apparently the director, approached Robin and motioned toward the house. From the same trailer a handsome young man, similarly dressed but with more a military cut to his clothes and wearing a wide-brim hat, came out and approached Robin and the director. While Robin walked toward the doorway, the newcomer, doubtless Duke James, was shown where to stand in front of the entrance arch.

As Robin spied Priscilla, he genuflected with exaggerated motion, smiled, and walked over to kiss her hand. "Why, my dear Priscilla, how charming of you to come see my humble performance. You'll stay and lunch with me, of course."

"Sorry," she said, "I must get back."

He smiled sadly, nodded his head with a shrug, and continued to the doorway.

"Why don't we go back into the manor where we can talk privately?" said Magnus to Priscilla.

"But, oh, I thought we were going to watch the filming."

"Ugh, that? That'll be going on all morning. It might take those dingalings hours to get it right." He gently ushered her to a side door and they entered the chapel. "Here," he said, manoeuvring her more aggressively with the bulk of his body, "let's sit on one of these benches."

Priscilla was taken back. She had come to see the filming, not Magnus Mandeville. Nor did she care for the idea of being alone with him in some isolated place.

"My dear Priscilla, don't look so concerned. You're a very lovely woman, you know, especially when you smile. Now wipe that frown away. I'm not going to hurt you."

"I know," she said, trying to decide how far she might let him go before giving him a karate chop. She forced a smile.

He reached for her hand and began softly, slowly caressing her fingers. She drew her hand back.

"Oh, no, dear lady, surely you don't think I'm going to try to seduce you here. Give me more credit, please. Do you think I'd throw you down on one of these hard wooden benches, or the stone floor? Give me some allowance for style."

"I, I, don't know." He was staring into her eyes and she didn't want to return his look, so she slowly moved her head to take in her surroundings. The chapel's ceiling was of dark wood supported by huge wooden crossbeams, the benches were dark but highly polished, and the stone floor showed uneven wear from many years of use. It was not a comfortable looking place, but yet had a sort of archaic beauty in its overall appearance.

Mandeville took her hand and again began stroking it. "There is a time for everything, dear lady. And this is the time for me to make you an offer you can't refuse."

Try me, thought Priscilla.

"Every beautiful woman dreams of being on television, and with Magnus Mandeville dreams can come true. Now, stop worrying. I'm just going to ask you to help me. We decided we need a new scene, and we're looking for two beautiful women to play the parts." He paused to let her get the full import of his words. "There," he continued, "now that didn't hurt, did it?"

In spite of herself, Priscilla suddenly began listening to him with interest.

"Now this is an earlier scene. Reginald Urquhart's son is engaged to Lady Pamela Zouche. The book describes how unfaithful he's going to be to her, but we can't do it that way on TV. We need to show, not tell. So we decided the best way would be to have a dance at Urquhart Manor with Lady Pamela present but with the young Urquhart dancing provocatively not just with one other attractive woman, but with two."

"Did they have dancing for couples in the late seventeenth century?"

Mandeville scowled. "Now don't give me that purist crap. This is entertainment, not an academic dissertation. Where was I?"

Priscilla felt as if she had become one more of his crosses to bear.

"Okay. All right. Young Urquhart goes from one babe to the other, almost ignoring his fiancée. The message will be obvious: if he behaves this way just before marriage, how will he be after? And that's where you and Gwen come in. They're not speaking parts, but you'll be dressed in beautiful costumes, you'll be dancing with both Robin Steele and Randolph Legend, and you'll be centred in a lot of close-up camera shots. Now, tell me, lovely lady, can you honestly resist that?"

Hmm, thought Priscilla, can I seize this bait and then run fast enough? "Hmm," she said, "I'll have to think. It *is* tempting."

"Would you like to see the costumes? Gwen also wants to, so why don't I put you two girls together. You know Gwen, don't you? She and her husband Tony have the gift shop and post office, and she also helps her mother at *The Case Is Altered*."

"Yes, I've met Gwen. And I think I'd like to see the costumes. Is Gwen coming this afternoon?"

"Didn't you see her outside? She was standing beside the make-up caravan. Come on." He led her to the door.

Robin, as Squire Reginald, was standing in front of the main doorway, and Duke James was facing him at the far side of the courtyard. The director, halfway between them, was shouting instructions first to one, then to the other. Besides the working crew, a large number of others had gathered to see the action. Some, dressed in late seventeenth-century military costume, were lounging about in the driveway, and Priscilla recognized several villagers among them. Gwen was leaning against a tree wearing baggy white slacks, red sandals, and a bulky used army jacket over a thin net blouse, her thick, honey-yellow hair spread out against the tree trunk.

Magnus motioned for Gwen to come join him and Priscilla, and the two women neutrally greeted each other. Gwen seemed to be trying to decide whether Priscilla's presence was a slight. Obviously she was not used to sharing the adulation men showered on her with another. Nor was Priscilla overjoyed at being cast an equal to Gwen. They were about the same age, same height, same figure, and same colouring, except for the hair. But there was a promiscuity reeking from Gwen's every motion that Priscilla could not identify with.

Without condemning the other, Priscilla shrank from being classed together with her. But that was ungenerous, she quickly told herself, and became ashamed of her thoughts.

"Think you can find it?" Magnus was saying to Gwen. "They seem to be getting serious out here now and I'd better watch. I'm a little concerned about Duke James—he's stoned again."

"I've been down to the cellar before," said Gwen. "You ready, Ms. Booth?"

"Priscilla, if you don't mind, Gwen."

Gwen smiled faintly. "Sure. I remember you from some years ago."

"You said the cellar?"

"That's where they keep the costumes. Robin showed me once, so I can find my way."

They entered the manor house and Gwen pointed to the front door. "Magnus is going to give old Glubb bloody hell if he doesn't fix this door lock soon." Leading the way through the banqueting hall to the kitchen, Gwen opened an old timber door and clicked a light switch. Nothing happened. "Lord love a duck, Glubb is going to find himself sacked. I'll get a torch. Robin showed me where last time." She was back in a minute with a two-dry-cell, plastic-encased flashlight in her hand. "We had to use this last time, but Robin said Magnus had ordered Glubb to repair the light. He's the laziest person." She led the way down the steps.

This was obviously the oldest part of the house. The steps were of stone, crudely cut, but worn smooth in centre depressions where hundreds of people had placed their feet thousands of times over the centuries. Blackened cast-iron conical frames attached to the wall had once held tarred flambeaus. The dripping of water could be heard and then an occasional animated scampering—mice? It was pitch black except for the circle of rather dim light projecting from Gwen's torch, but everything the light touched seemed so dark as to be shapeless. Spider webs were in all the corners. They were descending into nothingness, and Priscilla had no picture in her mind of her immediate environs. There was a stone wall on her left side, but what was on the other? Was there any bannister or rail or form of protection at all, or did the steps just drop off without warning, and how far down did they go? She was cautious about reaching over to try to find out.

"Gwen," she said, feeling a bit friendlier toward her companion.

"Yes, Priscilla," came the response in a tone similar to hers.

"Is this the cellar that they talk about in the pub, the one where there's supposed to be a 'Gray Lady'?"

"The same."

"Aren't you scared a bit?" said Priscilla.

"Who me? No, not me. I've fended off enough groping hands so I'm not afraid of anything that doesn't even have substance." But she didn't sound too convinced.

They went as far as they could straight down and then had to turn at a ninety degree angle for a few more steps to reach the bottom. Gwen moved the torch to scan her surroundings. They faced more ancient walls and three passageways, one to the right, one to the left, and one straight ahead.

"I think it's this way," said Gwen, walking straight ahead.

"But I thought you knew this place."

"Well, a lot's happened since Robin brought me here. But don't worry, Priscilla, the telly blokes have to come down here all the time."

"Do they ever come back?" asked Priscilla.

"Now don't talk like that. You're making me nervous." Gwen's voice implied a fright that seemed out of proportion to the cause. After all, they were just in a darkened cellar. There was nothing down there to really justify fear, was there?

"I'm sorry, Gwen." Lord, thought Priscilla, what happened to all my training? I'm supposed to be the brave one. Just the same, she wished Mort were with them.

They continued some thirty feet through the passageway, the sides of which were indented here and there by both alcoves and closed heavy wooden doors. In front, the total blackness was gradually penetrated by the torch's beam to reveal a dead-end wall.

"I'm not certain," said Gwen, "that this is the way. Perhaps we should have taken the left?"

You don't know! thought Priscilla. "Perhaps we ought to go back and get someone who knows the place to help us."

Gwen had turned around and was walking in the opposite direction. Priscilla let her pass by and then followed. They passed the bottom of the steps again and turned around to face the three-way division of corridors. There seemed to be a noise to their right, an eerie murmur.

"What's that?" said Gwen. "Maybe you're right. I think I've forgotten the way. Do you want to go back?"

Yes, thought Priscilla. But she said, "No! After all, there are only two other possibilities. Let's take the left, as you said."

Again they walked ahead a number of feet. In this corridor there was a number of open archways and closed doors on the right, but Gwen ignored them. "It's not in one of these side rooms," she said. "The corridor just opens into a big room, and there's a light overhead and all the costumes are on racks in the middle. We just keep going until we reach it."

"Are you sure?"

"Well, to the best of my memory."

Oh, great—uh-oh, what's that noise? thought Priscilla. "What's that noise, Gwen?"

There was undeniably a dull moaning noise coming from some place in front of them. Gwen said, "Robin told me there were always strange noises here, wind from some chimneys, water dripping, and things like that. He said it was all harmless, but just the same I don't like it. I don't think I believe all those ghost stories. But…, you know, there must be something to them if so many people have seen and heard them over the years."

After continuing a few more feet, their light showed them that they had reached the end of the passage, and there was no large room. They could go no further. The corridor existed solely to lead to the side rooms, and Gwen had said that the costumes were not in the side rooms. If she was right—and Priscilla was beginning to wonder now if she had ever been right—the correct corridor was the one they hadn't tried yet.

"I think we'd better get help," said Gwen, as she turned around and began to retrace her steps. "I don't like it down here. I don't like anything about this place. I knew we shouldn't have come."

I don't like it either, thought Priscilla, but she was determined to show herself stronger as Gwen displayed more weakness. No, we're not going to give up and show ourselves as a pair of silly, frightened females. "No," she said to Gwen, "there's only one more possibility. The costume room has to be down that third corridor and we're going to find it."

They started walking back. Again Priscilla heard the low moan, but tried to dismiss it. She kept telling herself that it was some effect of the wind outside, perhaps coming down an air passage. Even as she thought this, she seemed to sense a motion in the cold, moist air. Her skin felt clammy and the roots of her hair seemed electrified.

Suddenly there were simultaneously a loud crash, a flash of light, a shattering scream, and then darkness. The next second seemed divided into a million parts, each one moving with an unbelievable slowness. The darkness was everywhere. Movement of the cold, dank air seemed to increase. There was a noise. It seemed to be getting louder, crashing in a crescendo about her ears. Something touched her leg! She fought against screaming. Either control yourself, girl, she thought, or turn in your badge.

She heard another loud yell and the blood in her vessels surged with anxiety. "Gwen," she cried, "Gwen!"

"Priscilla! Priscilla!"

Then Priscilla realized that the loud yell had been Gwen, who seemed to be calling out from the floor. It must have been Gwen who had touched her. The torch had fallen. That was the noise. And it had gone out, or was broken, hence the sudden darkness. Gwen had dropped the torch. Or had it been knocked out of her hand? Priscilla had to find it. She knelt and with both hands searched the floor. It was hard, cold, gritty, scratchy. And then she touched something. The torch! She clasped both hands around it and stood up. "I've found the torch, Gwen." She heard a thud.

"I have the torch, Gwen. How do you turn it on?"

There was no answer. "Gwen. Gwen!"

She fiddled with the light using both hands. Her fingers explored the surface and eagerly sought any protuberance that could be the switch. There was a bulge on the plastic shell. The switch. She tried to move it back, front, sideways, and finally something happened. Somehow it turned on. The light cut through the darkness and focused ahead of her. Where was Gwen? Without thinking she swung the light around to the floor. There was a clump a few feet away from her. Instantly she recognized it as Gwen. And beside her was something else, something turned over with thin legs, wooden, a stool. Gwen had tripped over a darn stool.

Was she hurt? No, you fool, probably just passed out. Get a hold of yourself, girl. You're in a dark cellar and your companion has tripped and perhaps hurt herself and needs help. Give her some help, will you? Priscilla knelt down and rested the torch on the floor aimed toward Gwen. She felt Gwen's face and hands and gently massaged them. She could feel a stirring in the collapsed body.

"Oh, my leg!" said Gwen in a dazed moaning voice. "What hit my leg?" Then she lost consciousness again.

Priscilla picked up the torch again and looked up and around. The beam shone partly on Gwen's face and partly beyond her. The light penetrated the darkness in one of the side rooms, the massive wooden door being slightly ajar. In the dim illumination something inside that room was leering at her! It looked familiar! She aimed the torch higher to focus directly on the ghastly apparition.

Hideously, maliciously, murderously, the face was staring at her, and Priscilla half wanted to scream and half wanted to indulge in the luxury of joining Gwen and passing out, too. What did it want of her? It was almost bent sideways, as if trying to see her better. Involuntarily she thrust her face upward to stare back at the leer that was confronting her.

Again she heard a moaning, louder now, more real than before. Something clutched at her. She held her breath and pressed her lips tightly together to keep from screaming. She commanded herself to take rational stock of the situation, and in an instant she knew it was Gwen reaching for her, trying to speak again. She lifted Gwen's head, and Gwen briefly smiled at her.

"Oh, my leg, is it going to be sore! Where are we? Priscilla, is that you? Are we still in the cellar? What happened to me?"

Priscilla looked at her and then at the contorted face grimacing aslant some twenty feet away inside that horrible room, a face she now recognized. No, it was not a grimace, it was a tightly bound gag of white cloth.

"It's all right, Gwen. That is, we're all right, Gwen. Get yourself together. Can you be brave?"

"If you say so."

"Don't scream. Whatever you do, don't scream. Please don't scream. I don't think I could take it. But there's a dead man hanging in that room. I think we'd better go upstairs and get some help. We've found Giles Bacon."

Chapter *SIX*

"You and Joanna were right about Giles," Mort said to Priscilla when she telephoned to tell him about Bacon, "but are you sure you're not hurt?

"I'm all right, Jack," she said, smiling to herself for reassurance.

"How about Gwen?"

"Whole and sassy, except for a bruised shinbone."

"I'm glad it's nothing serious. By the way, Trevor Tremaine came through with the injunction, I'm free to leave The Deaconry, and will be over as soon as I can find another car."

Priscilla and Gwen were sitting in the banqueting hall, each silent with her own thoughts. As Mort came in, Priscilla jumped up to greet him. He put his arm around her, hugged her tightly, and stroked her shoulder. They strolled outside arm in arm as Priscilla told him all that had happened to her.

"Possible suicide?" asked Mort.

"With his arms and legs tied?" she responded.

"Ahh. You'd better tell me again in more detail. Start from the beginning, when you and Gwen first descended the stairs."

Everyone at the manor was in a state of shock. Actors, technicians, and spectators stood in small groups buzzing with hushed conversation. Magnus Mandeville nodded perfunctorily to Mort and said, "Do you know what this is costing me in terms of money and lost production?" The police, including some Scene-of-Crime Officers, were scattered over the premises.

Penhaligon arrived and Mort and Priscilla followed him into the hall. He was not happy. More to himself than to others, he commented, "It never seems to end, does it?" Then he learned the body had been moved. "This can't be. Who gave orders to move the bloody body?"

Magnus said, "After we cut him down, we thought there might be a slight chance he was still alive. So we moved him to see better."

Penhaligon turned to Priscilla. "As a policewoman, couldn't you have stopped them?"

Priscilla turned open palms to him. "What jurisdiction do I have here? After I showed them the body, two men cut it down and started carrying it away before I could say anything."

Actually, she thought, Magnus had been right. As long as there had been even the most remote possibility that Bacon had any life left in him, cutting him down to see was the right thing to do. But Magnus shouldn't have moved him out of that room, said the police officer in her. She hoped she'd never get more eager to solve a murder than prevent one.

Penhaligon went to examine the corpse, which had been placed in the butler's pantry, and after a few minutes returned to the hall. Asking Gwen to follow him, he took her into a small drawing room and closed the door. Twenty minutes later Gwen re-entered the hall and told Priscilla that she was next. Leaving Mort, Priscilla entered the drawing room and found Penhaligon in a more composed frame of mind sitting backwards on an armless chair. He motioned her to be seated. A plain-clothes man, introduced as Sergeant Arundel, was poised to take notes.

"You're a professional, aren't you?" said the inspector, "It would be gratifying if you could tell me something coherent about discovering the body. And I'd prefer not to hear anything about a Gray Lady."

"Did Gwen say she had seen a Gray Lady?"

"She said it must have been the Gray Lady, but you and I know that's silly, don't we? Please tell me your version."

Priscilla gave him a detailed account of her observations.

"You say you were not completely surprised?"

She quickly debated with herself as to how frank and expansive she should be in her answers to his questions. It was an interesting situation being on the witness side of a murder investigation, and she recalled people she had questioned who swore to facts which turned out not to be facts, who stupidly or intentionally evaded the real meaning of her questions, or who insisted on playing Sherlock Holmes and acting as if she were Inspector Lestrade. How she would have loved to have had witnesses trained to make accurate observations, volunteering nothing but pertinent facts, and giving answers precisely in accordance with the meaning of a question.

But would her frankness be appreciated by this impassive policeman? He had not exactly been rude to her earlier, but he certainly seemed to scoff at the idea of her being capable of handling murder investigations—or was she being too sensitive? She decided to give him the benefit of the doubt. "Well," she said in her friendliest voice, "when Giles was first missing, Joanna Gifford seemed worried sick over him. I had a bit more than intuition to go on because I've questioned many concerned women about missing husbands and sweethearts. Experience told me Joanna suspected that Giles might have met with foul play."

"I'll have to be the judge of that when I talk to Joanna."

Priscilla winced inside, but managed to keep the smile on her face.

"Now for motive, do you have any ideas?" he asked. "Is there a sex angle? a money angle? Who stood to gain by his death? What about Gwen Trelawney's story of Giles having had an affair with Joanna?"

Priscilla said, "I've already told you I know next to nothing about Giles Bacon. But Joanna acted as if she were more concerned about him than as just a writer, more as if they were or had been lovers."

"You were at the pub Monday night when he was spending money like a sailor?"

"I knew he was in the pub, but had no idea how he was spending his money."

"Well, again," said the inspector, "this comes from Gwen. It seems that Giles was not the generous type, but Monday night he started buying drinks for everyone. Gwen asked him when he had become the big spender, and he replied that he was about to inherit a lot of money. But you know nothing about that?"

Well, Priscilla thought, at least Penhaligon was volunteering something, but obviously he was not going to take this foreign female detective into his confidence and was not looking for any active assistance—which was what she wanted to give him. His concern for her was as a straight witness, just the facts, ma'am, nothing more than the plain, unvarnished facts. Priscilla let her smile slide into a slight frown and she shook her head in answer to his last question.

Penhaligon called to a police constable outside the door and told him to let Dr. Sinclair come in. Mort entered and again rushed quickly to Priscilla, anxiety showing in his face.

"I'm okay, dear," she said, resting her head against him."

"Knowing your reputation as a criminologist, Dr. Sinclair," said Penhaligon, "I'm going to put you in the picture as far as Bacon is concerned. It seems that Bacon was not a rich man. He wrote a series of historical novels some fifteen years ago which were moderately successful. Then it seems he couldn't write, or at least sell, any more, and he was working for an advertising agency when the television company decided to dramatise the Urquhart series. Even that didn't mean much money, because his contract with his old publisher had sold them all the rights in return for a lump sum. Thus he received nothing from the television sale or even from reprintings generated by renewed interest in his old works. His only benefit was a small sum as technical adviser during the television filming."

"But his old publisher gets a goodly amount," said Mort.

"The successor to the old publisher," said Penhaligon. "It seems the company was bought out by a syndicate that owns many literary and artistic companies. The interesting—and intriguing—fact is that the syndicate is mainly owned by Magnus Mandeville."

"That," said Mort, "sounds like a sure formula for success. Mandeville as television producer buys a literary property which enriches a company owned by Mandeville as syndicate head."

"But as far as this case is concerned," said Priscilla, "Giles would have seemed to have motive to hate or be envious of Magnus, yet Giles is the murdered one."

"We'll want to look thoroughly into the activities and movements of Mr. Mandeville in due time, won't we?" said the inspector. "Giles was obviously antagonistic toward him and that would have bred a reaction."

Mort said, "Giles told us Mandeville didn't like him and he reacted by disliking Mandeville."

"There, that's the sort of information we need, isn't it, Dr. Sinclair?" said Penhaligon. "Can you go into more detail?"

Mort repeated what Bacon had told him about Mandeville.

Priscilla, feeling left out of the conversation, opened her handbag and nonchalantly began examining her face in a mirror.

"Good," said Penhaligon, "this seems to establish that mutually bad feelings existed between the two of them. Now, tell me, when did you two last see Giles's car?"

Mort looked to Priscilla, who put down her mirror and gave a sign that she would answer for the two of them. Turning to Penhaligon she said, "When we first arrived in Treleggan his Volkswagen was in the middle of our driveway blocking us. We didn't notice when we went to the pub that night, but it definitely was not there the next time I looked, sometime Tuesday morning."

"Is that right, Dr. Sinclair?" Penhaligon asked.

Mort nodded his head in affirmation.

"I gather Giles's car is missing," said Priscilla.

"No, it's not, Sergeant Booth," said Penhaligon, "We know where it is now, all right. In the car park outside of here. It looks as if Giles disappeared for two days and then drove over here last night, but, according to my men, no one recalls seeing him."

Priscilla wrinkled up her face in thought. "I hope you don't mind my asking, Inspector Penhaligon, but do you think the person who murdered Giles is the same one who murdered Sylvia?"

Penhaligon allowed a slight, tolerant smile to appear on his lips. "If you overstep your bounds, I'll let you know, won't I?" The look he gave her said she had not done so yet and he hoped she would not in future. "To answer your question, it's too early to make a judgment. I've hardly begun the investigation into Giles's death and still have a lot of people to question." Turning to Mort again, he said, "I will say this, though, we have a witness who saw Mrs. Cawthorne on the path the day she died, and it seems she was not alone."

"Sylvia not alone?" said Priscilla. "Who was she with?"

"That is what I'd very much like to know."

"But your witness saw someone," said Priscilla. "Who is the witness?"

Penhaligon's expression turned blank, as if he were debating with himself whether he should answer her question. Finally he said, "A superannuated chef who lives at the housing estate on the other side of Pendorth. While walking from Pendorth he passed Mrs. Cawthorne as he neared Treleggan."

"You'll give us the details, of course, Inspector," Mort said, smiling in a confident way as Penhaligon hesitated.

The inspector half-smiled back. "Well, I suppose there's no harm in it. Our witness, Mr. Morgan, came around the bend of a hill and saw just a few yards away two people walking toward him. Mr. Morgan identified Mrs. Cawthorne, who was in front, from a photograph. The other person, a man, seemed deliberately to let himself get behind Mrs. Cawthorne and was partly hidden from view. It seems he had the hood of his anorak up and he turned his head away and put a hand to his face as Mr. Morgan passed. Morgan didn't think anything of it at the time. But he remembered it clearly when we questioned him yesterday. He couldn't describe the face, but he gave us a good description of the clothing, bright blue trousers and a yellow anorak."

"He didn't note anything at all about the face?" asked Priscilla. "But if he came on them suddenly, he must have had a quick view of the man before he turned away."

She felt Mort grip her hand tightly and realized he was warning her that she was being too persistent. Not feeling she was doing anything wrong, she made a mental note to discuss it with him later.

Mort said in a quiet, unhurried voice, "We're sure the thought has already occurred to you, Inspector."

"Well, yes, but remember his hood was up, wasn't it? Mr. Morgan was able to state that the man was clean-shaven and seemed to be of British origin, that is, ethnically."

Priscilla asked, "Tall, short, fat, bow-legged?"

Mort quickly intervened. "We don't mean to be interrogating you, Inspector. You've already been most kind in sharing your information with us."

"Quite, I understand. Our witness claims he was just average, meaning not tall, not short, not fat, not thin. Our witness seems to have been more observant of clothes."

"But didn't he observe anything about the way they were behaving?" said Priscilla. "Did they seem friendly? After all, he had to have seen Sylvia's face—did she seem worried or upset in any way?"

"You're rather determined, Sergeant Booth, aren't you?"

"I'm concerned, Inspector Penhaligon. Sylvia was my cousin, and like it or not we're involved."

"Our witness could only say that Mrs. Cawthorne was talking to her companion, she looked happy, and was even laughing a little. There's nothing more."

"Did your witness describe Sylvia?"

"Eh, what?"

"Physically. Was she tall, short, fat, bow-legged?"

"You seem to have put your finger on it, Sergeant Booth, haven't you?" Penhaligon nodded his head appreciatively. "He described her also as average in height and everything else."

"I'd hardly call a woman five-feet-ten average in height."

"Yes, that is a bit of a problem, isn't it? Our witness does not seem to excel in matters of observation."

"Anyway, this companion would seem to be a prime suspect," said Priscilla.

"He *is* a prime suspect, Sergeant Booth." Inspector Penhaligon got on his feet. "However, I still have questions to ask others in connexion with the death of Giles Bacon, and you must be leaving, mustn't you?" He hesitated, then said, "Like you, Sergeant Booth, I'm assuming for the present that both Sylvia and Giles were murdered by the same person, but we can't say for certain yet?"

As Mort and Priscilla reached the door, Penhaligon stopped them abruptly. "Oh, by the way, Sergeant Booth, have you by chance come across any diamond necklaces in your flat?"

"Diamond necklaces?"

"Expensive diamond necklaces," said Penhaligon. "Well, let's say just one expensive diamond necklace, one that belonged to Mrs. Cawthorne."

"No," said Priscilla. "Is one missing?"

"It seems that Dr. Cawthorne believes so. He reported to the London police that his late wife's diamond necklace, worth at least £50,000, was missing. He seems to think it was stolen."

Mort's face became animated. "Are you saying that Sylvia might have left a diamond necklace in her Treleggan house?"

"That would be one possibility, wouldn't it?"

Priscilla asked, "Are you acquainted with the terms of Mrs. Cawthorne's will?"

"If I were a competent investigator, I'd have to be, wouldn't I?"

"You would of course know the details of the will," said Mort. "Thus you're aware that if Mrs. Cawthorne left her necklace in the Treleggan house, it's part of her legacy to Sergeant Booth. I think the wording of the will was to the effect that Priscilla Booth was to inherit the house in Cornwall and all its contents without exception."

"Yes," Penhaligon said, nodding his head in affirmation, "I'm well aware of the fact. And Dr. Cawthorne, as you can see, has been well aware of the fact, too. On your way out, would you please ask Mr. Mandeville to come in. Thank you."

*　　　*　　　*　　　*　　　*　　　*

As they walked into the courtyard, Mort saw Priscilla kick a stone out of the way and mutter something under her breath.

"Were you swearing, young lady?" he said, knowing how she had been conditioned by her upbringing to eschew profanity, and deciding that making light of it might be his best way of handling her present mood.

"Not swearing," she replied. "Just a few 'drats' and 'darns.' But if anything could make me take up swearing it would be that smug, conceited, male chauvinist.... Well, I don't like to refer to police officers as pigs, but if there ever was a police pig, he's it."

"Now, now, temper, my dear Priscilla." He hooked his arm in hers and reached across with his other hand to gently massage her fingers. The trouble was that he could see both points of view. She was too experienced as a police detective to play the part of a simple witness in a murder investigation, but the inspector was not going to admit her to a level of equality. And, of course, it didn't help that he'd been impressed with Mort's lectures on criminology and looked upon Mort more as a privileged specialist. What Priscilla was forgetting was that she, too, must in her investigations in Bay City make decisions, conscious or not, on trusting some people more than others. Looking at the angry expression on her face, Mort couldn't make up his mind as to whether she was really irate or just playing with him, but with her next question he became convinced it was the former.

"And what's this business of me coming on too strong, I'd like to know?"

"I didn't say that."

"You were thinking it, don't lie to me, Mort. It's all right for you. All you have to do is open your mouth like a baby bird and he puts food in it. But he treats me like an ugly duckling."

"When it comes right down to it, neither of us has any right to expect to be treated as participants in this investigation, other than to answer questions on what we saw and heard."

They were approaching the car park and began walking in the direction of Mort's Ford Fiesta, which was closer than the Sierra. "How'd you get another car so quickly?" she said.

"Highway robbery."

"You don't mean you stole it?"

"I mean I paid a king's ransom to rent it from the only car rental place in Treleggan, the petrol station, where they refused to let it go for anything less than a week."

"Well, we can probably use two cars, especially if we continue making separate trips. This wasn't the way I had it in mind when I invited you here."

"Nor what I had in mind. Anyway, did you get the part?"

She didn't answer at first, but gradually she relaxed her grimace, her eyes losing their fury and even lighting up a bit, and then, as if involuntarily, a smile came to her. She couldn't hold back the laughter any longer and her good humour was completely restored by the time she said, "You suspected Magnus was going to make me some kind of terrific offer?"

"Or two."

"So far only one, but, you're right, there's a gleam in his eye. As to the first, he wants Gwen and me to get dressed up in costumes and play non-speaking roles in a ball-room scene."

"Tempting?"

"Mighty tempting, yes. But am I going to accept it?—reluctantly no. One, I think the price might be too high, and two, after coming across Giles's body like that, I just wouldn't feel right. Maybe I'm wrong, but that's me. It will be interesting to see what Gwen decides. On the one hand I think she'd normally give her eye-teeth for a chance like this, but on the other, in the cellar she acted as if she were one awfully scared girl—or was it just that, good acting? Now that you've diverted me into forgiving you, love, what'll we do next?"

"Well, as I said, neither of us has any right to be investigators in these murder cases. But there is a matter at hand that could rightfully occupy our attention."

"And that is?"

"Let's think about a diamond necklace worth more than £50,000, which may or may not be a part of all the paraphernalia you inherit along with a house."

Recognition suddenly came over her. "I'd forgotten about that! And perhaps we might think also about a Dr. Cawthorne who abruptly changes his mind and wants me out of my flat instantly—what do you make of that?"

"Undoubtedly a coincidence."

"Undoubtedly," said Priscilla, eyes glimmering. She paused a second, then suggested, "Race you to the flat, darling?"

"For once, my dear," he said in a deceptively casual tone, quickening his step as he spoke, "I'll take you up on that."

Chapter *SEVEN*

"All right," said Mort, closing the chiffonnier drawer in the bedroom. "It's not in any obvious place."

The mattress was standing on end near the window, and Priscilla was just closing the wardrobe door. They had been searching the house for several hours, but to no avail.

On the floor immediately above they heard footsteps.

"Think Dr. Cawthorne's doing the same thing?" said Priscilla.

"I doubt it. He's had a chance to go over that entire upstairs flat a dozen times since he's been here. And he's probably searched this one in our absence. He's probably in the same position we are, wondering what to do next. Here, help me move the mattress back."

"Then he might have found it."

"A possibility of course. But the police had already searched twice. Let's have tea and do some thinking." They went into the kitchen.

They sat in silence for a while as they sipped from their cups. Priscilla was the first to speak again. "Well, lover, I'm waiting to be led." There was a youthful eagerness about her that Mort at times found delightful and at other times somewhat daunting. She had pulled one leg up under her and was leaning across the table supported by her elbows to look into his eyes with all the admiration that a religious convert might bestow on a guru.

"First," said Mort, helping himself to a biscuit, "we don't know for a fact that the necklace is here. We're concerned with it only if it's in this house."

Priscilla suddenly became pensive and rested her chin on the back of her hand. "You know, Mort, I don't know if I'd want that necklace anyway."

"You can always donate it to your favourite charity. Or give it to Cawthorne if you want."

"Oh, no, I don't think I'd go that far."

"However, it's not the necklace *per se*; it's what the possibility of it being in this house implies."

"Meaning?"

"If Sylvia hid that necklace in this house and made her will so emphatic about your inheriting anything located here, she had a reason for it. Think now, you found it strange that she'd give you the house in the first place, much less throw in an extremely valuable piece of jewellery. Why did she do it? This is far beyond the kind of generosity that you were talking about. Was Sylvia trying to keep as much as possible of her estate out of her husband's hands? With her parents dead and no brothers or sisters, she should have left everything of more than minor value to Dr. Cawthorne. Why didn't she? Let's try to get inside her mind. There must have been some reason that made sense, at least to her. You knew her well, think!"

Something dropped on the floor above them. Mort lowered his voice to a whisper. "Do you think he can hear us?"

"Perhaps," Priscilla whispered back. "I don't know if the acoustics have the same affect in reverse, but down here, you can hear even normal-volume voices from upstairs."

Mort refilled their cups and led the way to the living room, where he turned on the television. Spreading out their copy of the *Radio Times* television schedule on the table, he said, "Which programme shall we give him?"

"*The Brittas Empire*," said Priscilla, looking over his shoulder. "I remember in London he said he couldn't stand Gordon Brittas."

"*The Brittas Empire* it is then," said Mort. "I think the programme's hilarious, but I suppose Dr. Cawthorne and I don't have the same sense of humour. Now where were we?"

"You were telling me to make like IBM: Think! What am I supposed to think about?"

He wished she would stop looking at him as if he were a sex object; role-reversal was disconcerting. "Think about Sylvia," he said. "Say she did hide the necklace in this flat, why would she want to do something like that?"

"Oh, she was always hiding things." Priscilla spoke with such spontaneity that she had obviously given her answer no thought. "At school we used to make a game of it."

"Where?" said Mort, suddenly demanding her attention with flashing eyes and imperative tone. "Where was Sylvia always hiding things?"

"That's it, isn't it? That has to be it! Oh, we had a lot of favourite little places where we'd hide notes for each other."

"Such as?"

"Well, such as taping notes on the bottom of a lamp."

"Have you checked the lamps in this place?"

"No, silly. We're not looking for a note, and you couldn't tape a diamond necklace on the bottom of a lamp."

"But if a lamp happened to be hollow...."

"You're right," said Priscilla, jumping up from her chair. "It can't hurt to try. But keep the television on so Mr. Nosey upstairs can't hear us. Because if we don't find anything here, we might want to make a clandestine entry and check out the lamps upstairs. After all, I'm supposed to inherit the whole house, and he's a squatter as far as I'm concerned."

They went to the only lamp in the living room, a Chinese ceramic one, and Mort held it up while Priscilla examined the base. Nothing there. He moved his fingers over the bottom to be thorough. There was a small hole in the centre that had obviously resulted from the moulding process. He shook the lamp and listened for any sound of a loose object. Priscilla stuck her index finger in and moved it around. Nothing.

They moved on to the bedroom. The bottom of the brass facsimile paraffin lantern was glued to a felt pad, and as Mort turned the lamp over to inspect the pad, Priscilla yelled in delight. "It's there, Mort, it's there!"

"Keep your voice down." He carefully set the lamp on its side on the bed and they examined the bottom. The felt pad had a rectangle cut out of the centre, inside which were some folded pieces of paper attached by transparent tape.

Priscilla gingerly removed the paper. "Let's see what we have here," she said. "Better, let's go in with the television."

Now even Mort's nerve ends tingled with anticipation. Priscilla, tightly clutching her treasure, sat on the sofa with Mort huddled closely beside her. She carefully unfolded the paper to open a two-page letter in small cramped handwriting, which she instantly identified as Sylvia's. Holding it jointly, she and Mort read it in silence:

> "Dearest Priscilla:
> "I write this because there have been attempts on my life and I'm afraid I'm going out of my mind. About a month ago someone tried to push me in front of a train in the London Underground. I and the few people I told at the time thought it was an accident and after a while I forgot about it, except that it made me realize I should have a will.
> "About a week later in London a car tried to ram me into a wall. I threw myself behind a tree and hurt myself badly, but saved my life. Accident again? When I told Frank, he laughed, said I was getting accident prone, and cautioned me to be more careful. I came to Treleggan to get away, but my attacker followed me here. I used to go walking daily usually by myself but one day when I was below the cliffs,

suddenly an avalanche of huge stones came tumbling down toward me. Fortunately there was a cave close by and I ran in just before the rocks hit.

"Now I was really frightened. Frank had been telling me that I was getting paranoid, and, truthfully, I didn't know if he was right or not. I was even afraid that Frank could have me put in an asylum if I behaved too strangely. Out of desperation I told two others about these incidents, but they too just laughed at me. Then I thought of you. You had been my best friend and you were a policewoman. I wrote you a letter but was afraid to mail it. Then I decided to write you again, but hide the letter so you would find it only if something happened to me. At least my death would be investigated.

"Yesterday I changed my will and gave you the house, thinking you would get bored long before thirty days and start remembering some of the things we used to do. I knew you'd find this letter if I put it under the lamp. I'm suspicious of everyone. Frank, Charles, Tony, Giles, Robin, Gwen, Winifred, Elspeth, even Joanna, I suppose I've hurt each one of them, but not in any way that should make them want to kill me. I know that God will forgive me for my sins, why can't they? I only trust Magnus because he has no reason to kill me, yet I dare not confide in him for fear he, too, will think I'm crazy. You won't laugh, my dearest Priscilla, because you will find this letter only after my enemy has succeeded. We did have fun together, didn't we?

Lovingly,

Sylvia"

* * * * * *

"Just the sort of lead we need, isn't it?" Inspector Penhaligon said with a guffaw of satisfaction the next morning. He looked tired. "I'd prefer not to have others know about this letter. You will cooperate, won't you?" He looked at the letter again. "I'll have to keep this, you know."

"Of course," said Mort, who had stopped on the way to the inspector's office to make a photocopy. "One thing emerging from the letter is that apparently Sylvia didn't intend to give Priscilla her diamond necklace. Otherwise she would have mentioned it."

"She could have thought about the necklace after she wrote the letter," said Priscilla.

"One thing is certain," said the inspector. "We've put out a description and if that necklace turns up anywhere we'll know about it. It could have been nicked from the house by the killer. Well, I needn't detain you two any longer."

"We'll say goodbye then," said Priscilla, making no effort to leave. "Oh, by the way, have you learned anything new?"

The inspector gave her a squinted look. "We have various leads the full significance of which has not been determined yet and we are of course making every effort to follow them up."

"Oh," said Priscilla. She smiled coyly. "I'm not a newspaper reporter, you know."

"I am quite aware of that fact, Sergeant Booth."

Still smiling, she asked, "Do you have an inventory of what was found on Giles Bacon's body?"

Penhaligon looked up sharply. "Why?"

"Since he was living in my flat, I could possibly make a connexion between his possessions and anything that belonged to the flat."

It was weak, but it worked. With reluctance, Penhaligon riffled through a file on his desk and produced a one-page inventory for her to see. Priscilla very carefully looked it over, passed it to Mort, then re-studied it herself. "Hmm," she said, handing it back to the inspector, "nothing special here."

"One would hardly have thought so," he said.

Mort took Priscilla gently by the arm, moved her to one side, and addressed himself to Penhaligon. "Mind if I ask a question? About when was Giles killed?"

Penhaligon looked up wearily and said, "Probably sometime between midnight and two o'clock Thursday morning. That's going mainly by body temperature and rigor mortis, taking into account the coolness of the cellar. We also have an analysis of stomach contents—he'd had a meal of fish and chips and beer—but, as you both know, stomach contents are vastly overrated as a means of determining time of death."

Mort agreed. "It's a popular, but untrue myth."

"But the last meal still can be important," said Priscilla. "You're checking...."

"Thank you for enlightening me, Sergeant Booth," said Penhaligon, looking more impatient with each question. "It would seem to be prudent to check places within a broad area where fish and chips are sold, wouldn't it? As it happens, we are also checking a few other things, but now if you'll excuse me."

"We'd better be on our way," said Mort.

"Thank you for your cooperation, Dr. Sinclair," said the inspector. "You, too, Sergeant Booth."

*   *   *   *   *   *

Priscilla drove the car back as if it were a hydrofoil, barely touching the road.

"Is there a need to live so dangerously?" said Mort.

"'Thank you for your cooperation, Dr. Sinclair,'" she repeated loudly. "'You, too, Sergeant Booth.' The cooperation's all one way, from us to him. He wouldn't give us the time of day. After all, how would he like it if he were in America and his cousin were murdered and he went to the police expecting to learn something from them?"

"You mean he'd get more cooperation there, such as from Captain Bumpus?"

"Well, I didn't mean Bumpus, of course." She paused, then said, "But he seems to like you, darling." Another pause, then in a provocatively sweet voice, "You don't think he has a crush on you, do you?"

"Don't be ridiculous," said Mort, his face reddening. "I think it's all in how you handle him. Perhaps he's a little wary of you as a fellow police officer, a little resentful over your way of insinuating yourself as an equal in the case."

"I do no such thing!"

"Well, in any event, perhaps I had better do the talking when we're with Penhaligon from now on."

"Welcome to him, Dr. Sinclair!" For emphasis she pushed her foot hard on the accelerator-pedal.

A car approached at equal speed, and then was behind them before they realized it. "Did you see that car?" said Mort, wiping his brow.

"Only in the rear-view mirror. Good thing for him the road widened at that spot."

"All right, let's take it a little easy now. How can we even think when you're driving like this? Do you want to discuss the case or not?"

Discussing the case was probably the only thing that would induce Priscilla to calm down. "Okay," she said softly, and the car slowed down accordingly. "What do we have?"

"Well, we now know that Sylvia felt a lot of people had reason to be 'displeased' with her. And of course what might cause displeasure in some people could cause hatred in others. In other words, we have an abundance of suspects. We can eliminate Giles now, but I think we should add Magnus Mandeville, in spite of Sylvia's apparent trust in him. That gives us nine people, a lot on the one hand, yet if we could start a process of elimination…."

"You sound as if we're actively pursuing this case," said Priscilla. "Are we?"

"Well, naturally we want to see it solved. If you mean are we going to start a counter investigation in competition with Inspector Penhaligon?—I don't think so. We have no authority, no mandate, and really no reason, considering that the police are competent and doing all they can. I think we could safety go home and feel that ultimately justice will prevail. The British police are neither stupid nor easily diverted."

"Oh, you're probably right, darling. I'm sorry I lost my temper. Forgive me?"

"Nothing to forgive, dear," he said. "Now what do you make of it?"

"The same thing you do, but haven't said. You've left out a few things. Either you're slipping or you're testing me."

"What have I left out?" Mort asked.

"One, the person seen with Sylvia on the cliffs was a man. That man did not report after her death that he had been with her close to the time she was killed. Ergo, either that man is afraid to report it, or, more likely, he is the killer. That would seem to eliminate the four females from our suspects. Two, whoever tried three times unsuccessfully to kill her was in both London and Treleggan and thus our killer most likely has the opportunity to go back and forth without looking suspicious. Magnus Mandeville is one of several who meet that criterion; in fact, he had to go back to London just this week. Three, Sylvia said she had confided in two people, but they just laughed at her. One could have been the murderer, but unless the two were in league with each other, one of them should have mentioned her prior suspicions to the police, but hasn't done so."

"Very good, except for the last. We don't know that one of them hasn't mentioned it to the police. Again, this is why we'd be so handicapped in this case—we'd be blindfoldedly trying to get ahead of the police, but they have all the authority."

On arriving at The Deaconry, they found two pieces of mail waiting for them. The thicker package contained research papers Mort had requested from a colleague in Oxford. The other was a letter for Sylvia. "What should we do with this?" he asked Priscilla, holding the envelope up for her to see.

Her hand swooped to relieve him of the object in question and she said, as her fingers quickly ripped open the flap, "Well, we won't be in a position to know until we see what's inside, will we?" She impatiently pulled out a single-page letter.

"It's from a firm of private enquiry agents," she said. "Messrs. Taywick and Runn apologize for delaying so long before responding to Mrs. Cawthorne's letter, but it had been inadvertently misplaced. They regret they would not be able anyway to assist her and suggest she contact some other agency. Well, what do you make of that?"

"Hmm, looks interesting," said Mort.

"So where do we go from here?" she said.

"We can wait until tomorrow to give Penhaligon this new little tit-bit—we probably gave him enough for one day. In the meantime, let's take it easy for the rest of the day. I'd just as soon do nothing but read and study and go to bed early."

"Oh, Mort, sometimes you make me so mad. Don't you have any curiosity?"

"Well, what would you suggest?"

She smiled. "Call up that detective agency and ask them what Sylvia wanted."

"Oh, sure. They're regulated by the authorities but they're going to answer questions from strangers about a woman who just happened to get murdered after she wrote them and they won't tell the police about our inquiry?"

She leaned back and lowered her eyes. "Oh, well, if you put it that way. But don't dig in too comfortably, darling. We have a dinner invitation tonight—at the Fitzpens—remember?"

Chapter *EIGHT*

Charles and Elspeth Fitzpen lived a little south of Treleggan in a large early Georgian house facing a secluded beach and the sea. It was close enough, Priscilla told Mort, to walk during the day if one wore rubber Wellingtons and were otherwise prepared for crossing pasture, rocks, sand flats, and sometimes a lot of mud, but usually it was better to drive around the long way. So they drove.

Helping Priscilla out of the car, Mort gave her hand a soft squeeze and said, "I suppose Charles will be dressed for dinner."

"Charles and Elspeth like formality," said Priscilla, "but he's also very considerate. He probably feels—correctly—that you didn't pack a tuxedo, and I suspect he'll be wearing a business suit like you."

Charles greeted them in a dark blue business suit at the entrance and ushered them through the reception hall into a drawing room that was well furnished with antiques, mostly from the eighteenth century. Their host explained that they were waiting for two other guests, Tony and Gwen Trelawney, and he no sooner poured the sherry than the Trelawneys arrived. Like Mort and Charles, Tony wore a blue suit, while the women showed more variety, Priscilla in a royal blue cocktail dress which set off her eyes, Gwen in a short form-revealing red jersey dress, and Elspeth in a silver lamé evening gown.

The dining room was formal with a table seating at least ten people, though set for only six tonight. Mort sat on Elspeth's right, and Priscilla on Charles's right. A maid wearing a white starched apron brought in the food.

"The house has been in the family for many generations," Charles told Mort, "though I had to do a lot of restoration. Priscilla's grandmother lived here as a young girl."

Mort, naturally interested in the family genealogy, asked the appropriate questions, but Charles was not a genealogist and deferred to Priscilla for answers.

Priscilla laughed. "I know I'm going to bore you all except Mort, so I'll try to keep it short." She proceeded to take the Fitzpen family back to the sixteenth century.

"I descend from Priscilla's grandmother's older brother, who was my great grandfather," said Charles.

Gwen resounded with ebullient laughter. "I descend from my mother, Winifred, but I don't think even she knows who my father was. Mum is such a dear. She has the kindest heart and never could say no to anyone, except when it comes to business. She remembers that her parents were Lewis and Mary Redruth and they came to Treleggan from Camborne, but that's all. Short genealogy, wouldn't you say?"

Elspeth frowned and began ringing a small silver bell. The maid came in bearing the next course, tournedos Rossini.

Mort covertly watched his hostess and tried to stereotype her. She had all the makings of a high-born bitch, being prissy, overbearing, snobbish, and intolerant of others. Yet she seemed also, at least in her less guarded moments, to have a look of kindness about her. She was, he felt, a woman whose main offence was in belonging to a different age, one who found herself confused, probably frightened, at the rapid changes which had taken place in Britain and the world during her relatively short span of years on earth. Moreover, Mort sensed in the way she looked at her husband, the way she joked with him, and the way she reached to touch him, that she seemed genuinely to love him. Charles and Elspeth were very much in love with each other, and Mort knew that could make up for a lot of things. He found it difficult not to be sympathetic toward lovers.

"I think you'll like the next wine," said Charles, as he began pouring from a bottle of Château Cheval Blanc 1986.

"Exquisite," said Mort, as he tasted the merrily glistening ruby red liquid. "I haven't had wine like this since I was on the diplomatic circuit some years back."

"I have a friend," said Charles, "who tells me what to buy as the vintners release it, then I lay it away until the time is right. Some might think it a bit early to be drinking this, but a fine St. Emilion can be drunk younger than a Médoc. Now we were talking about genealogy and that's an area where we'd all have to defer to Elspeth. Her line's in Debrett's."

"Oh," said Mort. "Sounds interesting."

"Her father, you see, was Squire Redvers and she was born at Penstead Manor. Her mother's grandfather was a baronet and so much of her genealogy is in the books."

"Were you born at Penstead Manor?" Mort asked Elspeth, immediately wishing that he had phrased it differently. Hadn't Charles just said that she was born at the manor?

"Yes," said Elspeth. "My brother, Baldwin Redvers, owns it now, but of course he's away."

"Her brother," said Charles, "is a career diplomat at the British Embassy in Athens. He has no need to live in the manor and it's rather an expensive white elephant. It was a godsend right after the old squire's death when the TV people wanted to rent it. I had to hurriedly make arrangements to remove some of the more valuable furniture to be sold at auction. Once the TV people leave, Baldwin is thinking of building a number of holiday chalets on the grounds for the summer tourists. It's a very lucrative business in Cornwall."

"Oh, no," said Priscilla, "he wouldn't do that!"

"Well, something has to be done," said Elspeth, looking tolerantly at Priscilla as she might when explaining new concepts to a child. "Paying the death duties took everything Baldwin had, and the estate costs more to keep up each year than it produces in income. It's either holiday chalets or selling it to a rock star or an oil-rich Arab. At least chalets can be torn down in the future, but if he sells, the manor's gone forever."

"Horrors!" said Priscilla. "That's what we call being between a rock and a hard place."

Mort turned his attention to Tony Trelawney sitting across from him. Rather handsome and pleasant, he was a biggish man, not exceptionally tall, but generous in size all over, giving an impression of indolence combined with self-indulgence. Mort had visited his shop several times and was impressed at the taste revealed in the displays of paperback books and audio tapes.

"I was noticing the books you sell at your store," Mort said to him. "Do you order the titles yourself, or do you get them from a distributor as a package?"

"Oh, I pick them from books I like," Tony said in a languorous tone.

"You're well read," said Mort, immediately hoping that he hadn't sounded too patronizing.

"Well, he should be," said Gwen. "He read for a degree at Oxford."

Mort looked at Tony. Tony smiled nervously and said, "Jesus College with Charles. I was a pass student." Then he made an apologetic little smile and added, "I didn't do much with my education."

"That's true," said Gwen. "All he learned in three years at Oxford was how to row a boat for Eights Week." She obviously intended the remark to sting, but Tony merely resumed his normal bland expression as if the words were as innocuous as "Please pass the potatoes."

Charles cleared his throat and said to Priscilla and Gwen, "You two ladies had a horrific experience yesterday."

Mort had expected the subject to come up earlier in the conversation. The Fitzpens had indeed been polite in not showing immediate curiosity about the finding of a corpse.

"Of course, I'm used to corpses in my profession," said Priscilla.

"I'm not," said Gwen, wrinkling her nose in disgust. "I've never discovered a corpse before. Could we just drop the subject until after dinner?"

"I'm sorry," said Charles. "I shouldn't have brought the matter up. You both have had a rather rum go of it."

Gwen's last remark had the effect of extinguishing much further conversation as the diners concentrated instead on the sherry trifle. When everyone had finished, Elspeth said they still observed the custom of the men and women separating after dinner, and perhaps it was time for the ladies to retire to the drawing room. Priscilla and Gwen followed her out.

Mort and Tony declined the cigars that Charles offered, but both accepted the vintage port. Mort sat back in his chair well out of the path of Charles's cigar smoke and relaxed. It was a good meal, good company, and the port was outstanding.

"Now I suppose it's all right to mention Giles," said Charles, as he looked from Mort to Tony.

Tony said, "Ahh, yes, I suppose so. Gwen's still very upset about yesterday. I'm sure you understand."

"Of course," said Charles. "Elspeth would be, too, had she been in that situation."

After Mort gave them the details of what he knew about Giles's death, Charles said, "I suppose that Priscilla as a police officer takes all this in her stride."

"Yes, to an extent," said Mort, "but it still affects her. Her mind just doesn't want to accept that Sylvia was murdered."

"Poor Sylvia," said Tony with a frown coming over his face, "my mind doesn't want to believe it, either."

"May I ask a personal question," said Mort. "I can't help but be curious as to why Sylvia put you both in her will for £500, and then took you out in the codicil. If I'm saying anything I shouldn't, just tell me and I'll be quiet."

Charles motioned to Tony, as if deferring to him to speak first, but Tony remained silent.

"Well for my part," said Charles, "I don't mind talking about it. Sylvia was a kind-hearted woman, but also a very lonely one. She was always wanting to give things to people. Elspeth and I were always receiving cards for all occasions from her, along with little presents, a box of chocolates, a bottle of Cognac, a pair of gloves—Sylvia was generous. I think she put me in her will to make a final present. Five hundred pounds is enough to make an impression and yet not an extremely extravagant bequest. It was a thoughtful gesture, and Sylvia was very thoughtful. Wouldn't you agree, Tony?"

There was a faint film of perspiration on Tony's brow and he wiped his hand across his forehead. "Oh, ah, yes, ah, I suppose so. Yes, Sylvia was always very generous and thoughtful."

"Frankly," said Charles, "it's easier trying to explain why she put us in than to say why she later took us out. Perhaps Tony can add to my thoughts on it, but, well, during the last few weeks of her life Sylvia was acting a bit strangely. It's rather delicate. I don't know quite how to say it." He seemed to be looking to Tony for help, but received none.

Charles looked so awkward as he talked that Mort wished he could prompt him or otherwise make it easier for him. He had just a suspicion of what Charles might be trying to say, but knew he could be wrong and so did not dare volunteer something which might not only be entirely mistaken, but also embarrassing.

Getting a little encouragement from his cigar, Charles said, "Well, Elspeth and I are very much in love and we're both very jealous of each other. I'm over explaining, I know, but I don't know how else to say it. I wouldn't have anything to do with any other woman and I suppose I had better say it straight out, Sylvia and I were never lovers. I was her cousin, her friend, her confidant, but we did not have intimate relations."

Tony coughed lightly, looked at his watch, and changed his position in his chair. "Do you suppose, ah, we should be joining the ladies?"

"Just a minute more, Tony," said Charles. "Well, I'll make it short and say that Sylvia was acting strangely and seemed not to trust me the way she used to, and I frankly think someone had been influencing her against me, as well as others, the others whom she dropped in the codicil, such as Tony."

"Ah, yes, that's probably it," said Tony. "You mean Magnus Mandeville, of course. Sylvia seemed, oh, ah, overawed at the glamour of the TV business." He stood up and led the way out of the dining room.

*   *   *   *   *   *

The ladies had been deeply involved in their own talk, Gwen finally deciding to discuss their discovery in the manor basement. Priscilla explained the details of finding Giles's body, and Gwen added a bit more to the explanation. They talked about the police interviews and then went on to other subjects. Somehow Sylvia's name could not help but come up.

"Sylvia was very generous," said Gwen.

"Perhaps too generous," added Elspeth.

"You mean she had lovers," said Gwen, thrusting her glance upward in a look of frankness. "I thought she was more or less discreet, except perhaps with Magnus."

"As long as she kept her hands off my husband," said Elspeth, "I didn't care, frankly."

"She and Charles were together a lot."

"They were cousins and good friends. But I was also Sylvia's friend and I saw her as much as Charles did."

"You mean there was never any opportunity for anything other than a platonic relationship between Charles and Sylvia?"

It was obvious to Priscilla that Gwen had turned the conversation to her liking and was not going to stop her jabbing.

"I mean," said Elspeth, "that I know my husband. I admit I'm a jealous woman, but I know Charles would never betray me. Other women might try, but in the end he'd be true."

"Suppose some woman succeeded?" said Gwen, with a merry twinkle in her eye.

Priscilla listened and was fascinated at hearing information usually obtainable only under cross-examination. It was apparent that an odd relationship existed between Elspeth and Gwen. Of course, they had in effect exchanged husbands and that was supposedly a tie between them, but there was something more. They could even have been sisters in a family of opposites. It was as if each perhaps secretly wished she could in some respects—certainly not all—be a bit more like the other. At any rate, the ties between the two women far transcended the words that passed between them.

Elspeth looked away from Priscilla and Gwen for a long time before answering Gwen's question and then said in a slow, even tone, "I'd slit her throat!"

"Oh," said Gwen, "I do believe you mean it!" She seemed delighted to have provoked such a strong response. This was a completely different Gwen from the one who had visited the cellar with Priscilla. It was as if the other one had been playing a role, but here Gwen could allow her real self to take over.

"And I suppose you'd do nothing if someone started playing around with Tony," said Elspeth, with a smug smile curving around the corners of her lips.

"When someone did," Gwen said, staring at Elspeth eye for eye, "I sent her a congratulatory card and wrote, 'Now you both owe me one.'"

"You would!" said Elspeth. "And what did **Sylvia** do when she received that pretty kettle of fine sentiments?"

As violently as the sudden change of pitch in Ravel's *Bolero*, the shift from the indefinite to a specific person rasped against Priscilla's nerve endings. She sat on the edge of her chair not daring to say anything for fear that she might break the mood of revelation that was permeating the room.

Gwen acted as if she were just continuing a normal talk. "Sylvia later said she couldn't imagine what I meant."

"And what did you do then?"

"I told her a joke," said Gwen. "Priscilla, did you ever hear the one about the Englishman and the Frenchman arguing over the meaning of *savoir-faire*?"

Priscilla shook her head. Elspeth looked as if she wished she could stop Gwen from continuing, but didn't know how.

"Well, one day in the pub an Englishman and a Frenchman were arguing about the meaning of *savoir-faire*. The Englishman said, 'If I came home and found you in bed with my wife, I would bow low and say, "Pray continue." Now that is *savoir faire*.' 'Oh, no, no, no,' said the Frenchman. 'Please allow me to enlighten you. If you came home and found me in bed with your wife, and if you bowed low and said, "Pray continue," now if I **did** continue, **that** would be *savoir faire*.'" Looking alternately at both other women, Gwen went on, "and at that point, I bowed low to Sylvia and said, 'Pray continue.'"

Priscilla laughed in spite of herself until she noticed how Elspeth, reminiscent of Queen Victoria, was staring unamused.

"It's time the men should be getting here," said Elspeth. "And your joke, Gwen, dear, frankly, is more the kind I would expect the men to be telling over their cigars and port."

*   *   *   *   *   *

When the men did join the ladies, it appeared all possible topics of conversation had been worn out. No one seemed to want to follow up on the various conversational gambits that one or the other would toss out and after a polite interval they decided by mutual agreement that it was time to end the evening.

As Mort and Priscilla reached their car, Charles, who had walked with them, said to Mort, "Could you call at my office tomorrow morning? It's Saturday, but I'll be there all day."

*   *   *   *   *   *

As they parked their car beside The Deaconry and got out, Mort and Priscilla heard footsteps coming up the darkened street. Priscilla grabbed Mort's hand as he stared in the direction of the sounds, his body and mind on total alert. The blackness was complete and he could make out nothing. The footsteps continued and became louder, closer.

"It's only me—Tony," said a voice. "If it's not too late could I come in with you and talk?"

They went inside and Mort and Priscilla waited patiently for Tony to begin.

"Well, ah, it's not as easy as I thought it would be. I was thinking to myself, you see, while driving back that I ought to explain, you know, about the conversation about Charles and me and Sylvia. You will excuse us, won't you, Priscilla?"

Priscilla was not sure if she was being asked to leave. She looked to Mort, and he motioned her to stay seated. To Tony she said, "You may say anything you wish in front of me. After all, my work in America has taught me discretion."

"Oh, ah, I didn't mean for you to leave. Do please stay. I meant I hope you'll pardon me for any, ah, er, indelicacy in what I have to say. You see the thing of it is that Charles was, I suppose, trying to be tactful and wanted to avoid saying that those people in Sylvia's will who were to receive £500, that is, Giles, Robin, and me, had been her lovers. All but Charles, and he's different. I mean Charles and Elspeth have a special relationship."

"We understand what you're saying," said Mort, adding to himself, but not why.

"Well, this is awkward, but I've told the police, and others know it, even Gwen, so I might as well tell you. When Sylvia first came to the village, she was, as we said, very lonely. She used to invite people to dinner and buy them drinks at the pub. She wanted to get people to like her. She had Gwen and me to dinner several times. One night when we were invited over, Gwen was sick, but insisted that I go to Sylvia's by myself. Well, there you have it, you see. We were alone, and I do have animal drives, I suppose you'd call it. One thing led to another, and we were in bed. And then we started meeting secretly."

"How long did this continue?" said Mort.

"Rather over two years, but she wasn't in the village all this time, just now and then. Sylvia apparently began, er, another affair in London with Giles Bacon, and that led to an affair with Robin Steele. When the television company came here, she was all engrossed with Robin, but she seemed not to want to tie herself emotionally to any one man. Even when an affair was ended, she always wanted to remain friends.

"You see," he continued, "in a moment of conscience I confessed everything to Gwen, and Gwen let Sylvia know that she knew. Thereafter Sylvia refused to have, ah, relations, that is, intimate relations with me. We remained good friends, but that was all."

Priscilla said, "You were disappointed when she terminated that part of your relationship?"

Tony had a puzzled look on his face as he glanced at his questioner, as if he were examining himself for an answer. "Yes, I suppose I was. But not to an extraordinary extent. You see, I try to live a simple life. I don't want to get caught up in all the complications and stresses that others seem to have. I didn't really pursue Sylvia. I suppose you could say that she pursued me. When she needed me, I was glad to be there. When she no longer needed me, at least in bed, I was willing to accept it. You see, I'm in love with my wife, and I don't go around looking for those things. It just happened. Yes, I suppose I was disappointed, but not angry, if that's what you mean."

"It all seems so strange," said Priscilla, "so unlike the Sylvia I knew."

"Well, I think I've said what I wanted to say," said Tony. "I wasn't trying to avoid mentioning my part in this, but I couldn't quite bring myself to talk about it in front of Charles, even though he obviously knows. So there you have it. I'd better be leaving. I told Gwen I'd just be a minute."

After Tony left, Mort and Priscilla compared notes on what had been discussed when the men and women separated after dinner.

"You know," said Priscilla, "I'm getting such a different picture of my dear departed cousin. It makes me feel that I never really knew her. And it's, well, just a little scary."

Mort said, "Yes, and I don't think we have the whole picture yet. Sylvia was obviously a many-faceted woman. But I'll tell you one thing, my sweet little angel."

"Yes, lover?"

"My appetite is getting whetted. I don't want to leave here until we get to the bottom of this whole thing."

"I just knew you'd get yourself involved if I gave you enough time," said Priscilla as she leaned over the back of Mort's chair to hug him. "Haven't I been good in not nagging? And now you're involved. So we're agreed? We're going to conduct our own investigation?"

"Well, I'm not sure that I'd call it our own investigation. Let's just say that while at all times behaving in a circumspect way, especially as regards local police authorities, we will pay more than ordinary attention to the exigencies of being personally assured that the murder of your cousin does not go unsolved."

"Right," said Priscilla. "We're going to start our own investigation. When?"

"Oh, I think we can wait until morning," he said with a grin.

Chapter *NINE*

"To make best use of our time," said Mort, over breakfast the next morning, "I suppose we should split up. Your cousin wants me to come to his office this morning and it will be interesting to hear what he has to say. Judging from last night, people around here don't seem to mind opening up in front of casual acquaintances."

"I noticed that when I was here before," said Priscilla. "I don't know what's happened to the much-storied British reserve, but I haven't found an abundance of it in Cornwall. Perhaps it's gone out with Dr. Bowdler morality, Agatha Christie sociology, and Oxbridge accents on BBC. Now, who do I tackle?"

For the first time that morning, Mort looked directly at his companion and suddenly became appreciative of the way she was dressed. Wasn't she looking very country-squire's-wife in her powder-blue cashmere sweater set and blue-and-gray plaid skirt? Somewhat distractedly he said, "Of course, there's Magnus Mandeville, not to mention Robin Steele. You said you decided not to accept Mandeville's offer of a bit part in the TV drama. How firm is that?"

"Not very. I could be swayed from it. I could tell Magnus this morning if you think it would help. He said they'd be filming today even though it's Saturday." Her eyes became lustrous as she added, "If he looks at me the way you're doing now, I shouldn't have too much trouble with him."

He quickly removed his eyes from her. "Hmm, well, being an extra would certainly give you a good excuse for gumshoeing around the manor. We can leave Joanna Gifford for the time being, though we certainly don't want to forget her completely."

"And the police?" said Priscilla. "Obviously you're the one to handle Penhaligon."

"By keeping him informed of what we find out, I'll have an excuse to discuss the case and hope that he'll reciprocate. But we don't want him to think we're conducting our own investigation. It must look as if we just come across information by chance, as has been the case up 'til now."

He paused to think. Half his mind was racing ahead to formulate a systematic way of having meaningful conversations with the various people they considered suspects, but the other half was still aware that the young woman sitting across from him was not only attractive and sexually desirable, but seemed to complement his temperament perfectly. Their conversation was smooth, effortless, and enjoyable, as if their minds were tuned to the same communications antenna. At times they seemed to anticipate the very words the other was about to say. This was the first time that they had shared a close domesticity and Mort was beginning to realize that Priscilla was one of the very few people in the world with whom he could feel entirely at ease at all times, morning, noon, and night.

Priscilla started carrying the dishes to the sink. "Is there anyone else we should have special interest in?" she asked.

Mort watched with approval the back of her lithesome body, her shapely calves, her trim waist under the cardigan, and the pert projection of her head beneath richly hued hair. He sighed to himself briefly, then said, "Let's think. I suppose Winifred Redruth, as owner of the pub, would be a good source for information. And there's Dr. Cawthorne."

"You take that one," said Priscilla. She looked at him sharply. "You make me feel something's wrong. Is my skirt on crooked or something?"

"No," he said, shaking his head, "nothing's wrong." Why don't you just say it? he asked himself. Say you're sitting here drooling over her. She certainly wouldn't be displeased to hear it. Instead he said, "I only mean that we should keep Cawthorne in mind. Is he still upstairs or has he gone back to London?"

"If he stayed upstairs last night, we would have heard him."

"There's also the unknown companion who was seen with Sylvia on the cliffs. Of course, that could turn out to be anyone of the people we've already mentioned."

"Any of the males," Priscilla said.

"I'd better leave if I'm going to see what Charles wants." At that moment he didn't especially want to leave, but he consoled himself remembering that there would be other times.

"Okay," she said, still looking especially lovely, "I'll be going to the manor. Don't expect me back soon. Who knows?" she said with laughter, "I might get a handsome actor or a powerful producer to treat me to lunch."

The thought was not comforting to Mort.

*　　*　　*　　*　　*　　*

Charles Fitzpen had a small suite on the upper story of Treleggan's only office building. The reception room was also the library and held floor-to-ceiling bookcases on three of the four walls. A secretary and a clerk shared the centre of the room, and the clerk immediately ushered Mort into Charles's empty private office, asking him to wait. "Mr. Fitzpen will be back in a moment, sir."

The view from the corner office was impressive. The sea outside the harbour was full of whitecaps, not a good day for small boats, but otherwise the sun was out and the fiercely colourful aspect of the village was as stunning as a Van Gogh painting.

"Coffee? Tea?" Charles had returned and motioned Mort to take a seat.

"Tea, thank you," said Mort. "What a beautiful view."

"I know. That's why in my heart I don't really want to move my offices to Truro. I'm happy here."

Charles thumped tobacco into a well-used bent bulldog pipe and began lighting it. "I hope you didn't mind coming here," he said. "It's not very important, but I seemed to have embarrassed Tony last night, and I thought I should explain."

"I don't think he was offended."

"No, he wouldn't be. He's very laid back, mellow, as Americans say. He'll probably live to be a hundred. It was just that I couldn't really answer your question about why Sylvia took us out of her will without alluding to certain friendships she had. You probably guessed that Tony had an affair with her. It's common knowledge and even his wife knows. Sylvia also had affairs with Giles Bacon, Robin Steele, and Magnus Mandeville, and in fact was more or less living openly with Mandeville at the time of her death. He was the only one at that time who seemed to have any influence on her."

"You had more influence with her in the past?" said Mort.

"Oh, yes, no question about it. Sylvia relied very heavily on my advice. She asked me to find her a suitable house in the village and I recommended The Deaconry. I did the conveyancing for her and dealt with other small legal matters. I said that she changed her attitude toward me a few weeks before her death, but it goes back further than that. I can't say exactly when, but for some months before she died she seemed to be confiding in me less and less, and I suppose, in retrospect, that she was confiding in someone else more and more."

"But her friendship with you was different from the others?

Charles laughed. "You mean that I was the only one who had not had intimate relations with her?" He laughed again, but seemed to be waiting for a response from Mort before continuing.

Mort hesitated, knowing that he was going considerably beyond any implicit leave Charles had given him to be discussing intimate subjects, though the other did not seem to mind. He thought back to Priscilla's remark about diminished British reserve in Cornwall. It was more than that, though, and he recalled Disraeli's saying, "Never apologize, never explain." People in Treleggan seemed compelled to explain themselves—it was an interesting sociological change; that is, if it had ever really been otherwise in the first place. His early years in Edinburgh had not prepared him for this kind of openness. Though more direct questions occurred to him, Mort decided to let the other speak himself out, so he merely replied, "Yes."

"It wasn't," Charles said with an embarrassed cough, "that Sylvia didn't try."

Mort looked at him attentively.

"I'm probably saying too much," said Charles. "But I started and so I'll continue with this one revelation. I was apparently the first one to whom Sylvia began making advances. She was lonely, feeling rejected by her husband, insecure, and so on, and I was here, frequently alone with her, an authority figure, and one she relied on. She hinted at first, and then began getting quite explicit with her advances, to the extent that I'd come over and find her in a robe, and after I'd come in, she'd drop the robe and show herself nude. She'd try to pull me…, well, why continue this way?"

He stopped talking and Mort wondered if he would resume without prompting, but was relieved to hear him start again.

Speaking more slowly now, Charles said, "I felt like an absolute cad rejecting her, but I was very much in love with my wife, I'd never been unfaithful to her, and I didn't intend to start. Besides, Sylvia was my cousin, and to me at least it would have been semi-incestuous; I know even first cousins marry, but that's not me. I told Sylvia there were strong psychological reasons for her feeling the way she did and that perhaps the solution was not to take a lover, but to divorce an uncaring husband. I knew, however, that she would never have considered divorce. Sylvia had a need to be the wife of an important man."

"Is Dr. Cawthorne considered an important man?"

Charles raised his head in the air in emphatic affirmation. "He's the cousin of the Earl of Bramber, he mixes in court circles, and it was expected that come the next honours list he would be Sir Frank Cawthorne."

"Was expected?" said Mort.

"Well, his wife's getting murdered doesn't advance his cause very much. I suppose his knighthood depends on how the case turns out. I don't mean that he would be considered a suspect, of course, but only that Sylvia's death must be completely resolved and there must not appear any scandalous reason for her being killed. In any case, there are quite a number of people who would consider him an important person."

"Obviously Sylvia did from what you say."

Charles held the bowl of his pipe in his palm and waved the stem as an extension of his forefinger to give full meaning to his words. "Sylvia would never have divorced him no matter what he did. Even if he tried to kill her. Believe me, being Mrs. Dr. Frank Cawthorne was vitally important to her."

The sky outside had suddenly darkened and nimbostratus clouds were following the coastline as they approached the village. The low-gliding layers would be bringing rain with them and Mort hoped it would not last long. He sensed his discussion with Charles was drawing to a close. The man might feel compelled to say a little more, but it was doubtful that he was going to open up new subjects. In fact, Mort sensed that he regretted saying as much as he had.

Charles let his pipe rest in an ashtray. "It's not that I didn't find Sylvia attractive or desirable," he said. "God! Why does one have to feel so apologetic about not being willing to commit adultery? You just can't understand the way my wife and I feel about each other. I know we sometimes make snide remarks in public, but we do that in private, too, almost as a game, but a private game. Elspeth means more to me than anything else on earth." He hesitated again. "Well, Mort, I'm not trying to tell you about the world's greatest love story. I just felt I owed you an explanation for the Pandora's box I opened up last night, and I couldn't give you one in front of Tony."

"You mentioned that Sylvia had been acting strangely for a few weeks. She seemed to reject everyone except Mandeville. Objectively, was he a good influence or a bad influence on her?"

"It must have been the port," said Charles. "I didn't mean to imply that Mandeville was a bad influence. The fact that someone rejects old friends for a new one naturally makes the old friends somewhat resentful, but that doesn't necessarily mean the new one was at fault."

"True in general, but I mean, do you have any objective evidence as to what kind of influence Mandeville had?"

"Yes, I understood that right away. That's why I did a little backtracking. Yes, I've been resentful toward Mandeville, and so have some of the others, but objective evidence…?" Charles walked over to the window.

"I infer there was something."

"There was one thing, but I don't know what it means. I was talking to Sylvia the day before she was killed—we were in this office, in fact—and the conversation turned to Mandeville. You might have heard that he had plans to film their television drama elsewhere, but at the last minute Sylvia persuaded him to change to Treleggan and Penstead. As it happened they were not bad places for his purposes, but he let Sylvia persuade him, even though they could have been completely unsuitable. I commented that she must have had some sword over his head to influence him to make such a decision, and she burst out laughing. She said—I'll see if I can recall her exact words—'Oh, if you only knew! He's the one who's holding the sword over me.' And she kept on laughing, as if it were all a big joke. But she wasn't happy, I could tell."

"And that was all?"

Charles turned away from the window and walked back to his desk. "That was all. She left immediately after."

"Have you told that to the police or anyone else?"

"No, I'd forgotten about it until now, and I suppose they didn't ask the right questions."

"Would you mind if I mentioned it to Inspector Penhaligon?" Mort had not made an appointment with Penhaligon, but decided now that he should do so promptly, for this new information would make a good addition to the wampum he intended to present him.

"No, I suppose not. I'll see if I can think of anything else from our conversation of that day that might be significant to him. Are you assisting him in this investigation?"

"I just happen to be seeing him this afternoon on other business. You're sure you don't mind?"

It was obvious that Charles wasn't quite sure what to make of the situation and perhaps was wondering if he had made a mistake in giving his information to Mort. "Perhaps I should tell the police myself."

"If you want to," Mort said. He could hardly have told him otherwise. "In any event, I'll mention it also when I see him." He decided that he had better act fast for it wouldn't do to have Charles mention a non-existing appointment to the inspector.

*   *   *   *   *   *

Mort telephoned from the pub and obtained a mid-afternoon appointment with Penhaligon. Then he walked up to the tourist bar to order lunch. Winifred Redruth was handling the regulars' side, but on seeing Mort she changed places with her barman and came to take his order.

"Would it be possible," Mort said, "to get two bangers with nothing else except two plain rolls?"

"For you, love," said Winifred with a provocative smile, "anything would be possible, anything your heart desires."

"Well, I wouldn't mind having a beer, too. A pint of real ale, please."

"Handle or sleeve?"

"Handle. I'm old-fashioned."

"I'll bet you run deep, too. Where's your lady friend? I didn't think she'd let a handsome bloke like you run loose."

"She said if I promised to be good, she'd let me out today while she went to the manor."

Winifred placed a large glass stein in front of Mort and said, "She doesn't know the risk she's taking."

"What, in letting me loose, or in going to the manor?"

"Well, I hadn't thought about that," Winifred said, as a serious wrinkle formed on her face. "I wish my Gwen weren't going over there all the time."

He'd said the wrong thing. Looking at Winifred closely, he noted that in spite of the beginning web of lines around the eyes and the corners of her mouth, she was not a bad looking woman. It was easy to see where Gwen's beauty came from. Winifred had a charming manner, she was playful but considerate, and she obviously liked being around people— it would hardly do for a pub landlord not to want to be surrounded by humankind. It was not an easy job to operate a pub, even though it seemed that everyone in Britain wanted to buy one.

Still, just as Winifred had to smile when serving beer, Mort had to probe even when drinking beer, and he said, "Has Gwen decided if she's going to accept their offer of a part? Priscilla went over to tell them yes."

"Bloody sods," said Winifred, just barely audible.

"Anyone in particular?"

She glanced sharply at him, then said, "It's the lot of them. I wish those bloody television people had never come here. We didn't have all this trouble before." The indignation in her voice changed to sorrow. "Gwen was always such a good girl. Lively, but staying in decent bounds. Of course, she didn't start this business of playing around. No, we have someone else to thank for that." Then, seeming to realize that she was saying too much to a virtual stranger, she responded to his previous question, "Yes, Gwen's going to accept the part. I'm sorry, I shouldn't have said anything. I'm supposed to be the utmost in impartiality."

"I didn't mean to pry."

Winifred nodded and smiled, brought him his plate of sausages and rolls, then left to attend another customer. Mort placed some money on the bar and walked over to an empty table.

*　　*　　*　　*　　*　　*

The pub was filling up with people. From the noise on the other side of the partition it seemed the regulars' side was completely full and some of the regulars even began overflowing into the tourist side. With Saturday a half-day of work for many, most of those now coming in would be people celebrating the end of their work-week.

Mort had not at first noticed anyone from the manor and he recalled that Priscilla had said they would be filming all day, business as usual. But suddenly he heard a familiar voice and looked up to see the callipygous Joanna Gifford standing at an angle beside him.

"Hullo," she said.

Mort observed that there was a good bit of personality in her eyes, voice, and smile. A bit of sadness also came through, but it did not seem a permanent part of her. After all, she had some sort of feelings for Giles, and it had only been two days.

"Could I persuade you to join me and let me buy you a drink?" said Mort.

"If you let me join you, I'll buy you the drink," she said. "All the other tables are taken." Before he could respond, she had taken his glass and asked, "What are you drinking?"

"I don't think it has a name. Locally-brewed real ale."

"Oh, one of those purists?" She didn't wait for an answer, but took long steps over to the bar.

She was wearing a knit dress which draped sinuously to reveal virtually every curve in her anatomy as she walked, and Mort watched with the satisfaction of *South Wind's* Bishop of Bampopo, who always took delight in seeing that which was the best of its kind. A work of art, he thought, his eyes still following Joanna. Then, as one thoroughly convinced that the cycle of the moon had some kind of influence over males as well as females, he told himself, it must be that time of the month or something. Not that Joanna affected him the way Priscilla did, *erotas* versus *agape*, and he was just admiring, not touching.

When Joanna returned she said, "We have something in common, you know, fellow Cantabrigians."

"I didn't know," said Mort. "When were you there?"

"I took honours in English in 1991, Girton. And you?"

"Trinity, Ph.D. in History. I'd rather not mention the year, else you might figure out that I'm almost old enough to be your father."

"I doubt that," she said. "You must have been very young for a Ph.D."

Mort nodded affirmatively. "But how did you know I was at Cambridge, too?"

She smiled, and Mort could see that there was a certain beauty in that smile. Joanna Gifford, he realized, grew on people—she was quite likeable.

"Frank Cawthorne told me. Apparently you met him when he arrived from London."

"You know Dr. Cawthorne?"

"Oh, yes, thanks to Sylvia." There was a look of pain, perhaps even distaste, on Joanna's face.

Until she mentioned Cawthorne, Mort had looked forward to a few minutes of idle conversation, no probing, pushing, fencing, but now all that had changed. He caught the nuance in her voice and knew that she could reveal more in response to adequate elicitation. "Does it hurt to think about it?"

"Not the way you mean." She shrugged and lowered her eyes in a thoughtful pose. "Still, I have guilty thoughts whenever I think of Giles. He was not a bad sort, intelligent and learned far beyond the simple stories he wrote." She was speaking as if she were alone and in a different world.

"But you knew Sylvia and Dr. Cawthorne in London?"

"London, oh, yes. Sylvia made me think of Giles. You see, I met Giles through her." She seemed pleased to note the widening of his eyes. She drank some of her beer and started to talk again in a more present tone, as if she had made a decision. "You see, I knew Sylvia before I knew any of them. I was on the staff of a literary magazine, and Sylvia and I belonged to the same literature appreciation group. Then she started inviting me to dinner, and Giles was there. It was a while before I realized that I was just the cover-up. She wanted Giles with her, but she didn't want her husband to know they were lovers. She wanted it to look as if Giles and I were paired, and I didn't mind although it was horrible for my self-esteem, because when I first encouraged Giles, I found myself rejected—I hadn't known that he was completely enamoured of Sylvia."

Mort's mind was trying desperately to record her every word. Though he didn't feel like another beer before driving to Truro, both their glasses were empty, and it was his turn to offer another round. She nodded yes, and he refilled both glasses.

"You said you thought Giles was rejecting you, but later you found out he, so to speak, had a previous engagement?"

"That's a nice way of saying it. Yes, I felt better when I learned it wasn't me he was rejecting. So I just went along with Sylvia and enjoyed being a guest. At any rate, I answered your question. I knew Dr. Cawthorne in London."

"But then things changed?"

"Well, when Sylvia took up with Robin Steele, my relations with Giles expanded into something more. Robin of course introduced Sylvia to others in the entertainment industry. It was Sylvia who persuaded

Magnus Mandeville to take me on as a scriptwriter and Giles as a technical consultant for the second Urquhart series. By this time our various relationships had become comical, a game of musical beds."

"I can guess the rest," said Mort. "Then Sylvia threw Robin over for Magnus."

"And I became Robin's companion, yes. Robin was handsome, debonair, and beloved by just about every woman in England, few of whom knew how shallow his little mind was. After the glamour had passed away, I regretted my decision, but was too proud, I suppose, to go back to Giles."

"Then after Sylvia's death?"

"Yes, yes, I became involved with Magnus. *Excelsior, excelsior, semper excelsior.* And Robin for consolation seduced Gwen. And now Magnus has thrown me over for Gwen, and I don't even have Giles to go back to. I don't count Robin. If you'll pardon me for saying so, I don't think I could take another night in bed with him and his mirrors. I mean if he were only looking at me in the mirror I might not mind, but he not only expects me to watch and admire his technique, he joins me in admiring it."

"You've not exactly had a happy life."

"I suppose it doesn't seem so now, but...well, it used to be happy when I was earning less money," said Joanna, as she started to get up. "I have to go now. It used to be happy," she suddenly blurted out, "before I met bloody Sylvia. I can't help but put it that way. Sylvia was my point of no return."

She picked up her pocketbook and thanked Mort for his company. "I didn't mean to tell you the story of my life. I suppose I'm lonely, that's all. I mean with Giles...we could sit up all night and discuss literature and poetry and music and history and world affairs, and everything—I miss him."

"Tell me, how did Robin feel about all this? I mean, he introduced Sylvia to Magnus and then lost her, and presumably he introduced

Gwen to Magnus and then lost her. How are relations between Robin and Magnus?"

"Robin could never be separated from the only person he truly loves, himself—anyone else is just an appreciative audience, including producers, whom he would never offend, for they give him life. As for Magnus, I never got to know how he really felt about anything, except making money, of course. Now I really must go."

She took a step away, then paused and turned. Coming close to the table again, she leaned over Mort and said in a quiet voice, "But I'll tell you one place where you're wrong. Robin didn't introduce Sylvia to Magnus. Magnus and Sylvia had known each other long before Sylvia ever met Robin, Giles, or me." She gave a cynical laugh. "Bloody Sylvia, it's always bloody Sylvia, isn't it?"

Chapter TEN

Mort drove the Fiesta to Truro and left it in the large multi-story car park behind the cathedral. It was a pleasant day and he enjoyed the walk to police headquarters at the roundabout on Tregolls Road. His only feeling of regret was that he might have to be deceptive with Penhaligon. As one who had long worked with the police, he did not like to hide facts from them or tell them half-truths. Moreover, from long experience he knew that working independently from the police would most likely backfire. Could he find a compromise? The duty sergeant rang Penhaligon and in a short while the inspector came out to show Mort to his office. Though he looked tired and irritable, his words and tone were friendly.

Mort told him first about Sylvia's letter from the detective agency.

Penhaligon asked, "You have the letter with you, of course?" He had Mort take a seat, but he did not sit down himself.

"Of course," said Mort, smiling. He had not bothered to make a copy, though he had written down the name of the detective agency and its address. He deposited the letter in the police officer's outstretched hand with the eagerness of a man happy to be doing his duty.

Penhaligon scanned the letter, then he put it in a file on his desk. "It seems I'll have to look into this, doesn't it? Thank you, Dr. Sinclair." He waited in polite patience as Mort's face indicated that he had more to say.

"Have you talked to Charles Fitzpen recently?" asked Mort.

"No, that may be one of the telephone calls I'm supposed to return when I can find some time. I'm also supposed to ring my wife, who will undoubtedly want to know when I'm coming home."

"I'm afraid I'm imposing."

"No, no, not at all, Dr. Sinclair, I didn't mean it that way. It seems that we just don't have enough personnel for all that we're expected to do. I can't even spare one of my sergeants to assist me on this one because they're completely occupied with other cases. If I seem impatient, it's because of outside pressures, but I always enjoy talking to someone with your knowledge and background. What can I do for you?"

"Can you get assistance from the Metropolitan Police?"

Penhaligon threw his head back in an emphatic snort. "There are reasons…politics…the chief constable…no, that's a non-starter, isn't it?"

Mort told him about what he and Priscilla had learned of Sylvia's alleged love affairs. The inspector made quick jottings on a pad of paper.

"More than alleged, it seems. Our investigation has shown that Mrs. Cawthorne was increasingly indiscreet in her affairs."

"You know then, for example, that Gwen Trelawney is aware of her husband having had an affair with Sylvia?"

"So it seems. And Tony Trelawney is aware that his wife probably had an affair with Robin Steele and more recently with Magnus Mandeville, and he doesn't like it at all, but doesn't seem to know what to do about it. It could become an explosive situation, couldn't it? Tony Trelawney is a mild-mannered, unassuming man with a strong sense of fair play. With his wife knowing about his relations with Mrs. Cawthorne, he might have felt he was not in a position to object to her affair with Robin Steele, but she might be going too far when she jumps from Steele to Mandeville. Is that all you have?"

Penhaligon was not telling Mort anything he had not already known. The inspector was being deliberately expansive to make a slight offering in return for information. It would not do to dismiss a cooperative visitor too soon, but now that he had given Mort a few crumbs, he could send him on his way. The meeting was not going as Mort had hoped.

"One more thing," Mort said, preparing to offer his final bit of wampum. "Apparently Mandeville had something to hold over Sylvia; it would be interesting to find out what. Significantly, it appears that she and Magnus knew each other years before they were formally introduced rather recently. I get the impression they tried to keep it secret, but were at times careless."

From the look on his face it was obvious that this was new information to the inspector. "Hmm," he said, "Mandeville has a rather dodgy background, you know."

"Dodgy?"

"No proven illegality, but he's been involved in some questionable financial activities." As if Mort's new information required a bigger *quid pro quo*, Penhaligon continued talking. "He was born in Liverpool and from nowhere suddenly became an egregious factor in the entertainment business. He originally spoke with a scouse accent, but trained himself to where he could almost pass himself off as a public school old boy, though he likes to pepper his conversation with Americanisms, having spent some years in the States. It seems that some businessmen trying to work with him have been squeezed and don't want anything more to do with him. Apparently he stops at nothing to get what he wants."

"And yet Sylvia felt he was the only one she could trust."

"She even invested money in one of his companies. We've had talks both with Mrs. Cawthorne's husband and her personal physician, and it seems she was not too stable mentally. I don't mean insane, just nourishing a few neuroses perhaps. Her doctor felt she was under some strain, but she refused to discuss it with him. He thought it had something to do with her parents. They left her a good amount of money, money that her husband insisted she manage by herself. Interestingly, it now seems that she didn't have half the money that Dr.

Cawthorne once believed. The bulk of her estate consisted of the Treleggan house and the necklace. There was only enough cash to pay her debts. However, we're arranging for an accountant to look into her bank transactions."

"Would I be too bold if I asked to know the details when you learn them?"

The inspector lowered his eyebrows and scrutinized Mort's face. "Yes," he said, "you would."

"Then I apologize," said Mort quickly.

For the first time during the visit, the inspector sat down and appeared to relax a little. Some of the weariness seemed to peel off his face, and, if Mort were not mistaken, he was letting himself become amused. "Don't, Dr. Sinclair. Perhaps in your position I might behave the same way, mightn't I? What you're telling me is that you and Miss Booth would like to participate in this investigation. I've suspected that for some time. Now I'm frankly not sure of your own status as one born in the U.K. but traveling under a U.S. passport. However, Miss Booth clearly has alien status and could be asked to leave the country at any time."

"I didn't think we'd gone that far."

In spite of his words, the look on Penhaligon's face was a genuinely friendly one. "You haven't—yet. It's just well to understand each other, isn't it? Now look at my position. We're not accustomed to having mysterious murder cases in Cornwall. Most of our work is time-consuming but routine…, crimes of passion…, today we're getting more deaths resulting from robbery…, or lager louts in homicidal brawls…, I don't have the manpower for a murder case requiring meticulous checking into hundreds of scattered details, and I recognize that you have much expertise in sophisticated criminal investigation. We have that also in the London Metropolitan, but all the way from the chief constable down to me, we're reluctant to call in the Met and let them run off with the case. So if you're asking me if I'll allow you to help me, the answer is yes. But it must be on my terms, mustn't it?"

Mort felt his own muscles relaxing and he allowed a faint smile to come to his lips. "And your terms are?"

The inspector continued his unblinking stare at Mort. "Your part in any investigation must be passive, not active. You keep your eyes and ears open, but you do not represent yourself as having jurisdiction in this matter. Privately you inform me of everything you learn, suspect, or can deduce. I will from time to time tell you of developments in our investigation, but will not feel obligated to divulge everything, only that which might put you in a better position to help us. Does that seem satisfactory to you?"

"Eminently so. Your terms are most fair. We're not competing in this and I'm not seeking any glory. Priscilla and I just want to see Sylvia's— and Giles's—killer brought to justice."

Penhaligon smiled. "Are you certain that's your only motive?"

"Why, yes, I think so. What else?"

"Oh, I might have said there was a bit of the thrill of the chase, the game being afoot, or some of those other nebulous things which appeal to people in the envious position of being able to select the cases they want to pursue."

Mort's relaxed smile stretched into a wide grin. "You may be right, but I wouldn't know; I haven't tried to analyze my motives. At least we've reached common ground and can agree."

"It would seem so, wouldn't it? In fact, I'll confide in you on a new development. We've found a second witness who saw Mrs. Cawthorne with someone else on the coastal path."

"Oh?"

"A retired army colonel saw her, it must have been some thirty minutes or so after she was seen by the chef. Colonel Billings was walking in the same direction as Mr. Morgan and he was able to identify Mrs. Cawthorne positively from photographs. Again Mrs. Cawthorne was in front and her companion, who was wearing bright blue trousers and a yellow anorak, had the hood up obscuring the facial features."

"Again not the slightest clue as to his identity?"

"His? Did I say 'his'? We questioned Colonel Billings thoroughly on that point, so thoroughly that he started to get a bit resentful, telling me that he damn well knew the difference between male and female shapes. Although he didn't see the companion's facial features up close, he would stake his reputation that Mrs. Cawthorne's companion was female."

Chapter *ELEVEN*

It being a lovely spring day, Priscilla threw her cardigan over her shoulders, fastened it with a clip, and started to walk to Penstead. As she proceeded along the road, a large black Daimler passed her, suddenly stopped, and backed up rapidly. "Going to the manor?" said Robin Steele, rolling down the window.

Priscilla smiled and, thanking him, scooted around the car to get in. As they drove, though he turned to look at her once or twice, he mostly kept his eyes straight ahead, perhaps, thought Priscilla, because he was a safe driver, or perhaps so he could better display his beautiful profile to her. They made polite conversation, but Priscilla was disconcerted to note how consistently he seemed to turn all her remarks back to himself.

She mentioned the filming and Robin said, "Yes, well, my scenes are over now. I'll be leaving in a few days."

She mentioned Magnus Mandeville and he said, "He's a great producer, really lovely. He was delighted to get me for this."

She mentioned how wonderful it must be to work on a location such as Penstead, and he said, "They gave me the best room, but it needs re-painting."

The once beautiful lawn at Penstead had been transformed into a scene of horror with straw-stuffed dummies suspended on scaffolds from the hangman's rope. A real man was on the gallows closest to Priscilla, his feet safely resting on a box while his head looked to the heavens with awestruck open mouth and the rope above him stretched taut, as if he were being pulled down by the weight of his body—the camera no doubt was focusing on him from the waist up.

"But have you shot the trials yet?" she said to Robin. "Don't tell me Gerald Mainwaring was here and I've missed him?"

"Well," said Robin, "his was really a minor part. All he had to do was growl savagely and remember to say over and over his one line, something to the effect: 'I hereby sentence you to be hanged by the neck until dead, etc.' Even then he bungled it enough times. It was different when I was playing Judge Jeffries on the stage. That was a real speaking part. They say that when Mainwaring gets a big part they have to break it into scenes of one line each for him. I wouldn't know, since he's never had the opportunity of playing a scene with me until yesterday."

"And you're finished now?" said Priscilla.

"I was hanged yesterday, so my part is finished, but I'll stay here for awhile in case they need re-takes." He parked the car and walked around to open her door. Suddenly turning off his profile, he gave her his full face and said, "Not that that's so difficult a thing to endure when there's such charming company around. May I buy you a drink? They've converted one of the drawing rooms into a bar, you know."

"It's a little early, isn't it?" Yet it was a wonderful opportunity to talk to him. Most of the others she recognized at the manor were all outside getting ready for more hanging scenes. As he coaxed her with face and words, she let herself be persuaded, "Well, perhaps a small glass of white wine."

Except for a locally hired barman, the drawing room with its bottle-laden bar at one end was empty. Priscilla took a corner seat at the far end while Robin brought over wine for her and a double whisky for himself. Somehow having a private drink with Robin Steele wasn't quite the exquisite thrill she would have imagined. Again, all conversation seemed to have one common end, some invoking of a scene Robin had once played. Priscilla began to realize that there was nothing behind the man, no substance, it was all two-dimensional, he was a piece of celluloid.

"Would you care to see my room?" he asked. "The bed is said to be one that Charles II once slept on. Did you see my rendition of the Merry Monarch in *The Witch of Whitehall*? I was told I was rather good. My room's the biggest one in the entire house, a corner suite, full of mirrors. I always like things to be light and airy and insist on lots of mirrors."

"I think I'd like another glass of wine," said Priscilla, needing more time to decide whether she should let herself be alone with him in his bedroom.

Robin dutifully procured them a second round, sat again, and brought his chair closer to her so he could reach over and hold his arm protectively around her back. While Priscilla delicately sipped her wine, his second double whisky quickly joined the first.

"You're drinking rather a lot, aren't you?" said Priscilla. "After all, it's not even lunch-time yet."

"I'm really a very disciplined drinker, you know. I absolutely refuse to drink until all my scenes for the day are finished. I'm not like Errol Flynn or Richard Burton, you know, at least not in that respect. Of course, I'm much too young to have known Flynn, but Rich once told me that when he flew into Gatwick with Flynn, Errol filled in a disembarkation card by writing 'drink' under Occupation and 'occupation' under Sex. Fortunately, as I say, there is nothing further scheduled for me, and I don't expect any retakes today. Now down your wine and I'll show you my room."

She could only stall so long. Did she want the opportunity for gentle interrogation or not? It was risky. Not that there was any danger in his forcing her into bed, for she was confident that her black belt in karate would be more than adequate in any contest of brute force with him. But if it came down to that, to perhaps having to break his arm or leg, or, worse, damage his beautiful profile, it would no doubt have, to say the least, a dampening effect on their future conversations. Nonetheless, with a final swallow of her wine, she decided to get it over with. They went up the staircase and walked to the end of the hallway, Robin carrying another double whisky in his hand.

"Do you realize," he said matter-of-factly as he opened the door, "that half the women in England would give their knickers to see the bed that Robin Steele slept in?"

Priscilla wondered why he modestly stopped at half. Then she looked around the room in amazement. A king-size bed occupied the centre of the room, and surrounding it on three sides was the largest collection of mirrors that she had ever seen in a relatively small area. Some were fastened to the walls, while others were of the stand-alone type allowing for adjustable angles of the glass, and one was even cantilevered as an overhead mirror. At first she lost her ability to speak, but seeing Robin looking eagerly at her for some reaction, she said, "Why, you have a crystal palace here, a—er, house of mirrors. And what a terrific bed."

"Would you like to see how soft that feather mattress is?" He swallowed his whisky, placed his glass on a dresser, and put his arm around her, pulling her toward the bed. One of his hands slid down to the hem of her skirt, trying to inch it up, while the other held her waist. His body pinned her against one of the mirrors, almost knocking it over.

She broke away, walked quickly to the other side where there was a gap between two mirrors, sat down briefly on the mattress, promptly got to her feet again, and awkwardly retreated to stand behind a wing-backed armchair. "My, it is soft," she said, wondering if they had reached the karate stage so soon. "Now I hope you didn't have any ulterior motive in getting me up here. I've heard all kinds of stories about you and my cousin Sylvia."

He was advancing toward her, but suddenly stood still. He smiled and momentarily glanced at himself in one of the mirrors. "It's true Sylvia has been here. She liked the bed, told me so. She was rather sybaritic, you know."

"She was in love with you?"

"I suppose she was." Again he contemplated himself in a mirror, nodding his head in satisfaction. A mixture of emotions seemed to pass across his face. "She was not a woman easy to please," he said, "but yes she was pleased with me, I suppose you would say." Briefly he became pensive. "Poor Sylvia."

"But what I can't understand," said Priscilla, "is why she left you for Magnus Mandeville."

The expression on his face now became one of shock at her lack of understanding. "Well, he was the executive producer, of course. He's the bossman, as you Americans say."

"What kind of a man is Magnus, anyway?"

Robin again was closing the gap between them and again his arm reached out, grabbing her cardigan as she tried to dodge. "Magnus, oh, I don't know. He has many interests. I suppose you might say that he's almost an American in his ways, except that would be ironic, considering that he was P.N.G.'ed when he was in America."

P.N.G.'ed? That was a new one. But she had no time to think about it, thinking instead of how quickly she could break away without stretching her sweater and how she could keep Magnus talking instead of groping. "But why did Sylvia leave you for Magnus?"

"I told you. He was the boss." He seemed perplexed.

Priscilla undid the clip on her cardigan and gracefully moved away, leaving the empty garment dangling in Robin's hand. "But you didn't mind?"

"Do you realise, dear girl, that at any given moment only ten per cent of the actors in England are productively employed? People like Magnus give us life. Besides, Sylvia had a husband anyway and I have a wife in London. No one had exclusive rights to Sylvia, just as no one has exclusive rights to me. We exist to gratify one another. Just as I could gratify you now. I didn't mind that Sylvia had past lovers or would have future ones."

"You mean Giles and Tony."

"Giles and Tony and Charles and Magnus. Sylvia described them all to me. She always used to confide in me; that is, before she started having those horrible delusions. Tony was especially pathetic, importuning her to carry on the affair after she had determined to break it off."

"Delusions? You mean suspicions? Was she suspicious that someone was going to kill her?" Priscilla filed away mentally the addition of Charles to the list, something to explore more fully later.

"No. Whatever put that idea into your head? She felt that some of us were questioning her too much about her past. She couldn't stand being questioned and became positively paranoic about it, finally retreating more and more into herself. She didn't like people like you, you know. You ask too many questions."

"I'm sorry, Robin, I didn't mean to. But I must go. Thank you for showing me your room."

His face became blurred like that of a disappointed little boy. "But you don't want to stay?"

"I'd like to, but Magnus asked me to see him," she said as she took her cardigan from him. "Surely you can understand that I can't keep Magnus waiting."

"Oh, of course," he said, looking in a mirror and stroking his moustache. "I didn't know you were here to see Magnus." He glanced at her from over his shoulder. "Perhaps some other time?"

"Of course. Perhaps some other time."

*   *   *   *   *   *

Magnus insisted that they have lunch together. "There's a fish-and-chips joint down on the bay that just opened this week for the season."

He drove his fawn Volvo estate wagon to the entrance of the manor, turned left, and continued downhill through the overgrown brush to the small village of Porthigan. The restaurant was on the water and, though there were tables and chairs outside on the wooden veranda,

Priscilla thought the weather was cool. Going inside, they found themselves alone, it still being early.

Priscilla begged off another alcoholic drink and asked for an orange quash. Magnus ordered the orange for her and a pint of brown ale for himself and fish and chips for both.

"Fish and chips," he said, "remind me of my childhood. No matter how rich I keep getting, I don't think anything will ever taste as good as the fish and chips my mum used to buy in Liverpool." He continued making casual conversation, discussing the problems besetting the filming, the quirks of some of the actors, the weather, which had been inordinately cloudy and dark, and the high extra costs for each day they were behind schedule. "It was a mistake to let Sylvia rope me into coming here."

Priscilla asked occasional questions but found that Magnus could easily parry them. She had the feeling that she was being transparent and that Magnus was laughing at her.

Then with the second round of drinks, Magnus suddenly stiffened, as if he were through playing games. "I'm a blunt man," he said. "Let's talk about you. I understand you're a police officer in the United States."

Priscilla said, "Yes, I'm afraid I can't help that."

"Have you been asked to work on this case?"

"No. The only interest I have is that I'd like to see my cousin's killer caught and tried. But I have no authority here, and the police are not likely to give me any."

"All right. But still you're curious. You have a lot of pent-up questions. Let me give you a scenario. Suppose I let you ask all the questions you want for fifteen minutes and then I'll ask you just one in return. That way you can stop your probing, and I'll either give you honest answers or refuse to say anything."

She was taken aback with his directness and thoroughly unprepared to start a cross-examination. It was better playing cat and mouse, she thought, so she wouldn't have to give herself away so much.

"Well, start asking," he said.

She desperately searched her mind for a place to begin. The waiter cleared the plates from their table, and she asked for a glass of water. Magnus called after him, asking if they had any spotted dick for dessert. No, only apple pie. Magnus looked at Priscilla, she shook her head, and he told the waiter to forget the dessert and bring him another brown ale. Priscilla continued thinking for a while longer, then blurted out, "Well, did you kill Sylvia?"

"Ha, right to the heart of the matter. No!"

"Do you have any idea who did?"

"Maybe."

"Who?"

"I refuse to answer that question because my idea is purely a guess. I don't know for a fact. But Sylvia was especially afraid of one person."

"Especially? But in general she was afraid of many?"

"She was apprehensive during her last weeks."

"Did she tell you she thought someone was trying to kill her?" Priscilla worried. Was she giving away too much by asking this question?

"She mentioned two attempts, but I suspected more."

Between questions she kept pushing her mind to come up with some kind of logical sequential probing. "Why did you think Sylvia was especially afraid of one person?"

"Because she'd ring me every time she was likely to be alone with that person. For example, she'd ring and say 'So-and-so wants to see me at my place and is coming over in five minutes.'"

"About how many times is 'every time?'"

"Ha, very good. About three times."

"Describe the other two."

He hesitated. "If you're going to do it that way, you'll get the name by the process of elimination. All right. Another time she telephoned and said that so-and-so wanted to meet somewhere. She was afraid to go and afraid to refuse, so she thought she'd go but let me know first who she'd be with."

"And the third time?"

"That was a few days before she was killed. She rang me and said she was going to take a walk on the coastal path with so-and-so."

"Have you told the police this?"

"More or less. And you're using up your time."

"All right. Another question. Why did Sylvia trust you above the others?"

"Silence," he said.

"Meaning?"

"Meaning I refuse to answer that one. And your time is almost up."

She tried to speed up her thought processes. What did she know about this man? He was born poor in Liverpool. He worked his way up in the business world. Hadn't she heard that once he had lived in the United States? She decided on that tack. "You once lived in the United States. What did you do there?"

"You always come back to me," he said, and he tried to smile as if he were flattered, but Priscilla sensed that he was not pleased with that particular question.

"I was in investments."

She had the feeling that he wanted to get off the subject, which made her want to continue it all the more. "What kind of investments?"

"Stocks, bonds, futures, puts and calls, the whole gamut of toys that investment bankers play with."

That didn't enlighten her. It merely confirmed that he was using the word 'investments' the same way she did. "Did you have your own company? What city were you in? When did you leave?"

From the look on his face she had really displeased him now. He hesitated, looked at this watch, then said, "Okay, time."

She gave him a pleading look. "Ah, but I asked those questions before the time was up."

He slapped his hand against his forehead and guffawed. "Ha, you're really in there trying, kid. But I've answered all that I'm going to."

"Very well. What do you want to ask me?"

Mandeville had finished his drink, and now he stood up abruptly to indicate that they should go. "I'll drive you back to Treleggan."

"You don't want to ask me the one question?" It was a little disappointing, for she had been curious as to why just one question and what it could be. He was clearly indicating displeasure with her and she suddenly feared that she might have severed any friendly relationship. She rose and followed him to his car, thinking all the time of what she might do to change the situation. He made no effort to open the door for her, and as she opened it herself, she said to him, "I want to be fair with you and think I should have the chance to answer your question."

"Forget it," he said, starting up the engine. "I already know the answer anyway."

"But what's the question?"

He looked in her eyes momentarily and shook his head. "Sure, but don't bother answering. I was going to ask you to sleep with me, but it's no longer a valid matter because I'd say no even if you said yes."

She started to respond by asking him if he found her so undesirable, but thought better of it. That would be getting on dangerous ground. She realized that she'd never been in a situation like this before and she didn't know what to say.

The silence was maddening to Priscilla as they drove back. Though Mandeville's appearance and manner were calm enough, she sensed that he was seething inside. What had she done to so offend him? She was only playing the little question-and-answer game that he himself had started. Something about his living in the States. He didn't deny he had lived there, but he definitely did not want to pursue that aspect of his life. Now that she knew his moods better, she belatedly recognized that he had also not cared for her question about why Sylvia trusted him above all others. He had not expected these questions. Or had he?

Had he learned more than he had given away? After all, he should have expected that she, a trained police detective, would ask pertinent questions. Nothing she said should have surprised him. But by showing him the kind of question she could ask, had she given him an indication of what he might be facing from the official police, from Penhaligon?

Had he really intended to ask her to sleep with him? It would have been rather crude of him to do it that way. But in spite of his position, power, and money, there was something about him that in fact bespoke crudeness. He was not a very likeable man. Then why had Sylvia rejected just about everyone else and trusted only Magnus Mandeville? That had been a strange relationship.

Why had Mandeville given Priscilla so much information? Well, obviously it didn't cost him anything if he had already told the police. And was he telling the truth? Did he give the name of the person he suspected to the police, or did he keep it from them, too? Would the police here allow him to get away with something like that, so many provocative answers and then silence? What would Mort do in a situation like this?

As they approached Treleggan, Magnus suddenly began laughing softly to himself.

"What's so funny?" Priscilla asked.

"Nothing. Just a case of *déjà vu*. I was reminded of another time when I drove a beautiful woman home along this road, another disappointing occasion."

Still trying to keep alive the question-and-answer game, Priscilla said, "Sylvia?"

"You betcha, dear little Sylvia. She was to stay with me that night at the manor and we had an argument. Because she couldn't drive at night, she had the chutzpah to insist after starting a fight with me that I drive her home. Like a fool I did." He paused, then said, "I could have made you walk, you know?"

"You wouldn't have done that. You're a gentleman." She meant the American meaning, but realized that in either case it was not quite the word she wanted.

"Me, a gentleman?" He took his hands off the steering wheel and clapped them together as he belched with loud laughter. Then just as quickly he frowned again. "You started off today by telling me that you'd take the part I offered you. I agreed then, but now I remember that part's already filled. You won't be needed. Oh, and therefore there'll be no need for you to come around the manor any more. Well, here we are, Sylvia's house. Good day, Miss Booth. I expect we'll see very little of each other in future."

CHAPTER *TWELVE*

As they walked to the pub after dinner, Priscilla and Mort exchanged information on their respective activities during the day. "I'd say you hit a nerve with Mandeville," said Mort.

"You seem to have made a good bargain with Penhaligon. At least, I hope it's good."

The clouds, flirting with the luminosity of the heavens, now covered moon and stars so that little light shone overhead and it was necessary to walk across the car park and green with great care. Mort continued, "Let's see what we have so far. First, one witness saw Sylvia on the coastal path with a male companion the day she was killed and a little later another witness saw her with a female companion wearing identical clothes. Which witness was wrong?"

"What I find awfully odd," said Priscilla, "is that the colonel, the more reliable witness, is so positive in saying Sylvia was with a female, and thus a female would have been the last person Sylvia was known to be with before her death."

"Meaning?"

"Meaning that my mind was set on it being a male killer. It's not easy to imagine a woman carrying Sylvia—not dragging her, but carrying her—a considerable distance to throw her off the cliff. But let's leave that aside now. What else have we?"

"Well," he said, "next we have Giles. He disappears Tuesday morning and he's killed early Thursday morning. Where was he for two whole days? And what connexion does his death have with Sylvia's death? Or are they connected in the first place?"

"Then we have Charles lying about his relations with Sylvia. Why not admit he had been sleeping with her like almost everyone else in the case. After all, being caught in adultery these days is as common as getting a speeding ticket." She tugged at her lip and said, "Oh, there, Mort, you see how horribly conditioned I've become. I never used to think of sex as something that's done as casually as saying hello."

He squeezed her hand lightly, then said, "Joanna thinks that Magnus knew Sylvia long before she met the others, though both Sylvia and Magnus acted as if they had first met in London shortly before the filming started."

"Sylvia's at the heart of this whole thing," said Priscilla. "I lived with her four years at college and yet the more I learn about her now, the more I feel I didn't really know her at all. She's a mystery."

"An enigma," said Mort.

"And let's not forget her husband. Cawthorne was the one wearing goat's horns. I wish we had more authority in the case. How I'd love to pull him in and rake him over the coals. Just occasionally I wish we could do things the old fashioned way."

"I thought Mandeville was the object of your wrath."

"Him, too! Oh, if I just had jurisdiction, I'd pull the two of them in so fast."

Mort laughed. "Of course you'd read them their rights."

"No, I wouldn't. I'd throw their rights out the window and get a piece of rubber hose and beat the truth out of them."

"How about thumb screws and the rack, too?"

"Why not?"

"Lord have mercy, am I glad I'm not one of your suspects!"

*　　　*　　　*　　　*　　　*　　　*

They entered the regulars' lounge of *The Case Is Altered* and found it full of people. Gwen was wearing an apron, but standing on the customer side of the bar talking to Elspeth. Priscilla thought she knew a few of the others by sight, but the majority were strangers to her. There was no table free, so she and Mort stood with their backs to the bar while drinking.

"Are you two ladies alone tonight?" asked Priscilla of Gwen and Elspeth, trying not to sound like an investigator.

"Charles had discussions all day with a barrister in Bristol," said Elspeth, "and will be staying overnight."

"Tony's spending the weekend with his parents in Bude," said Gwen. Facing Priscilla she asked, "Have you recovered from our experience with the Gray Lady in the cellar?"

"Mostly, I suppose. You don't really believe that was a ghost, do you?"

"No…and yes," said Gwen. "I don't believe it, but I'll never go down that cellar again. I suppose I'm all right though, except for that bloody bruise on my leg." She displayed a shapely though black-and-blue-marked leg to demonstrate her point, then she turned back to Elspeth.

Odd, thought Priscilla, for Gwen, in spite of her words' implying the contrary, didn't seem to have the slightest trace of fear; in fact she gave the impression that she wouldn't be afraid of anything. She had a defiant look about her, partly in her steady gaze, partly in the tightness of her lips, but mostly in the whole aggressive positioning of her body with right hand on hip, shoulders shoved forward, and one leg thrust out as if she were daring anyone to challenge her. Her attitude was different from what it had been on all the other occasions when Priscilla had seen her.

Priscilla casually walked to the doorway of the divider that separated the two bars and peered into the tourist side.

"Nosey?" said Mort, crossing over to stand beside her.

"Just curious. I'd expect more people in the large lounge."

"Well, it's not the full tourist season yet. Still, I would expect to see some of the television people here, especially on a Saturday night."

"Oh, they're having a party out at the manor. Robin invited me, but I declined."

They went back to the regulars' bar and ordered another round. The outside door opened, and a man walked in and stood by the wall looking at the bar. Priscilla nudged Mort.

"Magnus Mandeville," he said. "Why doesn't he come all the way in? Did you scare him off?"

Priscilla motioned toward Gwen and Elspeth. At that moment, Gwen looked in the direction of the doorway, smiled confidently, walked away without saying a word to Elspeth, took off her apron and threw it behind the bar, shouted a hasty goodbye to Winifred, and increased her pace as she proceeded over to Magnus. Opening the door with one hand, he took her arm in the other and guided her out. From behind the bar Winifred stared without expression on her face.

Speaking in a hushed voice Priscilla said to Mort, "Even though Tony's out of town, I think Gwen's being awfully bold in letting everyone know of her relationship with Magnus. After all, she could have met him outside. I'll bet every person here took in that little bit of provocative action, but she apparently doesn't care. And did you notice how Winifred was watching her?"

"Winifred was not the only one," he said. "Elspeth was staring a hole through her."

At that moment Elspeth approached them. "Do you mind if I join you. I don't like drinking alone."

Her glass was empty and Mort asked what she was drinking.

"Babycham," she said and thanked him as he held up her empty glass for Winifred to see.

"I hadn't expected to be left alone so abruptly," said Elspeth. "Gwen acts as if she's campaigning to be Sylvia's successor." Seeing Priscilla frown, she quickly added, "I'm sorry. I don't mean to be catty like that, either about Sylvia or about Gwen. Minding each other's business is a favourite pastime in small villages."

"It doesn't stop there," said Priscilla.

"I know, but it so pronounced in small places. I get caught up in it like everyone else, even before I know what I'm doing. You must think we're awful here, murder, open adultery, lust, and so on." Her fingers toyed with the opened bottle of Babycham that Winifred handed her.

"I think Treleggan is merely showing it's a part of the world," said Priscilla. "The world has changed tremendously in just one generation."

"Too much for me," said Elspeth. "I don't like at all the way we've become. The way I've become. I don't feel I belong in this age. Sometimes it makes me feel so desperate that I can't cope with it." She poured the Babycham in her glass and stared vacantly at the empty bottle.

"Yet you have that look of a survivor," said Mort. "I think in your own way you're every bit as tough as Gwen is in hers."

Elspeth's face brightened as she smiled back at Mort. "I take that as a compliment," she said.

Priscilla noted for the first time that once Elspeth freed herself from the severity of her normal countenance, she was quite an attractive woman, and Priscilla began to understand a bit more Charles's intense feeling for Elspeth. However, her metamorphosis was short-lived. As Mort continued to glance appreciatively at her, Elspeth bit her lower lip and immediately her face was restored to its characteristic disdain. She looked older and apprehensive, as if she were smelling bad fish. She tossed off the remainder of her drink and turned away.

"Thanks for everything," she said, walking to the door.

When she had gone Priscilla said, "I think she was terribly afraid she might like you, Mort."

At first he didn't seem to be listening, then he remarked, "That is one very interesting heap of contradictions. I think I was wrong, she's a lot tougher than Gwen."

*   *   *   *   *   *

"You know what is bothering me?" said Mort, as they made themselves comfortable in The Deaconry again.

They were playing Brahms's *Second Symphony* on their newly-acquired tape-recorder. Priscilla made some slices of French bread and butter and Mort got them two glasses of ale.

"The high price of beer?" said Priscilla.

"No, be serious. You know, we never completed our search. You said you and Sylvia had a number of hiding places. We found the letter she wrote you rather easily and then stopped looking. What were some of her other places?"

Priscilla put her finger to her lip and thought. "Well, sometimes we used books. The place to look was page 100, we'd often leave a note there."

The bookcase contained a hundred or more books that presumably showed the range of Sylvia's reading tastes. Cookbooks, crime novels, best sellers of recent years, Gothic tales of love and horror, travel books, a few on plants, some on art, several dictionaries and books of cross-word puzzles, some how-to books including several on painting, a few books of poems, and a few on investments.

He started on the top shelf and Priscilla on the next one down and systematically they inspected each book across the shelf. A quick opening flip followed by the turning of pages until page 100 was reached, a hasty glance to see if anything extraneous lurked between the open pages, and then the book was replaced and another taken. There was nothing in the top shelf of books or those of the second shelf or the third or fourth. Initial enthusiasm gave way to discouragement as they started from both ends of the bottom shelf.

It was only as they were close to meeting toward the middle that Priscilla shrieked. "Here's something, Mort."

He laid his book down and turned toward her. "What's that?"

"Three letters. Listen to this:

"Dear Sylvia:

I'm embarrassed about last night. It must not happen again. I'm not going to see you again until you promise that you'll behave. Elspeth would divorce me if she found out what happened between us. Get it out of your head that it's a personal rejection. It's just that I'm already married and happily so."

"There's no signature," Priscilla said.

"There doesn't have to be."

"So Robin was right," said Priscilla. "Charles was one of the boys after all. Let me read the second one:

"Sylvia:

I won't put up with what amounts to blackmail. We have slept together for the last time. If you can't give me assurances, then I will never see you alone again. And if you ever dare tell my wife, I won't be responsible for the consequences."

"No signature again," said Priscilla.

"But the same handwriting. Charles, the reluctant wooer."

A wry smile came to Priscilla's lips. "You can't help but feel sorry for him."

Mort snorted. "I did it in a fit of non-passion. She aroused in me feelings of platonic love and I had to kill her."

"Oh, be still. I'll read this other one:

"My darling Sylvia:
I can't go on like this. You're a sorceress, a witch, a demon. You've filled my life with more ecstasy than I'd ever known before. Please reconsider. Don't cast me off. I'm desperate. If I can't have you, no one will. I'll kill you first. Believe me."

"Still no signature," said Priscilla. "But this time it's obviously not from the same person."

"The handwriting's as different as day and night."

"From what we've been learning," said Priscilla, "it could have been anyone of half the men and boys in Treleggan."

"Presumably it's one of our suspects. Penhaligon shouldn't have any trouble in finding out whom it belongs to."

"Do we have to give it to Penhaligon?"

"We made a bargain with him, remember?"

Priscilla screwed up her face in protest, but she handed the three letters to Mort. They continued checking the few remaining books.

"Well, this is the end," said Priscilla, thumbing through a large volume of quotations. And then she yelled. "This is it! She held up an envelope and extracted a piece of paper. "It looks like a promissory note."

Reading over her shoulder, Mort summarized, "Winifred Redruth promises to re-pay Sylvia Cawthorne £20,000 interest-free in four semiannual installments of £5,000 each."

"And there's also a letter in the envelope," said Priscilla.

"Looks like a carbon copy." She read:

"Dear Winifred:
I have great need for the money now, and with sorrow I must ask you to pay up the arrears. You haven't given me back a penny yet. I hate to be demanding, but this is my last friendly request.
Sylvia Cawthorne."

"Notice the date," said Mort.

"The twenty-seventh of March. That would be...let me see, exactly one week before Sylvia was murdered. You don't think...?"

"We don't have proof of anything. All I'm thinking is that we were right to include Winifred in our list of suspects. I had hoped we could narrow the list down more than this. Now any more hiding places?"

They searched all other possible places, but found nothing.

"I don't think the necklace is here," said Priscilla. "I've racked my brain and I think we've found everything that Sylvia wanted us to find."

"That's a good point to keep in mind. All these discoveries we've been making are those that Sylvia led us to. And the more I learn about her the more I realize how complex she was."

"Meaning?"

"Even in death she's directing our moves. Let's hope that Sylvia's goal and our goal are the same."

"Meaning?"

"Meaning that this Sylvia we've been investigating just doesn't sound at all like the Sylvia you have been describing as your cousin and friend. I can't help but wonder if she deviously intended you to find these letters, too. Could she have been setting someone up? Suppose she really did commit suicide?"

Chapter *THIRTEEN*

Too excited to sleep, Priscilla and Mort talked the evening away, as if reiterated discussion by itself would solve the mystery, and they didn't get to bed until two a.m. Mort slept soundly, softly snoring to Priscilla's amusement. Priscilla lay on her pillow staring at the faint ray of moonlight projecting itself on the ceiling from behind the edges of the window shade.

Everything they discussed, every fact, every theory, every possible motive for every possible suspect, weighed heavily on her mind. Over and over the ideas circulated. From The Deaconry to Sylvia. From Sylvia to Giles. From Giles to Penstead. From Penstead to the cellar. From the cellar to her visit there with Gwen. The sounds, the motions of cool moist air, the darkness. From Gwen to finding Giles's body. Giles's body! Giles's clothes. His jacket. The pocket! What was in the pocket?

Now her mind raced back to the inventory Penhaligon had shown her. There was no newspaper on that list!

In her mind she saw a folded newspaper projecting out of the jacket's right pocket, slightly aslant as if it were ready to fall out. Fall out? That was it. If it wasn't there when the police took the inventory then it must have fallen out when the body was moved. Or could someone have taken it? But who? It was still in the pocket when she and Gwen had shown the others where the body was hanging. She and Gwen had followed Magnus out of the cellar with two men carrying the body immediately behind her and no one behind them.

She closed her eyes and squinted fiercely, knowing that with her training she should have a mental photograph stored somewhere in the recesses of her brain. Now she could see it, the scene fixed in her mind. The newspaper was no longer in Giles's pocket when they brought his body upstairs, she was sure. The police had certainly checked the area where the body was found. But if it had fallen elsewhere! Once out of Giles's pocket would it have had any significance for anyone? More importantly, could that newspaper still be there? In the passageway?

There was one sure way of finding out. "Mort," she shook him gently and turned on the light.

"What, er, what is it?" He blinked his eyes trying to adjust to the sudden disturbance.

Priscilla explained. "…and so the newspaper might still be there. Let's see if we can find it." She jumped out of bed and started dressing.

"Whoa, girl, whoa. Even if you're right, the newspaper might have nothing to do with this case. Anyway it can wait. And we have a pact with Inspector Penhaligon. We can get in touch with him the first thing tomorrow, or rather the first thing Monday morning."

That didn't suit Priscilla. She made a face and tried in vain to stir Mort's interest.

"Do you realize it's two-thirty in the morning?" he said. "Go back to sleep." And he lay down again, turned away from her, and sought to recover his violated slumber.

Disappointed, Priscilla pulled off her sweater and slacks, turned off the light, and threw herself down on the bed.

"That's better," said Mort half asleep, "only not so rough, huh?"

She tried and tried, but she just couldn't get to sleep. With her eyes closed she saw the newspaper now in some vague part of the cellar lying on the floor. Then she saw some phantom figure stoop over and pick it up. A match was lit. The newspaper went up in flames. The figure disappeared. She opened her eyes and felt cold and clammy.

Her hand reached toward Mort again, ready to grab his shoulder, shake him awake. But she stopped. No, she wouldn't be able to persuade him. Well, if he was going to be so darn stubborn, let him, but he didn't have any right to stop her. She slowly eased out of bed, felt for clothes and shoes, and quietly took them to the kitchen. A torch, a small one, was in the drawer. She turned it on briefly to test it.

*   *   *   *   *   *

The streets were empty. Priscilla drove to the top of the hill and headed toward Penstead Manor. It was three-thirty. There would not be much time. At this season it would be light in just a few hours.

She left the car in the park as far from the manor as possible, so the noise would less likely disturb anyone. Gwen had told her the day they went to the cellar that the front door lock was broken. Yes, she could open it. Her biggest problem was to enter without the door creaking. It was exasperating having to be patient, but very slowly she inched the door open. A rub here, a squeak there, but these noises were so slight they'd be inaudible to anyone more than a few feet away. Once she had slid it open, she was too impatient to ease it closed again, so she let it be, all the easier to make her egress when the time came.

What was that hum? She had a keen sense of hearing, but she was not sure if her ears were deceiving her. It was ever so slight, so soft. Was it an external noise, or was it something the mind heard when all else was quiet? On tiptoe she went into the kitchen and faced the frustration of having to coax the cellar door open ever so slowly so as not to make any noise.

Now the hum was louder; it seemed to be coming from the cellar. She eased past the door. Suddenly the hum stopped. She froze and time stood still with her. Her ears strained to distinguish between harmless though strange background sounds and noises of clear and present danger. From the top of the cellar stairs she could see nothing but pitch darkness, a black void. Just a hint of moving air creased her face and she heard faint indefinable noises. Her flesh gave way to goose pimples.

Coraggio, girl, she told herself, courage. She had come this way before with Gwen, and, yes, she admitted, it had seemed spooky then. But wasn't that Gwen? Hadn't it been Gwen transmitting her own fear? At least conveying a sense of fear. Whether Gwen herself had been really afraid or had just been acting that way for the effect it would have on Priscilla, she couldn't say, but she knew she wouldn't have been so fearful had it not been for her companion. But Gwen was not here. So why was she becoming so acutely apprehensive now?

What was that noise? Try to be rational, she told herself. There was no one else there. It was the conditioning everyone had throughout life to be wary of the dark in strange places. Then why didn't she use her torch? Of course, that was it, use the torch. No one upstairs in the manor could see it. She turned it on. Somehow it seemed so much dimmer here, but at least she could see the stairs this time. Again she couldn't see over the side, but she knew there was no guard rail on the right, it just plunged down to the stone floor.

Giles, that was why she was here. Again, moving moisture brushed against her face. She shivered and took the next step, carefully holding the torch in her right hand and using her left hand protectively to make intermittent contact with the cold wet wall. Was that a scraping of metal? She quickly covered the entire area in front of her with the torch, jerkily throwing the beam from side to side. It was no use, it couldn't penetrate very far. She was restricted to seeing just a few feet in front of her. The thought was suddenly terrifying and she tried to dismiss it. Did it make much difference how far she could see? Perhaps Mort was right, she should have waited.

Suddenly she was caught in a vortex of fear, the hairs on her body rising heavenward like the music of a requiem. She never cared for requiems. Mozart, Verdi she loved, but not when they wrote that kind of music. She wanted to turn and run but instead tried to silently hum something joyful, but only the notes of Mendelssohn's *Reformation Symphony* came to her mind. Martin Luther. She could see Luther rising defiantly: *Hier stehe ich....* Here I stand, I can do no other. It gave her a bit of comfort. She was there because she had to be there. There was no choice.

She reached the bottom of the stairs. How many were there? Thirteen? That was the hangman's number. But she hadn't counted. She didn't know it was thirteen. She pulled at the music to sing in her mind letting the syllables stretch out in a defiant mode: "A mighty fortress is our God." That was it. She was not especially religious, but it was good to think of an all-powerful, all-seeing **benevolent** deity above. Benevolence, that was what she wanted now.

They had moved Giles along the corridor from the left. No false steps this time, as with Gwen. She turned and proceeded toward the room where she had found the body. The corridor with its alcoves and recessed doors looked like a torture chamber. Mort had mentioned thumb screws and racks and she had said, "Why not?" How could she have been so cruel, even in jest? I'll be more considerate of others from now on, Lord, really I will.

She aimed her torch and saw that the door was still open. Cautiously she started to enter. Focusing the light in the centre where Giles's body had been hanging, she jolted, half-expecting to see that horribly leering face in front of her eyes. Nothing, the room seemed to be devoid of dead bodies.

She searched every inch of the room and finally convinced herself that what she wanted was not there. Then she turned and began to retrace her steps, going back slowly through the dark channel. Now she paid attention to the small alcoves on both sides. She had not been concerned with these on her previous visit. Some led into small chambers, while others were merely interruptions of the walls, small recesses used for storage. It was in one of these that she saw the stack of newspapers. She lunged to grab a top sheet of paper which seemed to blend in with the others, but yet was different because it was folded several times while the others were neatly stacked with just one fold. Her fingers disturbed the dust and she had to stifle a sneeze. But now it was within her grasp and she knew this was the one.

It was not a whole newspaper, but a single page folded several times to become just pocket-size. Suddenly she dropped the newspaper and turned off the torch. That was not her imagination, it was a real noise coming somewhere from behind her, somewhere down the end of the other central corridor. She paused and her prickling ears strained again to make out every decibel. Nothing now, only the aural sensation from the pressure of air that customarily defeated every pure silence. Even if there had been noise, it would not have necessarily been anything harmful. Of course, there would be nocturnal life in the passageways, mice certainly, perhaps other small creatures of the type normally found in hedgerows. It would not be unusual to hear real noises. She knew it had been real, but she gradually convinced herself that it portended no harm...she thought. Probably? Hopefully.

She again turned the torch on, picked up the newspaper, and gazed at her treasure, holding it up in one hand and using the free fingers of the hand with the light to unfold and orient it top-side-up. Awkwardly she focused the light. It was the first and second pages of a tabloid. There were many stories and a few photographs most of which she recognized as being of local Cornish origin, but her quick scanning showed nothing obvious bearing on the matters of interest. She searched for the date: 3 February. Exactly two months before Sylvia died. Was it significant? The paper had been old news when Giles was carrying it around in his pocket. And suddenly she knew when Giles must have found it.

The noise again! It was more than imaginary or harmless. Now she couldn't deny it and she trembled. There was someone else in the cellar with her! She knew it! No mistaking those menacing sounds. There were footsteps rapidly coming from behind her, no attempt to disguise them, accelerating, overtaking her, almost upon her. What did they want with her? Who was it? What was it? She tried to whirl around and confront her antagonist with her torch, but suddenly a fierce blow knocked it out of her hand. Terror! In the eternity of nanoseconds she felt the absolute horror of being attacked by the unknown, being menaced, being the helpless victim. She shrieked, but still tried to recall her training. She kicked out for a groin somewhere, anywhere, hoping to connect, but her knee only moved through vacant air. Something grabbed her arm tightly and pressed, squeezed, hurt her. She was spun around and lost all sense of equilibrium. The pain in her arm increased and there was suddenly, BANG! a fierce, excruciating blow, and then....

      *   *   *   *   *   *

"Priscilla," Mort called. He had thrown the covers off and was poised on one elbow in the bed. He sensed her absence from the room, and turned the light on for verification. He called again, got up, and went into the living room, then the kitchen, where he found her nightgown. He searched all over and finally was forced to admit that she wasn't in the house at all. Where could she have gone? Suddenly it came to him. You didn't, you couldn't have! Angry as well as concerned, he threw on his clothes and rushed out to the Fiesta. Making no effort to keep quiet, he pulled out the choke and gunned the car into the streets, up the hill, like a tornado heading for the manor.

The night was bathed in a hide-and-seek combination of brilliant moonlight peeking through splotchy clouds. As he sped through the outer gate, the silhouette of the manor house loomed up in front of him. Passing its car park, he instantly noted their Sierra behind the other cars and was glad to confirm that he was on the right trail; now he couldn't wait to get to the house. He drove through the archway to the courtyard and pulled up abruptly at the house's main entrance. Quickly he noted the open door and dashed in. Going directly to the cellar door, he found it open also, entered, saw dim light from below, and closed the door behind him. Just as the door closed, he heard a scream coming from the direction of the light.

"Priscilla," he called. There was muffled movement down there, several thuds, followed by a thump, and then he could clearly hear running footsteps. He let himself be guided by the dim glow of light, but it was too faint to be of much help. He groped for the light switch, found it, and pushed it to the on position, but no illumination followed his effort. The stairs were of stone and steep and he had never been down them before, in fact knew of them only from Priscilla. It would have been reckless to rush down the stairs blindly, but within some degree of prudence he descended as fast as he could, using the wall on the left as his guide and the luminous area below as a beacon. As he reached the bottom, his ears could hear fleeing footsteps straight ahead and he started to follow. But only a few yards away to the left his eyes made out a fallen torch still giving light. In the light was the vague outline of an unmoving body. He dashed to the spot, picked up the torch, threw the beam on the body, and yelled a curse as he recognized Priscilla.

Cradling her head in his arm, he gently caressed her cheek. He sighed with relief as he sensed her regaining consciousness.

"Mort! Mort! Hold me! What happened?" The light showed her face in a pained frown and she blinked while reaching behind with one hand to touch the back of her head.

"You're all right now, my darling. Don't worry."

"Oh, Mort, it was horrible. I was attacked and I think they were trying to kill me."

"They?"

"He, or she, or they, or it. I don't know. Ghosts aren't solid—they can't squeeze you until it hurts, can they? Oh my head. I think I was hit on the head, back here. Oh, it hurts terribly!"

As he saw normality coming back to her, he said, "What were you doing here anyway?"

"Oh, Mort, whatever you do, don't call me a little fool."

"I won't, my dearest, I won't."

"I found the newspaper." She explained in detail all the events leading up to the attack.

"Someone must have been carrying you as I arrived," Mort said. He helped her to her feet, and they walked back to the stack of newspapers.

"It's gone," she said, and she explained. "That was where I lost consciousness. I must have been carried a dozen feet or so."

"It looks as if someone was trying to take you elsewhere, but had to drop you when they heard me."

"Now that you mention it and now that my head doesn't ache so much, I think I've a pain elsewhere, too." She gently touched her rear.

They looked through all the corridors and unlocked rooms for the newspaper, but found nothing. Mort noted that the middle corridor, where he had heard the footsteps running away, ended at a blank wall. No sign of any exit. "Your assailant was running in this direction, but he's not here now. Do you remember anything about the newspaper?"

"Mainly the date. It was the third of February and I remembered that being exactly two months before Sylvia was murdered. But something else registered. Do you remember that first day at The Deaconry when Giles got us the beer? He was getting terribly drunk, but just before he left he went to the lavatory and took an awfully long time. He seemed to have sobered up instantly when he came out."

"I remember, go on."

"After he left and you were putting your things away, I went to the lavatory, and I found a stack of old newspapers there with one on top which had the front page torn off. Of course, I didn't think anything of it at the time. But now I remember that paper was also dated the third of February."

"Are you certain?"

"Mort, keep in mind, after all, I'm a trained police detective. There was a tabloid newspaper in that bathroom with the front page torn off and dated the same day as the tabloid front page I saw in this cellar just a few minutes ago. Do you doubt me? Oh, drat!—I threw away all those old newspapers."

"Not when you put it that way," he said. "Now let's go back to the assault. How did this happen to you? Assuming that your assailant was the killer, you were lucky to escape with your life. How did he—assuming it was a he—find you? Did he follow you from the village? Was it someone in the house who heard you going down to the cellar?"

She related in detail all her movements in the cellar and asked, "Could there have been an alarm system? I'm almost positive that no one could have been following me."

"Perhaps. Let's get you home and give you a chance to rest."

As they reached the top of the cellar stairs and rushed to the banqueting hall, they heard footsteps coming down the main stairway. The light turned on, almost blinding them, and Magnus Mandeville, dressed in pajamas and robe, confronted them, a look of scorn on his face. "I suppose you have an explanation for your uninvited presence here," he said.

Priscilla quickly spoke up. "I left my keys in the cellar the day we found Giles's body. I needed them desperately and didn't want to wake anyone."

Mandeville's face took on an amused smirk. "If I used that line in one of my productions, they'd accuse me of making pot-boilers. Now what were you really doing here?"

Mort said, "You heard her explanation. We apologize for entering this way but if you have any further questions, discuss them with our solicitor, Trevor Tremaine." Taking Priscilla by the hand, he walked to the door and left.

"Whew," said Priscilla. "Do you think he'll cause trouble for us with the police?"

"If I judge correctly, he won't. I think he likes having the police around even less than finding us here."

"He must have heard us in the cellar."

"I doubt that."

"But why," said Priscilla, "was he awake at four o'clock in the morning and apparently waiting for us to come up?"

"That, my dear, is one more among a myriad of unanswered questions. Perhaps he heard me come in—I was not exactly quiet about it. But I think it might be wise to find a way of looking a bit more into the background of Magnus Mandeville."

"Oh," said Priscilla, "that reminds me of something Robin Steele told me. He said Magnus spent some time in the U.S. where he was—what was the expression?—P.N.G.'ed. That's a new one on me, but Robin was so terribly busy trying to be amorous that I had no chance to ask him to explain, and I meant to ask you, but we've had so much on our minds. Do you know?"

"Declared *persona non grata*. Officially asked to leave and not come back."

Chapter *FOURTEEN*

Inspector Penhaligon was not in good humour when Mort and Priscilla called on him Monday morning.

"All right, I'm cheesed!" he said. "What the bloody hell were you two doing in Mandeville's cellar Saturday night?"

"Oh, that's it," said Priscilla, giving Penhaligon a pretty smile and turning to Mort. "You explain, Mort."

Mort didn't know where to begin, but Priscilla rescued him by speaking again. "Actually it's my fault, Inspector. Let me give you a full explanation and an abject apology. First, I made the visit alone. Mort stayed home sleeping. In fact, I'd asked him to accompany me but he wanted to wait until this morning when we could consult with you. Mort did not go back on his bargain with you, it was my fault alone."

"How did you find out?" said Mort, looking at Penhaligon.

"From Glubb, the handy man. It seems Mandeville jumped down his throat for leaving the broken door lock unrepaired for so long. But Mandeville said he didn't want to bring in the police, so Glubb called me on his own. Now, young lady," he said, turning to Priscilla, "I imagine you'd like to tell me all about it, wouldn't you?"

Priscilla told him what she did, her reasons why, and how Mort came just in time to save her. "I can only say that I had the most uncontrollable urge to look for that newspaper as soon as possible. Call it woman's intuition or whatever, but I felt that that newspaper would be gone before another sun rose. And we did come promptly to report to you."

As Priscilla talked, Mort studied the graying police officer to assess how much damage had been done. He was upset, but not irreversibly so by the cellar incident, especially since Mandeville himself had made no complaint. Priscilla, at great personal risk to herself, had found a significant clue and confirmed that some unknown person, probably the killer, was still engaged in mysterious activities. As Penhaligon became convinced that Mort had not betrayed his trust, his confidence in Mort seemed to be coming back.

"So it seems you had an encounter with someone who could be the killer," said Penhaligon to Priscilla. "But you can't describe the person in any way?"

"I wish I could, Inspector, but as it was, I was terribly lucky to get away with my life."

"Yes, yes, I see. I only wish you had told me first what you wanted to do."

"I'm terribly sorry I didn't tell you first, Inspector, and if you'll not let it interfere with your arrangement with Mort, I promise I'll never do it again. And besides," she said with a smile, "as we said on the phone, we have some other important information for you."

"Which is conditioned upon my forgiving?" said Penhaligon, starting to look uneasy.

"No, no," said Priscilla. "Mort, tell him everything. No strings attached."

"Well," said Mort, "we found more letters Sylvia had hidden in the house." He proceeded to describe them. When he finished, he placed everything in Penhaligon's hand.

The inspector took a few minutes to look at the letters. "It seems that one man has motive because Sylvia was too cold—no doubt Tony Trelawney; another because she was too hot—Charles Fitzpen; and dear Winifred—bless her soul—might escape paying her debt if she wanted to after Sylvia died. You're not suggesting a conspiracy, are you?" He was obviously pleased with the new tangible evidence they had given him.

"I'm not suggesting anything, Inspector," said Mort. "We are merely reporting to you what we found and doing so at the earliest practical moment."

"I'll have to question all three of them. Let me suggest...." Penhaligon turned abruptly to face Priscilla. "No, let me order you not to discuss these matters with any of those three people, nor with anyone else, until after I've talked to them."

"I see," said Priscilla. "I suppose there's no harm...."

"She means," said Mort, "that we're in perfect agreement with you. Perhaps after you've seen them, there's no problem...?"

"Perhaps," said Penhaligon, still glaring at Priscilla.

"Just one more thing, Inspector," said Mort. "How much of an investigation have you made on Magnus Mandeville?"

"A routine check of police files."

"Would it be possible to initiate a request for additional information? I would suggest you look for anything in the U.S."

"You're leaving something unsaid, aren't you?"

"All right," Mort said with smile. "I telephoned London this morning and spoke to a friend in the American Embassy. My friend said Mandeville is known to U.S. police authorities."

"Well, I could ask for an inquiry with American liaison." He paused as if to think. "Now here's something you'll find of interest. It seems Giles Bacon walked into a pub in Truro last Wednesday around 6:30 in the evening and ordered fish and chips and a bottle of strong ale to take away. He was alone. Where was he before then, and where was he between the time he left the pub and the time he was murdered? And why did he disappear in the first place?"

Mort and Priscilla seemed to be paralleling each other in opening their mouths and looking startled.

"Yes," said Penhaligon, "I thought you'd like that. We felt the same way." He paused. "And the identification was positive. The barmaid said she couldn't forget him because he kept flirting with her, winking and smiling all the time. He made her feel so uncomfortable that she called the landlord over, and when Giles saw him approach he hurriedly took his purchases and left."

"Interesting," said Mort.

"Puzzling," said Priscilla.

"Now if there's nothing more I can do for you two," said Penhaligon, "I have another appointment." He started to open the door for them.

"I have one more little thing," said Priscilla.

The inspector slowly relinquished his grasp on the doorknob.

"Is there any single place where I might see all the Cornish newspapers that were published on 3 February of this year? I'm sure that if I saw all the papers together I'd recognize the one from the cellar."

"Good idea. I'll be happy to get them, Sergeant Booth, and I'll ring you when I have them."

"Thank you, inspector. You're so helpful. Isn't he, Mort?" she said, smiling sweetly at both of them.

*   *   *   *   *   *

"Damn it, Priscilla," said Charles, "you know why I lied about Sylvia. I am—or at least was—happily married. I suppose Elspeth will have to find out now."

"That's not certain," said Priscilla. "After all, I'm not going to tell her and I doubt that the police will."

They were in the living room of Priscilla's flat and she was pouring tea. A tray of bite-size sandwiches was on the buffet.

Charles sat in an easy chair with his legs crossed. "But you know. And I assume therefore that Mort knows. Who else will the police tell?" He popped a sandwich in his mouth. "These are rather good. Chicken pate with walnut? Did you make them or buy them in a bakery?"

"Mort made them. He's awfully clever when it comes to fine food. But, Charles, did the police tell you how we found out?"

"They told me next to nothing. Just a brutal 'Why did you lie to us about your relations with Sylvia'?"

"I'm sorry. I'm partly to blame." She told him how she and Mort had by chance found his letters to Sylvia. "We had to tell the police or be guilty of withholding information."

"Oh? I see. Well, they practically accused me of murdering Sylvia to prevent her from telling Elspeth about it. They seemed convinced that I had done it and that the harder they were on me, the more likely I would confess."

"Oh, Charles, Charles. You're an attorney, you should know that's a common police technique all over the world. We're...they're that way with everyone. A murderer's conscience is unlike anyone else's. That's especially true if you distinguish the amateur murderer from the professional, from the hit man. Based on ample experience, the police hammer away at all suspects hoping that the guilty one will not be able to take the pressure. But they don't expect an innocent person to crack. At least not nowadays. Believe me, I know."

Charles laughed. "It's difficult to believe that you're a hardened copper at heart." He got up and put more sandwiches on his plate. After a look of hesitation, he said, "There's something I'd like to tell you, but I won't. On the one hand I trust you as my cousin, but on the other, you don't let me forget that you're also a policewoman."

Priscilla's face lit up. "You mean something you haven't told the police?"

"Yes. But don't ask anything else."

She could see he was determined. "All right. I'll wait until you're ready, if you ever are." She poured them both more tea. "Tell me, Charles, how did Sylvia take it when you told her you were absolutely breaking off the relationship?"

"I thought I'd already said. At first she threatened to tell Elspeth. I told her to go ahead. This was several weeks before she was killed. When she realized I was adamant, she just dropped the matter. She was no longer insistent, nor did she say anything more about telling Elspeth. She just acted as if there had never been any issue between us in the first place. We gradually became friends again. It was Sylvia's nature to want to be friends with everyone."

"But I understand she became morbidly suspicious during those last few weeks." She was not going to tell him about the letter Sylvia had written explaining her suspicions.

"Yes. That part's inexplicable. I suppose her suspicions included everyone, though perhaps one more than others."

"Who?"

"I shouldn't have said that. It's just my own feeling. I told you, I can't discuss it now. Perhaps later, depending on how things go. Please, Priscilla, don't press."

"Have another sandwich, Charles."

*   *   *   *   *   *

Mort was alone with Tony in his shop. He had bought a book and engaged Tony in a discussion about crime novels. Tony showed himself to be well up on the genre, though somewhat mystified at real-life police procedure.

"Ah," he said, "I thought I knew how the police worked, but I was surprised this afternoon when they called me in."

"Oh," said Mort, "about the murder investigation?"

"Oh, ah, absolutely. Well, I don't mind telling you, Mort, since you're sort of involved in the investigation anyway. The police probably keep you fully abreast of everything and you probably already know about this."

Mort said nothing.

"Ah, I see. Had you heard that they found a letter I'd written threatening Sylvia's life?"

Again Mort kept his silence.

"You're not saying. I'd rather thought that you and Priscilla probably found that letter and gave it to the police. Where else would they have obtained it?"

"Were they rough on you?"

"Rather. They accused me of murdering Sylvia, but they didn't arrest me. How can they do one without the other? I admitted I wrote her a threatening letter. I would have thought that with a letter like that in my own handwriting they would have arrested me—even though I didn't do it. You know, specifically threatening to kill someone? But they let me go. I just don't understand the police."

"They must have accepted your explanation."

"Oh, ah, do you think so? Of course, I told them that I wrote the letter in the heat of anger, but that I was incapable of murdering anyone. You must admit that it's one thing to write hasty words and quite another to throw someone off a cliff."

"Or murder an author?"

"Oh, yes, ah, Giles. I'd forgotten about him. The police mentioned him casually, it was Sylvia they were interested in. You know, I wasn't really in love with Sylvia. I love Gwen."

"That letter you sent made it look otherwise."

"That's what the police said. But you see it wasn't Sylvia as such that fascinated me. If you want to know, it was sex."

"Sex?"

"Yes. You know, the sexual experience. The act itself. You know I had been married to Elspeth before, and even though she looks a bit cold on the outside, in bed she's really not. And you know Gwen is a rather hot number. Even so, I'd never experienced anything like being in bed with Sylvia. I mean, I'm being frank, but she was dynamite. You know, bang!, fireworks, sirens, all that. I mean, she showed me a thing or two!"

Mort looked at him incredulously. "Are you saying that you weren't in love with Sylvia, but thought of her as a sex object to the extent of threatening to kill her."

"I'm glad you see what I mean, that I wasn't jealous. I probably misled you when I first told you of my relations with her, I mean, I suppose I was more obsessed with her than I admitted but I wasn't jealous. You see, I didn't care how many other lovers she had. I wasn't possessive or demanding or anything. Once she had trained me to get in bed with her, I just loved the sheer experience of it. That's all I asked of her, sex every now and then, nothing more. Then she dropped me cold after Gwen talked to her. You see, the sex act didn't mean that much to her. To her it was like shaking hands, and she didn't really care if she was shaking my hand or yours or Charles's or Giles's or Robin's or Magnus's or what. She always gave more than she received. She showed what she thought of me when she obviously found our relationship not worth carrying on if she had to suffer confrontations with Gwen because of it. Still, I couldn't have killed her. I had the hope that as we became friendlier again, we might eventually get together in bed again. You see?"

"No jealousy at all?"

"None. Even when we were out on the path the day she died, we had a very rational talk, and she stuck to her words, no sex now, but she agreed that we might someday resume."

Mort jumped inside but outwardly maintained his calm. He glanced at Tony and said softly in carefully composed words, "The day Sylvia died you were on the cliffs with her? By any chance were you wearing blue trousers and a yellow anorak?"

"Yes, those are mine. I probably wore them that day."

"What happened?"

"What happened? Oh, I just told you. Oh, you mean…I see, yes. Well, Sylvia told me she was going to take a walk, and I offered to go with her. At first, she said no, she wanted to be alone, but then she agreed. I told her I'd meet her after I asked Gwen to take care of the shop. Sylvia agreed to walk slowly and I'd follow. I told Gwen I was going out in my boat, then caught up with Sylvia as we planned."

"This was close to Treleggan?"

"Oh, yes, she hadn't gone very far. I told her why I wanted to talk. I pleaded with her to have sex with me if only just every now and then. She said she'd think about it. We might resume later. So I went back to the shop."

There was something so ingenuous, so artless, in Tony's way of speaking, seemingly so frank and straight-forward, that Mort was almost inclined to believe him. In spite of being an educated man, he seemed to have none of the dissembling about him that might be expected in even the simplest-minded person. In fact, he reminded Mort somewhat loosely of Dostoyevsky's Prince Myshkin, but Tony was not an idiot, not even an *idiot savant*. Could he actually be so devious as to be feigning? Was it all a mask to disarm and outwit others? But, from what others said, apparently Tony had always been this way—it was not a manner adopted after the murder of Sylvia. So he must not be posing in order to take suspicion away from himself. And yet, Mort wondered.

"When you returned to the shop," he said, "did Gwen say anything, or suspect anything?"

"Oh, Gwen? Well, no, she wasn't there any longer. Something happened, so she called Maggie, our helper, to take her place."

Mort screwed up his face and said, "Tony, did you tell Inspector Penhaligon about all this?"

"You mean about the walk on the cliffs? Well, no, but it wasn't Penhaligon who was questioning us, some sergeant of his. The inspector wasn't there. But, no, the sergeant didn't ask. He was more concerned about any enemies Sylvia might have had."

Mort thought quickly. He should tell Penhaligon immediately, but that might seem to be implying that the police hadn't examined Tony sufficiently. These things could be touchy. Finally he decided on a course. "Look, Tony, I am sure that Penhaligon would be interested in that walk.

If I were you I would contact him immediately and tell him that there was something you forgot to say when you were with his sergeant."

"I suppose it could be important. Do you think so, Mort?"

"I think you would be wise to give him a ring."

*   *   *   *   *   *

The next day Mort and Priscilla decided to take two cars into Truro. They'd be together to talk to Penhaligon, but then Priscilla wanted to visit the Public Records Office to do more genealogical research and Mort planned to drive to St. Mawes to see an old friend. It was mid-morning when they arrived at the car park and walked to the police building.

"It seems I have to thank you, Dr. Sinclair," said Penhaligon, as he ushered Mort and Priscilla into his office, "for sending Tony Trelawney to me."

Mort looked at him cautiously, not quite sure how that "thank you" was intended.

"No, I mean it," said Penhaligon. "I'd a lot rather have you discover that we missed something in an interrogation than have one of my superiors do it. As I said, we're overworked."

"I felt the important thing was to get that information to you as soon as possible regardless of how it was done."

"It really solves two mysteries," said Penhaligon, "doesn't it? And restores my faith in disinterested, creditable witnesses. Our retired chef saw Tony Trelawney on the path with Sylvia. Then our colonel saw Gwen Trelawney on the path with her. Tony and Gwen wore identical hiking clothes, as a man and wife might well do."

"Then you've talked to Gwen?" asked Priscilla.

"Not yet. She should be here shortly. Now as I said, I'll discuss with you the statements I obtained from Tony Trelawney, Charles Fitzpen, and Winifred Redruth. They confirmed the information from the letters you gave me." He went on to give details which, in the case of Tony and Charles, added nothing new to the talks Mort and Priscilla had respectively had with them.

"Very interesting," said Mort.

"But not exactly new to you," said the inspector, seemingly in good humour. "I take it you talked to them sometime after I did and learned the same thing, with the addition of what Tony said about being on the path with Sylvia.

Mort nodded in agreement.

"Then there's nothing more to be said." Penhaligon smiled.

"Well...." said Mort.

"Well, we haven't talked to Winifred," said Priscilla.

"Oh," said the inspector, "there are some places where even you fear to tread?"

"Well, we didn't exactly feel comfortable in bringing it up...." said Priscilla.

Mort said, "We would be grateful if you'd be kind enough to share with us what you learned from Winifred, Inspector."

Penhaligon laughed heartily. "It seems there's nothing sensational there. Winifred admitted that she had borrowed £20,000 from Sylvia to help meet the mortgage on *The Case Is Altered*. She had other pressing debts and wasn't able to make any payments. Sylvia let it go for so long and then suddenly told Winifred she needed the money and started pressing for arrears. Winifred went to the banks and the building societies to see about a new loan so she could repay Sylvia, but before she obtained one, Sylvia was killed. She admits her financial position is desperate; in fact, if she were pressed for repayment now, she'd have to tie herself to one of the big breweries by selling them a part interest in the pub."

"As a beer lover," said Mort, "I hope she doesn't have to. Who would be Sylvia's heir for the note?"

"Her husband, I suppose."

"Debatable. The promissory note we handed you was found in the house Priscilla inherited, where she was also entitled to all the contents whatsoever. Thus she is the legal holder."

"But Mort, I don't want that money," said Priscilla. "I couldn't feel that it honestly belonged to me."

"You would rather see it go to Dr. Cawthorne?"

"Well…."

Penhaligon smiled at the two of them. "In the light of Winifred's debts, it would seem to be a moot point, wouldn't it?"

"Still," said Mort, "in Cawthorne's hands that note could be a sword over Winifred's head."

"Oh, I hadn't thought about that," said Priscilla. "You mean if I have the note, I can extend the payment time as much as I want."

"Exactly."

The telephone rang; as Penhaligon put it down he said, "Gwen Trelawney's outside." He hesitated as he noted the reluctance of both Mort and Priscilla to leave. "You would like to sit in as I talk to her, would you?"

"If it wouldn't cause a parliamentary crisis and topple the government." Priscilla said.

"I'll have to see first that she has no objection. Let me speak to her."

Mort and Priscilla, left to themselves, looked at each other. Priscilla said, "He's being awfully decent."

"Well, he seems to trust us more. And we have been giving him some good leads."

The door opened and Gwen preceded Penhaligon into the room. She nodded to them and took the chair that Mort offered her.

Penhaligon sat behind his desk. "It seems, Mrs. Trelawney, that your husband has already told you what this is about."

Gwen gave him a weak smile. "Yes, Inspector. You want to know what I was doing with Sylvia on the path the day she died."

"It was you in the blue and yellow clothes, wasn't it?"

"Oh, yes. Tony and I have identical outfits." Then she hesitated.

"Would you please relate the events that led up to your meeting her."

Gwen lowered her head and rested it in her hand, then, after a short pause, said, "Tony asked me to mind the store. When I saw him going in the direction of the coastal paths, I thought he might be having a tryst with Sylvia, so I called our assistant, Maggie, and asked her to take over for me. I put my own hiking outfit on and ran across the fields to take a shortcut and get in front of them. There is a place in the rocks where you can view most of the path from Treleggan for a long distance, and I hid there."

"About what time did Tony leave, and what time did you leave?"

"I didn't check the time. Tony might have left around two o'clock, three o'clock, perhaps earlier, perhaps later."

The inspector was hurriedly making notes as she spoke. "So you wanted to spy on them?"

"You could call it that. Well, yes, it was spying. I wanted to catch them at it, you know, having it off."

"I have to ask why?"

Gwen's smile was broader now. "Tony always carps at me about my activities, my friends, who I see and what I do, so I felt that if I could catch him resuming his relations with Sylvia, I might be able to get him to dry up. I don't see anything wrong with that."

"I'm not here to make moral judgments, Mrs. Trelawney, am I?" said the inspector. "Now you waited and watched them walking on the path?"

"Well, yes, but they didn't go far. And they weren't carrying on, if that's what you want. They walked slowly, frequently stopping and moving their hands excitedly, as if they were having an argument. Then Tony turned and walked back toward the village, while Sylvia continued in my direction."

"Then what did you do?"

"Well, there was no need to remain hidden any more. I walked toward Sylvia, said hello to her, and started to pass. But she caught my arm and insisted that I walk with her. So I continued with her a while. She kept talking about Tony and told me what a pest he was, always begging her to screw."

"Did she put it that bluntly?"

"Oh, yes, there was nothing subtle about Sylvia. She as much as accused me of being responsible for Tony's forcing himself on her because, she said, I was always, well, having affairs myself. She said, 'If you'd only stop screwing around with other men and keep your own husband satisfied, then maybe he'd stop begging for sex like a starved child.'"

"Go on, Mrs. Trelawney. I imagine you didn't care for that."

"Ha! I'll tell you frankly, Inspector, at that moment I could've killed her. I'd always been faithful to Tony, until Sylvia got her hands on him, and he wasn't the one who started the begging. First she threw herself at him and then she cast him aside." Gwen sat on the edge of her chair and used both hands in a choking motion to emphasize the strength of her feelings. "I even thought about pushing her off the cliff right there, but I'm not a murderer. I just showed her two fingers and put in words what she could do with herself and walked back to the village, leaving her alone on the path."

"You didn't touch her?"

"No, I didn't touch her! Good lord, Inspector, this was more than a mile from the place where she fell, or was pushed. I didn't have anything to do with that."

"Did you see anyone else on the path?"

"Not a soul. Oh, I forgot, there was one man that passed us."

"And was Tony back in the shop when you returned."

She had been about to say something, but stopped abruptly. Penhaligon repeated the question.

"No. I suppose I expected to see him there, but Maggie was still handling everything. I let Maggie go and didn't see Tony again until supper. He said he'd been out in his boat because he wanted to get away and do some thinking."

"Did you come across him at all on your way back, or see his boat anywhere?"

"No, I didn't."

"Then you can't of your own knowledge say where he might have been during the period of several hours immediately after you left Sylvia?"

"Only from what he told me."

"What time did you get back?"

"Oh, I don't know, Inspector. I was so mad that I wasn't concerned about time. I was gone maybe an hour, maybe an hour and a half."

"Maybe two hours?"

"I don't remember. I think it was around three o'clock, perhaps a little after, when I started out. You might ask our shop assistant, though she's not very precise with time or money."

There were a few more questions which yielded nothing of value, and then Penhaligon let her go. After she left, he took a notebook from his desk drawer and began comparing a page with the notes he had just made."

Mort said, "You don't have any precise times as to when Sylvia started out on her walk that day?"

"It seems that we know only it was after lunch. The problem is that Tony was even vaguer than Gwen on time. If Gwen can be relied on, Sylvia must have been killed sometime later than three p.m."

"Of course Gwen could be lying," said Priscilla, "She could have gone all the way to Pendorth with Sylvia."

"Oh, yes," said Penhaligon. "She can't give either herself or Tony an alibi."

"But you seem optimistic."

"There's much that we don't know yet. We don't even know if we're dealing with one murderer or two, do we? And yet, I have a feeling that we're getting close to a solution."

Priscilla looked at her watch. "Mort, I have to go to the Public Record Office before they close."

"You go ahead. There is something else I want to discuss with Inspector Penhaligon."

When Priscilla had gone, Penhaligon said, "I'm glad you stayed. I have something to say and, in view of Miss Booth's sensitive feelings toward me, I'd prefer to say it to you alone."

"About that cellar business?"

"It's more than that," said Penhaligon, who seemed more disappointed than angry. "I'd asked you not to discuss the case with Charles, Tony, and Winifred until I said it would be all right."

"We understood the spirit of what you said to mean to wait until after you had talked to them, and we knew you already had. But in any event I just happened to be in Tony's shop and he volunteered to talk about his encounter with the police."

"And Charles just happened to be in Miss Booth's flat?"

"I don't know if she invited him or he came on his own."

"Well, what I mean is," said Penhaligon, "I can't have the two of you as both collaborators and competitors. I have superiors to report to, superiors who ask questions, and I can't lie to them. If Mandeville had made an official complaint against you about that cellar incident, I couldn't have ignored it or smoothed it over."

"I understand how serious it is."

"It's serious enough so that if anything else happens, I'll have to discontinue our informal arrangement."

Mort grimaced and nodded his head. "I'll try my best not to let anything else happen." He paused, cocking his head slightly to one side in a questioning glance.

"Well?" said Penhaligon. "You said there was something you wished to take up with me."

Mort gave an embarrassed little laugh. "Right," he said, thinking to himself that Priscilla was better at pulling off this sort of thing, "this might not be quite the time for it. But I was wondering if it would be possible to see some of your notes on the case."

Chapter *FIFTEEN*

"What's that noise?" said Priscilla, almost choking on her toast. "Don't tell me it's that horrid man coming back?" With disgust marring her features, she looked to the ceiling.

"You mean the good Dr. Cawthorne?" said Mort. Having finished his breakfast, he sat back in his chair to enjoy his paper. He had been reading the *Times*, completely oblivious of any unusual noise until Priscilla called his attention to the footsteps above.

"I mean the evil Dr. Cawthorne. This is **my** house. I won't have him here. He's still the Number One suspect in my book."

"I don't know if we can do anything about it at this time."

The noises upstairs had stopped. As Mort got up to remove the dishes from the table, they heard a tapping on the door.

"That's not Dr. Cawthorne's knock," said Priscilla.

Mort went over to open the door. The curvaceous Joanna Gifford stood in front of him dressed in a diaphanous white blouse and tight pink mini-skirt. The sight was so dazzling that he almost had to turn his eyes away. "You must want to see Priscilla," he said, bumbling his words."

"Either of you," said Joanna, "or both."

Priscilla walked over to join them at the door. "Won't you come in?"

"No, thanks. I just wanted to let you know that I'll be living above you for a while. I remember Giles told me that from your flat you could hear every noise upstairs. I thought I'd let you know who it was so you wouldn't be concerned."

Just the opposite was happening, thought Mort as he observed concern spreading over Priscilla's face.

"You'll be living upstairs?" said Priscilla.

"Frank suggested that it might be good for me to get away from the manor."

Priscilla looked at her searchingly. "Dr. Cawthorne?"

Mort asked, "Is Dr. Cawthorne back at Treleggan?"

"Not now, but he'll be coming back Friday night."

"He'll be staying upstairs?" asked Priscilla.

Joanna's face turned red and took on a flustered look. "Oh, we're old friends. Excuse me, I must go." And she turned and hurriedly walked away.

Mort, peering over Priscilla's shoulder at the departing Joanna, could not help but admire the lines of her body, the shapely legs, the undulating hips. Then he caught hold of himself and began instead to wonder if there could have been any ulterior reason for her paying them a visit.

There was something incongruous about her relationship with Frank Cawthorne. She had told Mort that Sylvia was her friend and had used her in an attempt to cover up her involvement with Giles. But now it turned out that Cawthorne was also her friend. How and when did this come about?

"Well, I like that!" said Priscilla as Joanna disappeared.

"Somehow I don't think you do," said Mort. "Interesting, though, that they're **old** friends."

"Meaning?"

"I wonder how old. How friendly were they when Sylvia was still alive?"

"Oh, I see," said Priscilla. "Yes, of course. With Sylvia dead, Joanna could have a clear path to the wealthy doctor."

"Or Dr. Cawthorne could have a clear path to the very sexy Joanna. I told you about my conversation where she showed she and Dr. Cawthorne had obviously been discussing us."

"Oh, I don't think she's so sexy." Priscilla took quick steps toward the kitchen.

After a few seconds Mort said, "Any more tea out there?"

From the kitchen she yelled, "I'm making it now. By the way, I'm getting some wonderful material on my genealogy. Not so much in a direct Fitzpen line, but in one of the other families, Prowse. I think I may have found a royal line."

"Good luck. Shall we have a quick recap on the case?"

She brought in the tea, poured their cups, and sat down looking more relaxed. "That might be helpful. You start."

"Well," he said, "let's examine those twin perennials, motive and opportunity. First we are assuming that the person who murdered Sylvia was the same person who murdered Giles. We are handicapped because we don't know exactly when Sylvia died and we don't know where Giles was for some two days before he was killed. As suspects we'd have to include from the village, Charles and Elspeth Fitzpen and Tony and Gwen Trelawney, and of course, with that promissory note business, Winifred Redruth. From the television company we have Magnus Mandeville, Robin Steele, and Joanna Gifford. From London we have Dr. Frank Cawthorne. Any others?"

"I don't think so, nine suspects, some more likely than others."

"Let's take the shotgun approach and hope we can narrow down the possibilities later. As far as Sylvia's death is concerned, Charles had motive because Sylvia threatened to tell Elspeth about their affair. Elspeth had motive because of that affair. Tony had motive because Sylvia spurned him. But did Gwen have sufficient motive?"

"Gwen admitted in front of us," said Priscilla, "that she felt like pushing Sylvia off the cliff."

"She had motive enough. And Winifred could have had motive because with Sylvia dead there was a hope of delaying the repayment of her £20,000 debt. Funny with Magnus Mandeville, we're assuming that he had a motive, but we don't know what it was. He's the mysterious one. Apparently he knew Sylvia long before anyone else, except her husband, or perhaps he knew her even before her husband. Yet apparently he and Sylvia wanted to keep their previous relationship secret. Why? At any rate, let's say he had motive. Robin Steele puzzles me. What motive could he have had? Jealousy?"

"Not unless he's a better actor than I think he is. He's too much in love with himself to be jealous of anyone."

"Could he be feigning?" asked Mort. "Could he have killed Sylvia out of jealousy because she threw him over for Magnus? Sylvia's letter had him among the people she had hurt."

"By all means, keep him in. Now Joanna, well, we've already discussed her. If she were after Dr. Cawthorne, Sylvia would be in her way."

"We'll certainly keep her among our active suspects. That leaves Dr. Cawthorne, who had at least two motives. Sylvia made a cuckold out of him, or perhaps he wanted her out of the way so he could have Joanna. But the question that nags at my mind is, have we covered all the possible types of motives? We're assuming that Sylvia's sexual promiscuity is at the root of the whole matter, except for a financial motive in Winifred's case. Is there any hint or indication whatsoever of anything else?"

"I'll be glad when I can see those newspapers. In the cellar I skimmed all the headlines and saw nothing that seemed related to this case, and yet that newspaper seems significant."

"Newspaper, a possible clue. Anything else?"

"Let's go on to Giles."

"All right, but we have to keep in mind here that a second murder can always be a fall-out from the first one."

"Giles could have learned who murdered Sylvia, or possibly the murderer thought Giles had learned something."

"Exactly," said Mort. "The intriguing question is where was Giles from the time he was last seen on Monday until he walked into the Truro pub Wednesday evening? Was he hiding from someone? At any rate, we can't eliminate any of the nine from having motive as far as Giles is concerned."

"For Giles, motive is murky."

"Right. But we do have a better understanding of the time of death in Giles's case than in Sylvia's. When I stayed with Penhaligon yesterday he let me see his notes where he summarized what each suspect was doing on the occasion of both murders. I made mental notes and then wrote them down as soon as I left." He took a notebook out of his pocket.

"You didn't!" Priscilla's face glowed.

"Penhaligon assumes that Sylvia was killed between three and six p.m. on a Monday, but it's not so certain, while Giles was apparently killed between midnight and two a.m. the Thursday morning after we arrived."

"Let's see," Priscilla said, looking over his shoulder. "'Cawthorne—In surgery a.m.'?"

"Cawthorne was in his surgery in London during the morning of the day that Sylvia was killed. In the afternoon he said he took a drive in the country by himself to relax. He was last seen in London around three o'clock. In other words, no alibi for the rest of the afternoon. However, the only way he could conceivably have come from London in time to kill Sylvia would have been with an airplane, and airplanes, even private ones, leave records, but there is no record of him taking one. Penhaligon has checked all the local airports for arrivals."

"Hmm, I see," she said with an air of disappointment."

"Now as far as Giles's death is concerned, Cawthorne says he was alone in the upstairs flat Wednesday night. Yet I can't recall hearing him during that night. Of course, he could have been very quiet, but in any event he has no tight alibi."

"You're saying it was probably impossible for him to murder Sylvia, but he could easily have had time to kill Giles."

"Yes, that's about it. Now let's take Charles Fitzpen. He says he was in and out of his office in Treleggan all afternoon the day Sylvia died and then went to Falmouth for a business dinner. Because of the indefinite timetable regarding Sylvia's death, we'd have to say that it was quite possible he had the time to do it. But on the night Giles was killed, Charles says he stayed at Bristol on business, and the police have confirmation he was registered in a motel there and was seen in the bar when it closed at midnight. He couldn't have made it to the manor in time except again by airplane."

"But does that mean Elspeth was by herself that night?"

"You're going too fast, but yes. Elspeth was at a bridge party all afternoon when Sylvia died and she went from there with another woman to church, where they helped prepare meals for the poor; she has a perfect alibi from noon until nine that night, when Charles returned from Falmouth and picked her up at the church. On the other hand, Elspeth has no alibi at all for the night Giles was killed."

"I hope they're not all going to continue in this pattern, because so far, realistically, we're eliminating everyone."

"Well, let's see. Joanna Gifford says that she was alone in her room at the manor making script changes the afternoon Sylvia was killed, so no alibi. But when Giles was killed she was down by the beach with almost all the other television people filming their night scenes and didn't finish until after 2:00 a.m. Then she and some of the others had a nightcap in the bar and were together until two-thirty."

"Hmm," said Priscilla again. "No alibi for one, good alibi for the other." A frown appeared on her face. "But, but, could any of the television people have disappeared for a few minutes and gone to the cellar to kill Giles?"

"Penhaligon doubts it. It would have taken more than just a few minutes to arrange Giles's hanging. You don't say, 'Excuse me while I go spend a penny' and then retrieve a tied-up prisoner from wherever you've been hiding him, take him to some other room, throw a rope over a pipe, string him up, then hurry upstairs and say, 'There, that didn't take a minute, did it?' And Penhaligon questioned each person at the manor extensively about the movements of all the others there, including Robin as well as Joanna. All of them have their time accounted for until at least two-thirty."

The look on Priscilla's face said she clearly didn't like the fact, but would accept it, at least tentatively.

"Let's go on," said Mort. "Magnus Mandeville says he was wandering all over the manor the afternoon Sylvia was killed. He can get several people to say they saw him here and there, and it would be difficult to find periods of more than half an hour when he was unaccounted for, not enough time to go from the manor to the cliffs on the other side of Treleggan and back. Regarding Giles, though, Magnus's secretary confirms that he left his London office at 6:00 p.m. Wednesday; however, no one saw him the rest of the time. He says he spent Wednesday night alone in his London flat to get some sleep before driving back to Cornwall very early in the morning. In fact, he arrived just shortly before you showed up that first time you went to the manor. Of course, Magnus could have set out earlier than he said, and thus he really has no alibi for Giles."

"Is this leading up to something weird, Mort? Are you going to tell me we have no viable suspects at all?"

He laughed. "Let me go on. Winifred was alone in her pub taking inventory the afternoon Sylvia died. She closed the pub at 2:30 p.m. and reopened it at 5:30 p.m.; no alibi between those times. When Giles was killed, however, she and Gwen stayed in the pub that night long after closing in order to talk things out, Winifred being concerned about Gwen's behaviour. Unless she and Gwen were in on it together, they both have good alibis until after 3:00 a.m."

"So Gwen seems to be eliminated, too."

"Robin's next, let me cover him. He was being filmed until 2:00 p.m. the afternoon Sylvia was killed and then he drove by himself to Treleggan and later went to the pub when it opened at 5:30 p.m. He conceivably would have had the opportunity. But as far as Giles was

concerned, Robin's continual presence at the night filming is well veri-
fied, so he has an alibi there."

"Now do we come to Gwen?" Priscilla asked. "But you've already
eliminated her as far as Giles is concerned, since she was with her
mother at the pub all night."

"Exactly. Of course, we know about her movements on the cliff paths
when Sylvia was killed and she does not have an alibi there. In fact, she
was the last known person to have seen Sylvia alive."

"So we come last to Tony, who of course had no alibi for Sylvia's
death. He could have hidden behind some rocks and waited until Gwen
turned back to the village, and then he could have followed Sylvia and
thrown her off the cliff. He didn't return to his shop until much later."

"Yes," agreed Mort, "Tony has no alibi as far as Sylvia is concerned.
Regarding Giles's death Tony stayed in the pub until it closed at 11:30
p.m. and then he went home and was alone until Gwen returned."

"But you said she was with Winifred cleaning up the pub until 3:00
a.m."

"Exactly. Tony has no alibi in either case, and in fact he's the only suspect we know of without some kind of alibi."

"Aren't the police going to arrest him?"

"Now think as a policewoman, Priscilla."

Her eyes became abstract for a number of seconds and then she said,
"Of course. There's no proof whatsoever that it had to be one of those
nine who did the killings. Some other person as yet unknown could
have done one or both of them." She paused to think a bit more. "And,
of course, there could be two murderers, either separately or as a conspiracy. Robin Steele, just as an example, could have killed Sylvia, while
Magnus Mandeville could have killed Giles. Or Giles could have killed
Sylvia and then someone else have murdered him. So that leaves us
where we started."

"Perhaps," he said.

"Perhaps what?" replied Priscilla with irritation showing in her voice.

"Perhaps a defending barrister might believe that, or a judge, or a jury, but...."

Her face suddenly blossomed into a wide smile. "But you and I don't believe it for a single second, do we? I think I'm on track again, Mort. Being out of my native element, it takes me a little more time, that's all. It's one of those nine suspects. I'd bet my promotion to lieutenant on it."

CHAPTER *SIXTEEN*

The rest of the week was uneventful as far as the murder case was concerned. Mort and Priscilla sieved through the flat once again in an effort to uncover any more of Sylvia's possible hiding places, but were finally convinced that they had exhausted that particular gold mine.

Priscilla spent her days mostly doing research for her genealogy at the Public Record Office. Through Charles Fitzpen she obtained introductions to other kinfolk, some of whom were very helpful. Mort used the material sent him by his Oxford friend to write some draft chapters for his book.

Toward the end of the week Inspector Penhaligon showed a different facet of himself when he invited them to his house for Sunday dinner. Priscilla was delighted, feeling it indicated greater acceptance of her by this stand-offish detective.

Penhaligon lived with his wife, Emma, in a small detached house on the edge of Bodmin Moor. Mort and Priscilla learned that Penhaligon had a first name, Geoffrey, with Emma referring to him as "my Geoff." She was a pleasant woman, taller than her husband, and an outstanding cook. She seemed determined to stay as happy as possible in her difficult position of being an overworked policeman's wife. "If only," she said, "my Geoff can get promoted to chief inspector before he retires. It means so much. He works so hard, does my Geoff." Geoff, thoroughly embarrassed, quietly said, "There, Emma, we should accept things as they come along, shouldn't we?"

The Penhaligons took them for a Sunday drive in the afternoon to tour the moors, see Jamaica Inn on the far side, visit a deserted tin mine, and view the prehistoric man-made rock formation known as Trevythy Quoit. The Treleggan double murder case was not discussed at all until late afternoon when Emma was in the kitchen preparing tea. It was then that Penhaligon said, "Oh, by the way, Sergeant Booth, any time you'd care to call, I have your newspapers."

She thanked him. "I don't know what I expect to find, but I don't think it will be a waste of time."

"Incidentally," said Penhaligon, addressing himself this time to Mort, "I'm in your debt again for that tip on Magnus Mandeville. We checked with American liaison and learned that a number of years ago Mandeville had lived in the States, where he was selling shares in international gold mines. It seems he was not too scrupulous and there were a lot of complaints against him from people who felt they had been cheated."

"I heard that he was booted out of the U.S.," said Priscilla.

"Yes," said Penhaligon, "but not for that reason by itself. He had a partner and a mistress and it seems there was an attraction between the two which was not to Mr. Mandeville's liking. At any rate, the partner and mistress were found dead in a cabin which had been burned to cinders in northern New York. Their bodies were almost, not quite, beyond identification. The interesting fact is that they both had bullets in them and had been killed before the fire started."

"Ah," said Priscilla, getting excited. "You mean the police there thought that...."

"The police arrested Mandeville and charged him with murder, but later released him because they didn't have enough evidence. However, as an alien he could be—and was—deported from the country as undesirable."

"There's a ruthlessness about that man," said Priscilla, "that I...."

"I can be ruthless, too, can't I?" said Penhaligon. "We've questioned Mandeville about his early relations with Sylvia, but he has not given us completely truthful answers. And he's been evasive in other matters— he clearly does not like to co-operate with the police. But I think we can say that this is another case—if you'll excuse the pun—that has altered."

"How?" said Priscilla.

"When he returned from the States, he had made some money, but he was not the newsworthy man he has since become. Now suppose some of our sensationalist tabloid newspapers should learn of his arrest for murder and subsequent deportation? As one who trades in part on reputation and trustworthiness, what might happen to his business interests, his credit rating, etc.?"

"It makes my stomach turn even to think of it," said Mort.

"Exactly," said Penhaligon. "As I said, I can be ruthless, too. Tomorrow I'm going to talk to Mr. Mandeville, and I think he will—as the expression goes—come clean, don't you?"

Chapter *SEVENTEEN*

The following morning Priscilla and Mort were paid a visit by their upstairs neighbour, Joanna, this time wearing short flaring shorts and a loose-fitting blouse and looking distraught.

"I'm always bothering you," she said in a tearful voice. "I'm sorry."

It was just the right appeal to overcome Priscilla's reservations about Joanna's overly generous display of flesh. She invited her to come in, but the half-sobbing woman declined, saying merely, "Have you seen Frank?"

"Dr. Cawthorne?" The name came out of Priscilla's mouth distastefully.

"Yes, Dr. Cawthorne. Do you have any idea where he is?"

Priscilla said no and turned to Mort, but he shook his head. She asked Joanna if she wanted to talk about it.

Joanna's face perked up—she obviously did. But she said, "I must return. I'm waiting for someone to telephone me back about Dr. Cawthorne. But would you care to come up and have tea?"

"We'd love to," said Priscilla, not bothering to consult Mort and putting an arm loosely around Joanna to reassure her.

On entering the upstairs flat Priscilla remembered that this, too, would soon belong to her, and she looked around to make a mental inventory. Sylvia had obviously decorated the two flats in identical fashion, but the upstairs one showed more signs of wear and damage. Of course, a variety of tenants coming and going would not have given the place the care that an owner would.

After making them tea Joanna sat down and said, "Frank—that is, Dr. Cawthorne—had planned to come down from London Friday night. But here it is Monday morning and he hasn't arrived yet. I telephoned his house but there was no answer. I rang his office and he wasn't there—they said they'd call me back, that's what I'm waiting for. I'm so worried, especially after what happened to poor Giles."

"You think Cawthorne has met with foul play?" said Mort.

"I don't know what to think," she said, tears overflowing from the corners of her eyes. "I've had such hard luck. I'm no good for myself or anyone else." She broke out in open crying.

Priscilla moved over to the sofa where Joanna was sitting to try to comfort her. "Perhaps," she said, "it would help to start at the beginning—that is, if we aren't prying too much."

Heaven forbid, thought Mort.

Joanna reached for a tissue and dried her eyes. She drank a little tea, rearranged her position on the sofa, and tried to smile, but not too successfully. "Well, it all began when Magnus threw me over for Gwen. And the way he did it! He kept accusing me of being unfaithful, of still having relations with Giles and Robin. That's why I didn't tell anyone the full story about Giles; Magnus would have used it as confirmation that I had been too friendly with him."

"The full story about Giles?" said Priscilla. "Well, there's nothing stopping you from telling it now."

"I suppose not. All right, the Monday before he died I telephoned Giles and asked if I could see him in the morning to discuss some script changes. I wasn't sure how receptive he'd be to this, seeing as how he didn't like Magnus. But he said he'd be delighted and, in fact, there was something important that he wanted to discuss with me. I asked him if we could discuss it over the telephone. He said no, but he'd give me something to think over. How would I feel about coming back to him if he had sufficient money?" She paused and looked first at Mort, then at Priscilla.

Seeing that she was holding their attention, Joanna went on, "He told me he had in mind some place like Majorca, where we could afford to live a life of ease while he wrote some best sellers. I didn't know what to tell him, except I suppose I asked him where he was going to get all the money. He told me that when I came over in the morning—that was the morning when I first met you because he wasn't there—we'd discuss the possibilities. I thought it strange because just the previous day he said he had almost no money and was relying on the success of his new, uncompleted novel to make a living. I thought perhaps he had sold his book in the meantime for a sizeable advance, but somehow I don't really think that was it."

"About what time was this on Monday?" asked Mort.

"I don't remember. Late afternoon or early evening. When he disappeared, you can imagine how my mind worked. I wondered if he had become involved in some illegal activity, perhaps some gang activity, and had endangered his life. When I learned that he'd been murdered, I was scared to death. My first thought was to wonder if they were after me, too. But I was also concerned about my relationship with Magnus because I needed him then more than ever. He was getting more and more infatuated with Gwen and finding fault with me, and I was afraid to say anything."

Priscilla patted her on the shoulder and could feel her trembling. "Did Giles say anything else that Monday when he telephoned? Anything at all?"

"No, it was a short conversation. Oh, but there was one strange thing he said. Now what was it?" She closed her eyes and wrinkled her forehead. "Yes, I thought it mysterious because he said something like this, 'Strange how the wreck of one man's life becomes the beginning of another's fortune.'"

"Were those the exact words?" said Mort.

"As exact as I can recall. They were just about the last words he ever spoke to me."

"How does Dr. Cawthorne figure into all this?" asked Priscilla.

"I was trying to tell you. What I feared, happened. Shortly after Giles was murdered, Magnus told me we were through. And he said if I wanted to keep my job I'd better not cause trouble. Then by chance I came across Frank the last time he was here, and, as I said, we were old friends."

Something in the expression "old friends" put Priscilla on alert, but she felt she should not pursue it at this time. Nonetheless Joanna seemed compelled to purge herself.

"I might as well tell the truth," she said to Mort, "which I didn't quite do when we were together that day at the pub. I told you how Sylvia would invite me to dinner as cover for her affair with Giles. Well, it was a bit deeper than that. Sylvia was using me as bait for Frank to take suspicion off herself. Yes, Frank and I had an affair, and I knew what was going on, but Frank didn't. He thought Sylvia didn't have the slightest suspicion about us, when all the time it was Sylvia who had arranged everything."

"Whew!" said Priscilla. "I never knew my dear cousin could be such an awful little schemer."

"You don't know half the story," said Joanna. "But that's another matter." She was actually smiling a bit now. "Your tea's cold. Let me freshen it." She walked to the kitchen.

"You're feeling a bit better now," said Priscilla, as Joanna returned with full cups of tea.

"Much better, thank you," said Joanna. "It helps to talk. Where was I? Oh, yes, I had met Frank in the village as he was leaving for London and I poured out all my woes to him; that is, about Magnus. Frank suggested that I might be more comfortable in his—I mean, your—flat, and he said he had the right to let me stay here. He promised he'd come down again Friday night and cheer me up. We'd have a great time, just the two of us. He's really a most interesting man. I know sometimes he seems abrasive, but he's really very nice. I like him. But now I'm so afraid for him."

"Why don't you ring his office again," said Mort. "They might have telephoned when you were downstairs."

Priscilla moved back to her chair as Joanna walked over to the telephone. Suddenly there were heavy footsteps on the outside stairs. The door was flung open and Cawthorne appeared in person.

He stared at Priscilla and Mort briefly, then said, "You obviously weren't expecting to see **me** come through that door."

"We were just leaving," said Priscilla. "Come on, Mort."

Cawthorne held up a huge hand and motioned them to sit down again. Softening his voice, he said, "No, please stay. I have something to say that concerns you. But first, let me apologize for my boorish actions over the necklace—I mean, my trying to evict you so rudely."

Priscilla looked questioningly to Mort as she slowly took her seat again, while Mort, remaining standing, reached to take her hand in his. Joanna clearly didn't know what to make of the new event. When Cawthorne first appeared she had started to go to him, but when he held up his hand, she stopped moving, took a few steps backwards, and waited.

"Sit down, please, Joanna. I must apologize to you, too, for not being able to let you know I wouldn't be coming Friday, but everything happened so fast."

"I was so worried, Frank," said Joanna. Now she started again in his direction, and this time he extended an arm to her.

"Let me go on," said Cawthorne. "I've been so confused by everything. First, Sylvia's being murdered. Then I learned she left this house to you, Miss Booth. That didn't bother me much, but when I couldn't find the necklace and realized it might be in this house for you to inherit, I was hurt. And I had earlier learned that Sylvia didn't have near what she had led me to believe in her bank accounts and investments. Again I wondered if she had left money in this house and you might inherit that, too. I couldn't understand why Sylvia in her will was spiting me so. Perhaps I hadn't given her all the attention she wanted, but in the main we had a pleasant and friendly relationship."

Priscilla said, "We found neither jewels nor money in the house, Dr. Cawthorne. And please believe me, I never wanted to take anything away from you. I even felt guilty about inheriting the house."

"I don't disbelieve you. As for money, I knew that Sylvia should have had far more than we could find. Last week I decided to make my own investigation. I flew to Canada, where Sylvia's parents had died. I talked to their attorney and that was a revelation. They left her next to nothing!"

"Nothing?" said Priscilla. "But the necklace, and all?"

"It took all her father had just to give her an education—I believe it was at university that you two got to know each other well, Miss Booth. He died shortly after she returned to England, and the mother died a few months later. The parents had lived almost entirely on his pension. There was nothing left. There was no family heirloom. Sylvia had a very valuable necklace, but it was not from her family, and I have no idea where it came from or where it's gone now. Nor do I have any idea where Sylvia obtained her money, for she indeed had a fair amount at one time, even paying all cash for this house." He seemed finished with his explanation and drew Joanna over to the sofa, where they sat down.

"It appears more and more," said Priscilla, "that the most mysterious thing about this whole business is Sylvia herself. I don't think any of us ever really knew her."

Joanna sat upright and said, "The only person who really knew Sylvia was Magnus Mandeville, and he won't tell anyone about their previous relationship."

"That's what you think," said Priscilla.

"What?" Joanna appeared startled. "No one can get Magnus to say anything he doesn't want to say."

"Well," said Priscilla, "I have inside information—and I'm don't think there's any harm in telling you—but the police are interrogating

Magnus Mandeville today, and they have enough on him to get his full cooperation. If Magnus is the clue to Sylvia's mysterious past, we'll soon find out."

"Oh my god!" said Joanna. "Oh, no!" She put her hands up to grasp her forehead.

"I don't understand," said Cawthorne. "Why should you be so upset, Joanna, if we get some answers to this whole conundrum?"

"Because," said Joanna, raising her voice, "it can bloody well hurt others. It can hurt me and it can hurt you."

"You're being ridiculous," Cawthorne said.

Mort said, "You apparently know more than you've been telling, Joanna."

There was a long silence as she sat with an irresolute expression on her face before responding. "Let me tell you something else about your precious cousin, Miss Booth. Do you know where she obtained her money? She came back to England with nothing. All she had were family connexions and an education, her looks and her wits, but no money. What do you think she did? She became a prostitute in Mayfair." She paused to let that bombshell take effect.

Priscilla and Dr. Cawthorne gasped at the same time.

"I, I, I can't believe that," Priscilla said.

"Oh, it's true, all right. Not just any prostitute, mind you, that was not for Sylvia. She became a high-class call-girl and you can believe she was very much in demand. She was also an entrepreneur and quickly realized that the person owning the business made most of the money. You're right about her having money, Frank. Even after buying the necklace and house, she was loaded."

"She wrote me," said Priscilla, "that she was in the catering business."

Joanna laughed loudly. "It was catering all right, but she served something other than canapés and hors d'oeuvres. She had a posh call-girl business, perhaps the best in London. Believe me, I know. She had a way about her and she had all of the charm and *savoir faire* to make it work. She joined various literary and artistic groups, where she scouted out other well-born, well-educated, cultured, but moneyless girls like herself. That's how I first met her after leaving Cambridge."

Frank Cawthorne made almost a painful sound as he looked at Joanna in amazement. Priscilla stared at them both with unbelieving eyes.

Mort said, "You're telling us she recruited you into her select group?"

"Exactly, and guess who was my first client? Magnus Mandeville. He already knew Sylvia and had her come see him frequently. By this time she no longer personally accommodated many clients, having become very selective, but Magnus was big enough, important enough, for her to give him anything he wanted. When from time to time he wanted variety, she'd send one of her newest girls to him, and that was when I met him. So Magnus and I are old friends, too, so to speak."

"So this is what Charles meant about Magnus having a sword over Sylvia's head?" said Mort. He looked over to see how Cawthorne was taking all this. Not very well.

"Yes. How Sylvia would laugh if she could see us now."

Frank Cawthorne was noticeably shaken. "I can't believe all this. Sylvia? My wife Sylvia?"

Joanna said, "After Sylvia saved enough money, Frank, she yearned for respectability again, and that was when she met you. You had position and wealth and were still unmarried, and she decided she was going to marry you. It was easy enough to get you in bed, but she had to convince you that she was close enough to being your social equal. She had the gentry background, and from her 'catering' business she had enough money—all she had to do was combine these two facts. Obviously she was successful at it, for you married her."

"Well, yes, I did. She had me convinced that her parents were well off. She lived well, had a luxurious flat, expensive clothing, and then when her mother died she told me she had inherited a family heirloom, the expensive necklace, plus some money and some trusts. Everything dove-tailed, and I accepted every word she said. I can't believe I was taken in by her."

"I'm sorry, Frank," said Joanna, "but you **were**. A lot of people were taken in by her."

"Does all this have to come out publicly?" asked the doctor. "I mean this sordid affair is past history. It can't have anything to do with the murder case, can it?"

Mort said, "First, it certainly could have something to do with the murder case. At this time the police don't even know what the motive was for two killings. Any fact about either victim is pertinent to their investigation. Second, when Inspector Penhaligon finishes interrogating Magnus Mandeville he'll know everything that we just heard, possibly more, and he'll be obliged to make a complete report. There is no way on earth this sordid affair, as you put it, can be kept a secret."

Frank Cawthorne was looking more and more uncomfortable as Mort spoke, even a little greenish, thought Priscilla. With his mouth open he stared vacantly ahead, then suddenly said, "Oh my God! Oh my God!" He put one hand to his mouth and another to his stomach, stood up, and rushed to the bathroom, slamming the door shut behind him.

Priscilla stared after him in amazement. "I can see how he'd be shocked at all this, but I should think being a surgeon and all—you know, nerves of steel—that he'd be able to show a little more restraint."

"There's more to it than meets the eye," said Mort.

"Meaning?" said Priscilla.

"He just lost a knighthood."

Chapter *EIGHTEEN*

"It seems you and your lady friend already have all my information," said Inspector Penhaligon. His tone was one of playful irritation, as if he were trying to remind Mort of the bounds.

"In the spirit of our cooperation I thought it best to tell you what we learned from Joanna Gifford and Dr. Cawthorne before asking about Mandeville," said Mort in the inspector's Truro office.

Mort was by himself, Priscilla remaining at the flat with Joanna. Dr. Cawthorne had changed his mind and decided to go back to London, though he told Joanna she could stay in the flat "for a day or two" if she wished.

The day was heavily overcast with dark clouds rolling in from the sea. Mort, sitting in front of the desk, was relieved to note that Penhaligon's reservations about their co-operation were gradually oozing away. The liaison relationship, necessarily delicate in the beginning, seemed to have been strengthened by the personal bond which had developed between them, especially since Sunday at Penhaligon's house. Nonetheless, Mort felt it was best to keep as low-key as possible.

When Mort finished his story, the inspector said, "I can add to that. When Mandeville returned to London after deportation, he had ample funds to go into business with new partners, buying up small companies in the entertainment field. It seems he met Sylvia when she, as a call-girl, was sent to his London flat. She pleased him and he continued seeing her. She decided to start her own business, but it was

Mandeville who lent her the money to do so. She bought a town house and was off to a good start as the Mayfair Madam, so to speak, but again it was Mandeville who sent her many of his business associates, especially rich foreigners, so that the new enterprise could prosper. When she wanted to marry Cawthorne, Mandeville arranged to have a group of men buy her out, increasing still further her savings and investments. It seems she retired with several hundred thousand quid, plus property and jewels.

"During her marriage to Cawthorne she still saw Mandeville on discreet occasions. Cawthorne, of course, introduced her socially to a number of important people. She was able to chain her acquaintances, and eventually she and Mandeville agreed to hide completely their earlier relationship. By the time she started taking up with Giles, her new friends were unaware that she and Mandeville even knew each other, until she was later properly introduced to him at some society function."

"Of course Joanna knew," said Mort.

"Yes, she would, wouldn't she? When I questioned Mandeville, he mentioned her, but only reluctantly. He denied that anyone else knew. It seems that while he was filming the first Urquhart series on the north Cornish shore, he would quite secretly visit Sylvia in Treleggan, so he was not a stranger to the area, and that's why he didn't need much convincing to change his mind suddenly and film the second series at Treleggan and Penstead Manor. He says that Sylvia did not know he had been arrested in the States and then deported, so she had nothing she could hold over him, but he of course knew enough about her to wreck her marriage if he were so inclined. Thus he points out that Sylvia might have had something to gain by killing him, but he had no motive for killing her."

"No premeditation, perhaps," said Mort. "But there are such things as crimes of passion and so on. Not to mention the possibility of his lying. Where did Robin Steele find out about Mandeville's deportation from the U.S.?"

"They knew each other during Steele's Hollywood period, but Mandeville had sworn him to secrecy, and he was being indiscreet when he told Miss Booth. Sylvia trusted Mandeville because he already knew so much about her, but she was cautious in adding to his knowledge. She told him of the two 'accidents' endangering her life in London, but did not tell him about the Treleggan attempt. Mandeville told us essentially the same as he told Miss Booth, that he thought Sylvia was afraid of someone. She telephoned him on three occasions to let him know that she was going to be alone with that person. This was more detailed than his earlier statement—he's a very reluctant witness."

"Surely he told you," said Mort, "what he would not tell Priscilla, the name of the person Sylvia feared."

"Oh, yes, he told us that all right."

"And that person is?"

The inspector smiled and said, "Would you care to guess?"

Mort laughed. "I'd guess it was Tony Trelawney."

"Rather obvious, isn't it? Tony Trelawney. I even suspect that Sylvia telephoned Magnus on the day she was killed to say she was going for a walk with Tony, but Magnus denies it and there's no way I can prove him wrong. Not that he would want to protect Tony so much, rather he instinctively just doesn't like to co-operate with the police."

"And Tony is the only suspect without a good alibi for both murders."

"That makes him rather interesting, doesn't it? We've been soft with him so far pending a detailed investigation of his past, any previous offences, sex troubles at Oxford, complaints against him anywhere, other women reporting fear of him. Thus far nothing. However, we're about to ask for his further assistance, and he won't be cosseted this time."

"Tony's your chief suspect then?"

"It would seem so, wouldn't it? Before you leave, I have one more interesting item for you. We've found the necklace."

"You have?" said Mort, beaming. "Had it been pawned?"

"Something rather similar. First, it seems that Sylvia bought the necklace at an auction for fifty thousand quid after her mother died and shortly before she married Cawthorne. Now the necklace has turned up in the hands of a collector who bought it from a dealer whose reputation is not as scrupulous as one might wish. We've gone over the details *ad nauseam* with this dealer, but he's sticking to his story. An American or Canadian sold him the necklace for twenty thousand."

"I see. No doubt the seller could have obtained much more if it had been a completely above-board transaction. So your dealer was not too concerned about where the seller got the necklace in the first place."

"That seems to be the case, doesn't it? In fact, our dealer claims he never saw the man. The seller telephoned him and made all the arrangements over the phone and then sent a messenger to deliver the necklace and receive the money."

"Incredible! There are actually people who would deal that way?"

"If they thought they might profit enough out of it. He sold the necklace for sixty thousand a fortnight after he laid his hands on it. Not a bad profit for keeping his mouth shut."

"But the chance he was taking! The necklace was obviously stolen and with Sylvia's murder surely the police would be onto him?" said Mort.

Penhaligon smiled. "Not exactly. It seems all this happened three months before Sylvia was killed!"

Mort, who had trained himself never to show much surprise, couldn't help but exclaim, "My god!"

"He had two visits from the messenger a week apart. The first time he examined the necklace carefully and then made numerous discreet inquiries to learn if it had been reported stolen. Only after he had satisfied himself on that score did he agree to pay the seller."

"The seller was obviously desperate," said Mort. "But that raises the question of whether the necklace was stolen in the first place. Sylvia had at least three months to report it missing, but apparently didn't do so."

"There is no record of her making any such report."

"Do you know if it was really an American or Canadian?"

"Our shrewd dealer says only that the man on the telephone making all the arrangements spoke with that sort of accent."

"And the messenger?"

"It seems he was all bundled up with hat over his eyes, scarf around his neck, and speaking with a cockney accent. Size average, age thirty to sixty, and our dealer remembers nothing more. My super says that if I make more progress like this I'll be back to where I started. He was not very pleased when last I saw him."

*   *   *   *   *   *

"Mort, that's weird!" said Priscilla. He had just come back from Truro and was telling her what he had learned.

"My word for it exactly."

"Dr. Cawthorne would have had access to the necklace, and if he sold it Sylvia might not have wanted to tell the police."

"That's one possibility. Another is that she might have given the necklace to Magnus Mandeville, or he might have stolen it. With his hold over her she would not have reported it. Or she could have needed the money and sold it herself, using some male friend to front for her."

Priscilla laughed. "Must be something in the water here. At times you're not thinking too clearly either."

Mort looked at her in surprise, then said, "Of course, you're right. Sylvia owned the necklace and would have had no need to sacrifice it for a fraction of its true value. That's the salient point. Whoever cashed in that necklace was willing to take a loss in return for having the matter covered up. Someone presumably sold it without Sylvia's consent or knowledge, yet she never reported it missing." He paused. "By the way, how's Joanna."

"I fed her lunch, then gave her a sedative and helped her get to bed. I think she'll be all right. She says that when they finish the Urquhart series, she's going to use her credits to get a job in another studio where she can start anew. She doesn't want to be around Magnus any more."

Mort shook his head. "Damn it, with all the pieces we have to this puzzle, we should be able to see a part of the picture."

"Maybe some of the pieces aren't right-side up. Maybe we're not looking at them the right way."

"All right, how are we looking at them?"

Priscilla smiled. "Well, for a start, we're sort of assuming that Sylvia's death had something to do with sex or jealousy or something like that, aren't we?"

"Sort of. What other motives could there be? Someone stole her necklace but she didn't find out until three months later? Then she confronts the thief, who murders her? Or there may be a business matter. Perhaps she started some new business and double-crossed a partner, who killed her for revenge. Perhaps in spite of Mandeville's denial, Sylvia threatened to expose his shady past and he killed her to silence her. Perhaps Cawthorne found out about her past and decided to divorce her the quick and dirty way."

"All unsupported speculation, Mort."

"All right, but with Giles I think we're on firmer ground. There are indications that he might have learned who killed Sylvia and tried to blackmail him—or her—but only succeeded in getting himself murdered. What other motives could there be?"

"Could it be," she said, "that Giles killed Sylvia and then someone, husband, lover, whatever, murdered him for revenge?"

"Good try, but it doesn't fit well with Giles's dreams of sudden riches. Let's take a new tack. Suppose Sylvia and Giles were both killed as part of a single master plot?"

"That's a novel idea. Let's see. What did Sylvia and Giles have in common?"

"They had been lovers once. They were both associated with the television company in one way or another. They'd both known Joanna for a long time. They both had strong, though opposite, emotions about Magnus Mandeville. That seems to cover it, doesn't it?"

Mort was looking out the window with his chin cupped in his hand. Suddenly there was a noise from above. They heard a toilet flush, then footsteps crossing the floor. Mort looked toward the ceiling."

Priscilla said, "Joanna going to the loo."

"Of course," said Mort loudly. "Giles lived upstairs. Giles and Sylvia had this house in common. Any significance there?"

"I don't know. Is there?"

"I don't know either. There's something in the manner of Giles's death that bothers me. This is the kind of feeling I get when my subconscious mind's at work trying to solve a problem. I can't quite break through."

They were interrupted by Joanna knocking on the door. On being invited in, she said, "I just thought I'd let you know I'm moving back to my room at the manor. I don't feel like staying here any more."

Priscilla told her she understood, and when she was gone commented to Mort, "She's probably right. Now would you mind going to Truro again? It would be nice if you'd accompany me while I look at those old newspapers."

*　　*　　*　　*　　*　　*

The variety of small local newspapers printed in Cornwall was surprising, though most of them were weeklies and that kept the number down. Only four were dated 3 February. Priscilla spread the four front pages on a large table in front of her, turned to the second page of each, turned back to the front, and then gasped.

"Oh, Mort, this isn't going to be as easy as I thought. After all, I only have a vague recollection of what I saw that night and all these newspapers look the same. Look at that—there's something about local politics on every first page. And I remember there was a picture of a fire, but three of these darn things have pictures and stories about the same fire. And that car crash is in all of them. And the shipwreck. And I remember something about the new airport. I also remember seeing a picture of a girl in a swimsuit, and—wouldn't you know it?—all four have girls in swimsuits. And just for perversity's sake, here's a story about the filming at Penstead Manor, yet that's one that I don't recall at all."

"Be calm, darling. Let's go through this systematically. There's a story about a fire in three papers, so we can eliminate one. And of the three, the new airport's only in two so we're narrowing it down. Is there any way you can decide which of these two is the newspaper you saw?"

"No, but the girl in the swimsuit is vaguely familiar. I think she's one of the local girls working as an extra out at the manor."

"What else might be significant? I think we can dismiss the articles on local politics. Now this paper has the story about the TV company at Penstead and even if you don't recall seeing it, it has a fifty-fifty chance of being in the right paper. Remember, we're looking for something that might have activated Giles. The story mentions Magnus and Robin, but gives us nothing new."

"How about the car accident?" said Priscilla. "A man from another county was killed in a crash and—look here, Mort—the police found bags of cocaine in his trunk."

"Drugs? Let's keep it in mind as a possibility. Now the shipwreck took place just a little south of Penstead Manor and the police suspect it was a terrorist bomb. Let's file that one, too, in our mental data banks."

"On that fire in an historic house in Truro, witnesses said they saw what looked like a ghost in the middle of the blaze."

"I suppose we can't ignore it," said Mort. "Anything else?"

"Mort, look at the list of investors in the new airport. One of them is Magnus Mandeville."

"Well, well, what doesn't he have his hand in? Obviously a good possibility. If there's any significance at all in the newspaper you saw, it's probably one of these stories: TV extra as a local bathing beauty, the filming at Penstead, drug dealer dies in car accident, shipwreck possibly caused by terrorists, ghost starts fire, and Magnus invests money in local airport."

*   *   *   *   *   *

On leaving the pub that night, they noted how dark it was without the moon. Instead of cutting across the green and car park, they clung to the verges, sensing their way more than seeing it. As they turned into Haunted Lane, Priscilla suddenly lurched forward. Trying to catch her, Mort threw himself forward and whipped the air with his hands, but she wasn't there.

"Owyowwww!" Her yell was terrifying. Then after another couple of seconds. "Darn and drat!"

"Are you all right, are you okay, darling?"

"I tripped over this darn wheelbarrow some stupid lout left in the middle of the road. Oh, my poor leg." She had not fallen to the ground but was suspended over the wheelbarrow.

Mort helped her to her feet and put her arm around his neck. Then putting his arm under her shoulder he was able to help her hobble on one foot back to the flat.

"Let me wash this dirt off," she said.

When she finished, she and Mort inspected the bruise, which had now turned into a huge welt, but the skin was not broken and Mort doubted that the leg was seriously injured.

"You're going to have a sore leg for a week or two and then you'll be as good as new."

"And that was a brand new pair of pantyhose ruined," she said. "Or tights, as they say here."

"*T'evrika!*" Mort yelled.

"Tevya…you mean, as in *Fiddler On the Roof?*"

"*T'evrika!* *T'evrika!* That's modern Greek for Eureka as in Archimedes," he said. "First person singular of the past tense of the verb "to find" with a neuter pronoun in the accusative in front. Bless the man who left that wheelbarrow out!"

"I'd bless him more if he'd hit you over the head with it."

Chapter *NINETEEN*

Mort drove to Truro by himself early the next morning for a talk with Penhaligon, returning in time for lunch with Priscilla.

"At last I feel we're getting somewhere," he said, as he helped her set the table.

"You'll share your thoughts with me of course," said Priscilla.

"Of course," he said, with a touch of vagueness in his tone. "When they jell sufficiently. I'm not even sure I can put them in words at this time."

"Since when have you ever been at a loss for words? Usually I get a lecture and have to yell 'Enough!'"

"Mind you, I don't have the answer yet. But I'm getting a completely different picture of how Giles might have died, one that could possibly lead us to the killer."

"How?" she said, perking up her face in an excited look of anticipation.

Though he knew more than he had said, some of it was so unformed in his mind that he didn't fully understand it himself. It was not unusual when he was mentally juggling various elements of a complex problem. Part of his mind would be labouring unconsciously as he slept or as his more aware mind was diverted by everyday thoughts. What was fermenting in those particular brain passageways was sometimes vaguely known to him, or more often just felt. It was like trying to recall a dream on awakening only to find that it was hidden behind some hazy film of soap-suds.

"Time of death," he answered like a robot in words of monotone. Then in a more normal voice, he said, "You know how important—and sometimes how frustrating—time of death can be in a murder case. We normally assume that the victim died at the same time the murderer took the action to kill him, but that's not always true. We're going to need Penhaligon's full co-operation."

The telephone rang. Priscilla answered it and listened without comment. Putting her hand over the mouthpiece, she said to Mort, "It's Penhaligon. How do you invoke him like that?" After listening further, she said, "Yes, of course. He's here with me now. I'll tell him."

She replaced the handset. "He wants to see you at his office. May I come, too?" She followed him out the door, though with a puzzled look on her face.

The road to Truro wound around gentle hills and tidal streams through high hedgerows and occasional dark vales of densely growing trees. As they waited in the car for a farmer to move his cattle from one pasture to another, Priscilla said, "One of the great attractions of Cornwall is its unhurried ways. It's not for people who want to rush around all the time."

Mort didn't necessarily want to rush around all the time, but at this particular time he was impatient to get to Truro. As the last cow sashayed out of the roadway, he eagerly sped away.

"You know," Priscilla said, as they drove around a bend and suddenly had presented to them a sweeping checkerboard vista of lush green uphill pastures divided by hedgerows, "I wouldn't mind retiring here, living in my little two-flat house. I suppose I could even combine the two flats into one if I wanted to. I don't know that I would, but there's always the possibility. You know, if I had children and needed extra room."

"Aren't you a little young to be thinking about retirement?"

"Well, I meant if I left the force. Wouldn't it be terrific to settle in a place like this and be free to write books and just enjoy life?"

"I didn't know you wanted to write books. I'd encourage you if that's what you want, but you never mentioned it before."

"Well, I meant if someone wanted to write books."

"Oh, I see." He was silent for a while and they soon came out to the main highway. "This whole liaison concept," he said, "is so fragile—I know from my diplomatic experience. Each side wants to give as little, and get as much, as possible. When you start obtaining something extra, it's like walking on eggshells. Just one little wrong word can ruin everything."

"Am I being warned, or something?"

"Why, no, of course not. What made you say that?"

"Oh, I just thought you were tactfully telling me to keep my mouth shut in front of Penhaligon."

Mort laughed. "No such thing. I was just talking in general."

"I see." She smiled and twisted a finger around her hair. "I'll go back to thinking about how nice it would be to retire here."

He took his eye off the road momentarily to glance at her. "Isn't there a bit of inconsistency in that? You talk about leaving the force and yet your major objective in life seems to be your potential promotion to lieutenant."

"That's not so inconsistent. After all, I might make lieutenant and then resign shortly after."

"Sounds iffy. And you have no assurance of making lieutenant before retiring for old age."

She abruptly turned her head away from him and stared silently out the window. After a minute or two she said in a voice just above a whisper, "Well, I was just thinking out loud."

*   *   *   *   *   *

Inspector Penhaligon was listening. He took notes and asked an occasional question, but mostly he just listened as Mort spoke. When

Mort finished the inspector said, "With respect to the money, it seems she made a number of large withdrawals over the past two years. She usually dealt in cash, I suppose a conditioning from the company she used to keep, the fast money crowd. Her husband says she liked to keep a locked steel box in her bedroom with a large amount of cash in it. But she virtually depleted her bank account and it seems no one knows what she did with the money."

Mort asked, "And the payments into her account?"

"I have them here, but see nothing suspicious about them."

"When did she last rent out the upstairs flat before Giles took it, and to whom?"

"The last rent receipt before those for Giles was from the previous summer. Now about letting you see the entire file on the case, that might be awkward, mightn't it? All the more so since there are of course items on you two in there. At the time I didn't know you...."

"Or trust us?" said Priscilla.

"Well, er, not as much as I do now."

"But you do trust me now?" said Mort.

"Certainly. If it were just a specific report, as you requested last time.... Well, I suppose I can let you, Dr. Sinclair, look through the entire file in my office for a few minutes. But I should remove a few papers first, shouldn't I? Perhaps Miss Booth might have some errands to do in town while you're looking at it. I'll go back and get a cuppa, but I can't stay away more than fifteen minutes. That's all I can allow you." He took a file from his desk drawer and started shuffling through it.

"Half an hour?" said Mort.

Priscilla looked up and smiled at the inspector. "Perhaps instead of having tea in a back room you and I might go to a teashop. I'll bet you could recommend the best one in town."

Penhaligon couldn't stifle the hint of a smile. "Let's go, Sergeant Booth. I'll be back in thirty minutes, Mort." He removed a few papers from the file, locked them in his drawer, and left the file on his desk.

When they were gone Mort started speed-reading through the file, determined to make a first pass on the entire contents and then come back and take notes in more detail on selected items. He was just barely able to carry out his intentions in the allotted time and was turning the back cover to close the file as Penhaligon returned.

"Where's Priscilla?" asked Mort.

"She went to the bank and said she would meet you at the car park in fifteen minutes."

Mort looked at his watch. "Fifteen minutes? That will just about give me enough time to explain my theories, which have been strengthened considerably thanks to your letting me see the file. I won't hold anything back, and I'd like to see if it all means the same to you as it does to me."

Penhaligon, nodding affirmatively, said, "I'm completely at your disposal."

         *   *   *   *   *   *

On the way back to Treleggan, Mort was for the most part lost in deep thought. But after some tactful prodding from Priscilla, he said to her, "The key to this case is your house. Sylvia probably stumbled across some information and she was murdered because of it. Then Giles must have come across the same information, which also let him know who killed Sylvia, and he probably tried to blackmail the killer. So he had to die, and the killer couldn't afford to muff it as happened in the three unsuccessful attempts on Sylvia's life. Much more than in Sylvia's case, time was of the essence in getting rid of Giles. And I think here the significant thing is the way Giles died—though that hasn't been confirmed yet. We'll know more when we see Gwen."

The Case Is Altered closed at two-thirty in the afternoon, and Mort and Priscilla arrived there at two-fifteen. Gwen, wearing a long apron over a short skirt, greeted them as they entered.

Mort said, "Gwen, could I look at your leg?"

She smiled and lifted her leg to place it on a chair. "Any time you want," she said. "I wouldn't do this for just anyone, but I'll do it for you." It was a shapely leg, bare of stocking, and her mini-skirted pose was quite revealing, not to mention embarrassing to Mort.

"Not that one," he said. "The other one."

"Mort, for heaven's sake," said Priscilla, "what do you think you're doing?"

"I'm sorry," he said. "When I get an idea sometimes I pursue it too fast without explanation. Let me explain to both of you. Gwen, am I right that this mark is what's left of the bruise you got when you were in the cellar with Priscilla and discovered Giles's body?"

She looked puzzled. "Yes, that's the one."

"Do you remember what shoes you had on that day?"

She reflected on the question. After some vacillation she looked up at him and said, "No, I don't think I can."

Priscilla spoke without hesitating. "You were wearing red sandals without stockings that day, Gwen. Do you remember? Do you have more than one pair of red sandals?"

"I've only one pair of reds, and I do recall now that I was wearing them that day."

"Could you get them and put them on?" asked Mort.

After a bit more of rapid-fire persuasion from both Priscilla and Mort, Gwen started for her flat above the gift shop. Winifred, preparing to close, looked up concerned as Gwen left, but the latter motioned to indicate that she would be returning in a few seconds. Winifred acknowledged the message with a cautiously faint smile.

"I take it," Priscilla said to Mort, "you want precise measurements, that's why you want the same shoes."

"Right."

When Gwen returned wearing red sandals Mort took a tape measure from his pocket. Understanding his purpose, Gwen started to lift her leg to the chair again, but Mort indicated that he just wanted her to stand still. He knelt and carefully measured the distance from the floor to the centre of that part of her leg where the still faint ochre-magenta bruise remained.

With his eyes Mort motioned to Priscilla to double check him. "Fourteen and a quarter inches," he said, writing the figure down in a notebook."

Priscilla said, "Where to now?"

"We're meeting Penhaligon at the manor."

"Oh, I see. I didn't know."

Mort turned to face her and took her hand in his. "Oh, Lord, I forgot to mention it, darling. I'm sorry. Forgive?"

She smiled. "Of course. Well, then, let's go."

But first Mort walked over to the regulars' side to ask Winifred, "Just before Giles moved into Sylvia's upper flat, had anyone else been living there?"

Winifred smiled him her willingness to be cooperative and then thought on the question. "Yes, I seem to recall.... No, I don't think I remember any particular person there, and yet I have a vague idea that the flat was occupied."

"Would you know who had it?"

"No, I'm just thinking of seeing some lights occasionally in the upper flat at night, but I don't think I actually saw anyone there. Perhaps someone else in the village might know."

*   *   *   *   *   *

Inspector Penhaligon was already at Penstead Manor when Mort and Priscilla drove up. A uniformed police constable standing guard at the door told them the inspector was expecting them in the cellar. They found him with two other uniformed constables and a plainclothes man. Though the overhead lights had been repaired, they were using powerful electric torches to aid them in their search.

Penhaligon greeted them. "Did you get your measurement?"

"Fourteen and a quarter inches," said Mort.

"Fourteen and a quarter inches here," said Penhaligon, looking at his notebook. He led the way and pointed to a stool near the wall.

"Recognize that, Miss Booth?" asked the inspector.

"It looks like the stool that Gwen stumbled over when we were here together."

"It was important," said Mort, "to establish whether the stool was upright or already knocked over at the time Gwen bumped into it. The height of the stool exactly matches the mark on Gwen's leg, so now we know the stool was upright."

"And," said Penhaligon, "as we discussed, there were faint traces of dirt on the top of the stool. I've had samples taken for the laboratory. If that dirt matches the dirt we scraped off Giles's shoes, your theory will be confirmed."

"Our theory," Mort corrected him. "It's conceivable that Giles could have kicked the stool just before he died and it rolled out the door, but in that case it wouldn't have been upright. The killer was not present at the time Giles died, but he returned later and moved the stool, placing it upright outside the door. We've been looking for someone with no alibi at the time of death, but we should have been looking for someone with no alibi a number of hours before Giles died and again a number of hours afterwards."

Priscilla looked at them both. "Are you suggesting that the killer persuaded Giles to hang himself? It doesn't make sense."

"I'm suggesting," said Mort, "that Giles was killed in one of the most vicious but ingenious ways imaginable."

Inspector Penhaligon said, "We've questioned both the barmaid and the publican. They admit on prodding that perhaps Giles wasn't trying to pick up the barmaid, that he might have been silently pleading with her for help."

Mort turned to Priscilla. "Giles was not alone that night when he went into the pub in Truro. His captor went in with him, but probably a second later, so it would look like two customers arriving independently. The other person had some powerful means of persuasion, perhaps a gun in a pocket. That person would have ordered a beer or something and stood near, but not too near, while Giles ordered his food and drink. When Giles was ordering, his back being to his captor, he tried with facial motions to let the barmaid know he was in trouble, but she misunderstood and called the landlord over. On seeing this the companion must have immediately motioned Giles to leave, and poor Giles had no choice."

Penhaligon nodded in agreement. "The girl and the landlord think that someone else came in just about the same time Giles did and left just about the same time."

"But why?" asked Priscilla. "Wouldn't the killer be taking an awful risk? And why would Giles cooperate?"

Mort said, "To extend his life a little longer. Giles was living on hope. As long as he could stay alive, there was always a chance of rescue, and so he would be reluctantly co-operative with his captor. Why was the killer doing this? Well, I suspect again that it has to do with time of death." As another thought came to him, Mort turned to Penhaligon. "Have you found the secret entrance yet?"

The inspector looked glum. "No. We've not been searching long, but wherever it is, it's not very obvious."

"We could save a lot of time checking directly with Elspeth Fitzpen, since she used to live here."

"Right," said Penhaligon. "I'll telephone her."

*   *   *   *   *   *

The three of them drove to the Fitzpen house in Penhaligon's police car. Charles received them at the door and showed them into the living room. Elspeth walked over and greeted them. "I hope you don't mind, Inspector," she said, "but after you talked to me I thought it might be advisable to have my husband present, and so I telephoned him."

"I should have suggested it myself," said Penhaligon as they took seats. "Either of you could probably tell me, but I thought of you, Mrs. Fitzpen, because you lived in the manor."

Elspeth nodded in agreement.

"We know there's a secret entrance in the cellar," said Penhaligon, "but it's been a bother to find. It probably leads to the beach somewhere, as did so many of these hidden passageways common to ancient houses in these parts."

Elspeth nodded. "Would you rather tell them, Charles, or shall I?"

"You go ahead, darling, and then if they want I'll go over and show them the secret door."

"Well," said Elspeth, "it's not that secret. There are many people around here who know about it. In fact, that's why we had to install a lock; otherwise who knows who might be able to enter the house secretly from the beach?"

Priscilla said, "I vaguely remember Sylvia once mentioning some underground passageway between the manor and the sea."

"No one knows exactly when it was constructed or why," said Elspeth. "In fact one theory is that it was prehistoric and later the manor was built over it to take advantage of its being there. Certainly a lot of tunnels were used during the Civil War when parts of Cornwall went back and forth between Cavalier and Roundhead. Later it could have been used for smuggling purposes, the free-traders being able to take their goods directly from the beach to the house without having to pass over land. In my time it was just a curiosity, something we used to play in as children—there's nothing like a secret passageway to excite the imagination."

"Where's it located?" asked Penhaligon.

"It's directly under the kitchen, of course, the oldest part of the house. After you make the right turn to get to the bottom of the stairs, you go straight ahead. Go as far as you can until you reach a brick wall. The door is in the wall and revolves on a round shaft from ceiling to floor. It's easy to push open except that you have to reach up to the ceiling and disengage the lock we installed. Charles will show you if you want to see it. You won't mind if I don't go, will you?"

*   *   *   *   *   *

Charles drove his own car and Mort, Priscilla, and Penhaligon followed in the inspector's. On the way, Priscilla said, "So the night I was hit on the head my assailant escaped through a hidden passageway. But I don't understand where he, or she, came from. Are you suggesting that whoever it was might have somehow learned that I was there and come in from the beach, or was it someone living in the manor who came down the stairs?"

"Neither, my pet," said Mort. "I think your assailant was already in the cellar before you arrived, and it had nothing at that time to do with you. You rudely interrupted the murderer with your rash actions."

"Already there? But not because of me? Then why?"

"You said that when you opened the cellar door for just a moment or so you heard some kind of whirring noise."

"Yes, I remember that. There was definitely some kind of weird vibrating...."

"Motor noise?" he said.

"Yes, it could have been a motor. You know, a clothes dryer or a vacuum cleaner or something like that."

"I'd say a vacuum cleaner. The killer was doing a little clean-up job when you interrupted."

"And I walked in on him! Mort, you don't think he was really going to kill me, do you?"

"Perhaps not when you first came in, but after you'd seen that newspaper…? There was no way the killer could tell what you had learned from the paper. From the killer's point of view you might have been able to understand the whole thing."

"So I was as good as dead if you hadn't come along, Mort. Who?"

They entered the grounds of Penstead Manor and Penhaligon parked the car as close to the house as he could. Charles Fitzpen helped Priscilla out, while Mort hurried around to join Penhaligon.

Priscilla repeated, "Who?"

"That's what we're going to find out," said Mort in a determined tone, "before this day is ended."

Chapter *TWENTY*

"It seems," said Inspector Penhaligon, "it might have been a good thing that Miss Booth interrupted the killer. That is, considering she was not badly injured. The point is that she might have prevented the killer from sweeping up evidence."

"I'm glad," said Priscilla in an unusually sarcastic tone, "to have been of some humble service."

They were in the manor cellar again, and one of the police constables was running a vacuum cleaner over the floor of a room which had been locked. When he finished, he carefully removed the bag and placed a sticker with writing on it.

"Send it to the laboratory for analysis," said Penhaligon.

"What on earth are you doing?" asked Charles.

Mort said, "Looking for traces of drugs. I'd thought that smuggling was ended in Cornwall, but the inspector tells me I'm wrong, only it's changed to bringing in drugs."

"Drugs?" said Charles. "In Penstead? You must be joking."

"Guessing," said Penhaligon. "Perhaps we're wrong, but we'll see, won't we? The answer will be in the lab reports."

Suddenly another answer came to Priscilla. "The newspaper! It's the article about the drug dealer who was killed in a car crash, isn't it?"

Mort nodded. "Now we know where the cocaine came from." He looked puzzled. "But didn't I tell you before?"

"You most certainly did not! Do you realize how much you've been leaving me out in the cold?"

One of the constables came out of an adjacent room and walked over to Penhaligon, saying, "This room has been recently cleaned, sir. There's hardly any dust at all."

"Good," said Penhaligon, "that's the one to concentrate on. Keep in mind that the person who last cleaned it may have been interrupted." Turning to Charles, he said, "Now then, Mr. Fitzpen, if you'd be kind enough to show us the tunnel."

It was just a few feet to the end of the corridor. Charles put one hand against the wall. With his other he took a silver pen from his inside jacket pocket and said, "Any thin round object will act as a key to release the spring lock." Raising his hand overhead to touch the rough wood and stone supports, he moved it around slowly and explored the top. "It's here somewhere, but it's been years since I had occasion to use it."

Penhaligon, Priscilla, and Mort waited while he continued his efforts.

"I don't know if I can find it," he said. "These rocks all feel…no, this one's it. I'm inserting the pen and now I can feel it releasing the catch. There!" With a bit of effort he moved his hand to the right and then brought it down so he could use both hands to push the doorway. The entire wall moved slowly around revealing a vast blackness on the other side. "The passageway is about a quarter mile long," said Charles, "but I don't know what condition it's in. It doesn't go directly to where the sea is closest to the manor, but opens behind a thicket on one of the creeks. You can get fairly close to the other end by road."

Taking one of the torches, Penhaligon briefly explored the beginning of the passageway. Priscilla could see that the roof was made of large stone slabs extending over the walls, which consisted of smaller stones tightly fitted together. The floor was of hard pressed dirt. Although there were a few cobwebs blocking the passageway, they looked relatively new, as if older ones had been torn down in recent usage.

Turning to Charles, Penhaligon said, "There's no need to detain you any longer, Mr. Fitzpen. We're going to explore the tunnel, but you're free to leave. We're grateful for your help."

"Do see that the door is secured again when you finish," said Charles as he turned to go. He walked back to the steps.

Priscilla looked to Mort and Penhaligon to see how they were going to proceed.

"Do you want to come with us or wait here, darling?" said Mort. "We don't know what we're going to find in there, but at the very least it's going to be messy."

She was torn in her mind. Though one aspect of the lady within her had reservations about ruining a costly dress, her instinct as a police-woman was to accompany them. Just briefly she wondered if they were hoping she'd stay behind.

Mort looked at her. "We're only going to see where it ends and then come back as soon as possible. Honest, darling, you're welcome to come if you wish."

With misgivings she decided to stay. As Penhaligon and Mort disappeared into the passageway, one of the constables offered her a small chair. She thanked him and sat down. As she did so, her eyes caught a gleaming piece of metal on the floor beside the open tunnel doorway. Something silver. Charles's silver pen.

He had just left, but he had to walk to the car park. She could easily catch him if she hurried.

Charles was opening his car door as she shouted to him. He looked at her and smiled, cupped his hand to his ear, and started walking toward her. She met him halfway and gave him the pen.

"It looks awfully expensive," she said. "I knew you wouldn't want to lose it."

"Thanks. It's sterling silver, a gift from a client. Weren't you going to explore the tunnel with the others?"

She laughed. "They didn't want me to get dirty."

Charles joined her in laughing. "I'll tell you what. I'll take you in the car to where the tunnel comes out. That way you won't get dirty and won't they be surprised to see you?"

It didn't take her long to decide. "Terrific! Let's go."

*   *   *   *   *   *

"I don't think I've ever been in your car, Charles," she said, as she entered the black Rover.

"I like it because it has a powerful V-8 engine. Allows me to put on the speed when I have to travel."

Quickly starting the car, he took the rough manor road as fast as it would allow and then zoomed out of the gate and darted into the road to Treleggan.

"You didn't even pause to look!" said Priscilla, shocked at someone else's reckless driving. "If another car had been coming along then, we'd have been creamed."

He didn't reply, but kept his foot on the accelerator and sped through the narrow road. Then, slowing down just a bit, he headed the car into the smaller lane that led to his house.

"Charles, where are you going? This can't be the way. Why are you going home?"

"Be quiet. I have to get something first." His tone was snappish, his face pained. Braking abruptly at the circle in front of his house, he brought the car to a halt and jumped out.

Priscilla lurched forward and for once was glad that she had buckled her seat-belt, for otherwise her head would have gone up against the windscreen. "What on earth are you doing, Charles? Ouch, let go of my arm, you're hurting me."

Having opened her door and grabbed her arm, he reached across to release her seat-belt and pulled her from the car. His action was so fast and so violent that she almost fell on the ground, and he had to give her support. "Shut up, you fool! Do as I say or I'll kill you."

Her eyes widened with fear and horrible thoughts raced through her mind. He pulled her roughly to the house, through the hallway, and to the room he used as his office. Throwing her into a chair, he said, "Stay there! Don't make a move."

Opening a small safe, he first removed a pistol and placed it in his jacket pocket, patting the pocket as he glanced quickly at her. Then he began sifting through envelopes and papers, selecting some and stuffing them into his other pockets. Finished, he spun around, grabbed Priscilla by the arm again, and started to leave the room.

Elspeth was standing in the doorway, an expression of astonishment on her face. "What are you doing, Charles? What is going on?"

"No time to explain, dearest. I have to leave the country. I'll contact you and you can join me later. You're innocent, so they can't touch you. They'll probably watch you for a while, but later you can get out."

"Watch me? Who's going to watch me? Where are you going? Why is Priscilla with you?" Understanding came over her face in a single wave. "I knew it, you killed Sylvia, didn't you?"

He pushed her aside as he yanked Priscilla by the hand and jolted her into following him. "The police are after me. I did it for you, darling," he said over his shoulder. "Priscilla's my insurance in case the police catch up with me."

Elspeth's mouth closed and she collapsed like a marionette with the strings cut, slumping into a chair and remaining motionless.

Charles pulled Priscilla through the hall to the outer door. As she dug her heels into the carpeting to slow her progress, he turned and slapped her face, saying, "God damn it! I'm desperate, don't you see? I don't want to kill you now, but I will if you make me." He grabbed her by the throat with both hands and began firmly squeezing until she could hardly breathe. "Now, will you come willingly?"

She nodded her head as much as she could in agreement and gasped as he released his grip so she could get her breath. She could feel the warm moistness of blood trickling from the corner of her lips where his hand had struck her. Was this the time to use the methods she had been taught? Could she sufficiently injure him in the one chance that surprise would allow her? He would surely kill her if she failed. Or should she go along with him and hope that a better opportunity might present itself before he had no more need of her? Given the right chance, with her black belt in karate, she might even overpower him, but suppose he had a black belt, too?

She guessed that he ultimately intended to kill her. There was no way he could leave the country with her or force the authorities to let him escape alone. Somewhere, he would get rid of her and try to go abroad in disguise. Shouldn't she act before it was too late? A kick in the testicles with all her strength might work. *Coraggio*, she told herself, *coraggio*.

He was preceding her and there was no chance to deliver her planned blow. The way he was moving her at his side, with his hand fiercely clutching her arm, dragging her and causing her excruciating pain, left no opportunity for her to put up effective resistance. Would she have the strength left if that opportunity came? If he turned just briefly toward her as he opened the front door, could she sufficiently recover her balance, firmly plant one foot on the floor, and thrust her knee with adequate force to disable her much taller antagonist?

As they rushed through the hallway, she wondered if he would exit by thrusting her in front of him or continue dragging her behind. The door opened on the left. Good, that favoured his having to put her in front. She calculated the different factors, the distance from the door, the number of seconds before he'd open it, and the way he'd have to turn to manoeuvre her through the opening. Her first leg out would be the left, the one she would need to brace herself against the door jamb. That would leave her more powerful right leg free. She knew she would have to put all her strength into that one blow. It couldn't be just a kick. When she released her leg it had to transfer 120 pounds of well-trained, well-toned body into the tiny circle of her knee, and she dared not miss.

He reached the door and opened it with his right hand as he still tightly clutched her right forearm with his other hand. He turned almost facing her as he opened the door more fully and brought her from slightly behind to almost standing beside him. In that split second he unknowingly offered her one chance at the target. She fell back knowing that with the door jamb there to support her she was now in position to deliver maximum strength.

The computer in her mind suddenly amended her programmed actions. He wasn't open enough, and yet by a quick movement of her arm that he was holding onto, she might just be able to force him to face her a bit more. Violently thrusting her arm to her right, she made him respond just as she wanted. He opened himself up to her. Even as he did so, her knee was cocked and readied so as to connect not where his nether parts were at that precise moment, but where they would be when he recovered his grip and stopped moving. She put everything she had into it and released the juggernaut of her knee toward the softness of his groin.

Oh, Lord, he hadn't moved enough! Her knee connected with his thigh and must have hurt him tremendously, but not enough. It was not the same as hitting the groin! Only momentarily did he release her arm and then just as quickly he restored his grip, only more painfully this time. "You bloody bitch!" he yelled, as he squeezed her arm relentlessly, simultaneously raising his right arm with clenched fist ready to smash into her face. Now she came face to face with the consequence of failure. She could see in slow motion the blow coming toward her and she winced and held her breath to prepare for it, fully knowing that no preparation could be adequate to save her.

Chapter *TWENTY-ONE*

Somehow the blow failed to connect. There was a disturbance outside. There were noises, a car braking, doors slamming, angry voices shouting. The hand that should have smashed her face now had a gun in it and was pointing it out the door. As Charles moved to get better aim, she could suddenly see that Mort and Penhaligon were running up the pebbled driveway at full speed, now just a matter of yards away, with Mort slightly in the lead. Oh, great, she thought, they're not even armed!

The gun in Charles's hand looked like a 9mm Biretta, at that distance just as deadly as a cannon and far more accurate. He was aiming the pistol point-blank at Mort. He couldn't miss. He caressed the trigger as one well trained; no rash actions for him, no jerking his finger wildly in panic, he was calmly preparing for two murders. Three, counting Priscilla as a separate victim when the other two were finished.

Her eyes suddenly brightened. A second chance! Charles had turned his attention away from her to sight down his shoulder at his two attackers, leaving himself exposed once more. If she could only ignore the pain in her knee. How stupid of him! He'd had all the time he needed to shoot her first and then casually execute his two male attackers.

Time expanded to fill consciousness, every second seeming like a minute or more. As he glanced at her, she knew that he knew it was too late! He could swing his pistol over to fire at her, or he could ignore her and kill the two on-rushers. Her or them, not both. Now even that moment was gone as he hesitated just a split-second too long.

The adrenalin performed faithfully. The pain in her knee gone, she shifted her weight to her left foot, pumped every ounce of energy her body was capable of into the powerful spring action of that small bent right knee, and again let it be converted into a destructive battering ram. As she released it, Charles could see what was happening, the knowledge was there in his face. He tried to recover, to take the simple movements necessary to block it, but it was too late even for that. Her knee was perfectly on target this time. His yell of pain was horrifying.

As if part of the same action, she followed through with double karate blows to his stomach and back neck, grabbed his arm, turned her back and threw him over her shoulder to a supine position. Her unbroken action continued as she leapt atop him and simultaneously recovered the gun to point it now at the middle of his face.

Charles's blood-freezing scream had almost stopped Mort and Penhaligon in mid-step. Recovering instantly, they continued their charge to the open door, where they encountered a completely helpless Charles in great pain on his back, Priscilla straddling him. He no longer had the advantage of size and weight, but was outmatched by this lithesome woman who now had the initiative and would have been in charge even without the gun. He was unconditionally defeated.

"Great girl!" said Mort. "You saved our lives."

"Lovely, lovely!" exclaimed Inspector Penhaligon, helping a dazed Charles to his feet.

"You mean I finally did something right?" she said, handing the pistol over to Penhaligon.

*   *   *   *   *   *

"You mean you knew all the time we were in the cellar that he was the one?" Priscilla asked in amazement several hours later as they sat in

Inspector Penhaligon's office and the two men explained what had gone on. Priscilla had been taken to hospital, where a doctor examined her and determined that no serious injury had occurred. Penhaligon had obtained a statement from Charles Fitzpen, but Mort and Priscilla had not seen it yet.

"We didn't have the evidence," said Mort, "and so we needed to provoke him into giving himself away. The caretaker had already told us how to open the door to the tunnel."

"But he could have killed me."

Penhaligon said, "When we didn't find you on coming back from the tunnel, we knew that you had to be with him. We had roadblocks all over and quickly learned by radio that he had not reached the main road, so we thought he must have gone to his house. We lost no time in coming after you."

"You shouldn't have done it, Priscilla," said Mort. "Oh, my darling, I'm so glad you're safe, but you shouldn't have accompanied him."

"Oh, sure," she said, as she shifted her thoughts from what Charles had done to her to think more of what Mort had not done. "Why didn't you warn me? The two of you had all that knowledge, but you couldn't trust it to me."

"I had started telling you the details, but it wasn't until Geoff and I compared notes today that we realized what must have happened. Then events were moving too fast."

"Too fast to tell me the one important detail? Couldn't you just have given me some inkling that Charles was the one? It might have saved my life, you know."

"I hadn't thought of the possibility of your going with him. You know how oblivious I am to everything else when I'm concentrating."

Penhaligon said, "Well, it's over now. We have our man and he's made a full confession which confirms in the main what Mort and I had worked out."

"He did confess then?" said Priscilla, letting her curiosity override her anger. Stall, part of her mind told herself. Don't let it go too far and say anything you'll regret. You've been through a harrowing experience and you need time to sort it all out. "I suppose it's all right for me to be given some of the details now," she said, making her tone as sarcastic as possible.

"Of course," said Penhaligon.

"Darling," said Mort, "you'll feel better after you've had some rest."

"Is that supposed to mean that I shouldn't be told now?"

"No, of course not. I didn't mean anything like that."

Calm down, she told herself. She took a deep breath and then said, "So my cousin Charles Fitzpen is the killer—and believe me, that hurts, too. Well, tell me about it."

Mort turned to Penhaligon. "You explain," he said.

The inspector looked back at him for a second, then smiled and said, "It seems the motive was the usual one, money, added to ambition and love. As with Sylvia, his parents gave him a good education, but little more, except for a dilapidated house. That beautiful house of his was just about falling down at the time he inherited it. He married Gwen and lived there in something close to squalor. As his law business gave him income, he began improving the place on a modest scale. After he divorced Gwen, he married Elspeth, the local squire's daughter. She brought him no money, but her family connexions made him very conscious of social status."

"I see," said Priscilla. "This of course was before I met him three years ago, for he was already married to Elspeth then."

"It seems he was really in love with Elspeth," said the inspector, "and he promised her a life more comfortable than she had had either at the manor or with Tony. She was ready to divorce Tony because he couldn't fulfil her ambitions. Charles lived expensively, entertained on a lavish scale, let Elspeth buy anything she wanted, and kept putting more and more money into making his family's house a second manor. Obviously he couldn't go on like this, and soon he was embezzling funds from his clients, and then embezzling even more from newer clients to pay back old ones. Then his cousin Sylvia came to Treleggan."

"And Sylvia, my dear cousin," said Priscilla, "was accustomed to getting any man she wanted, and she wanted Charles."

"That would seem to be the case, wouldn't it?" said the inspector. "Because she was a cousin and in love with him, she trusted him, and he used her to pay his debts. He spurned her love, but succeeded in getting her to give him more and more money. In fact, she just about depleted her savings for him. He still needed more, so he persuaded her to let him use her necklace as collateral for a loan. Actually he didn't borrow money, but sold the necklace outright at a tremendous loss, he was that desperate. Sylvia thought he could always get it back; that's why she didn't report it missing. But selling the necklace was to no avail, he still needed more money."

Mort said, "And it was around this time that he became involved with cocaine smuggling."

"Exactly," said Penhaligon. "Charles's father-in-law had just died with Charles as executor of his estate, but there was little cash, so this didn't help solve Charles's financial problems. One of his clients from London was a drug dealer and—you know how crooks can sense a fellow crook—he soon determined that Charles was desperate for money. He suggested that the manor might be used as a temporary storage site for a large shipment of cocaine. Charles agreed and he sacked all the manor staff except Glubb, the caretaker, who, being convinced of ghosts, would never have gone into the cellar by himself. The cocaine was brought in by sea and transported via the tunnel to be stored in one of the cellar rooms, where it was repackaged into small bags for reshipment to divers places."

"Don't tell me," said Priscilla, some of her self-assurance coming back. "All of a sudden Sylvia says, 'Guess what, love, I arranged with a television company to lease the manor for a very attractive amount, only they have to take it over immediately. Isn't that wonderful'?"

"Sylvia thought she was doing Charles a favour," said Penhaligon, "but actually she put him in a horrible position. So he had to think fast. He asked Sylvia to let him use her upper flat, but confidentially, she mustn't tell anyone. He told her he needed a place where he could get away occasionally to do his work. If he used his office at night, his wife would find out and bother him there. He needed a private place that no one, not even Elspeth, would know about. Sylvia presumably agreed because she felt that if she could have Charles in the same house she would have greater opportunity to press her love for him."

"So Charles was then able to go to the manor," said Mort, "under the pretext that he was moving out some antique furniture before the television company arrived. Of course, he also moved out the cocaine shipment and transferred it to the upstairs flat. Now I'd suppose that this was the time when he finally succumbed to Sylvia's charms and reluctantly became her lover."

"Exactly," said Penhaligon. "He didn't want to take the slightest chance that Sylvia might see the rather large drug shipment, which he had placed in all the cupboards and wardrobes. So if Sylvia attempted, for example, to spend an evening in his flat, he would instead agree to spend it in her's, anything to keep her away from the upstairs. Thus for a time he became her paramour. He tried to get the London client to remove the drugs immediately, but the gang wasn't ready and told him to jolly well keep himself under control or he might get hurt. So Charles very nervously awaited word from them. In the meantime he found himself at Sylvia's mercy. Also Elspeth was beginning to suspect something, which of course added to his problems."

"Poor Charles," said Priscilla. "You can almost sympathize with him."

"What I don't understand, though," said Mort, "is why he was so reluctant to become Sylvia's lover. She was attractive and he didn't seem to have many scruples."

"You wouldn't," said Priscilla.

"Psychological problems, according to him," said Penhaligon. "He really did have an aversion to what he thought of as incest and couldn't forget that Sylvia was his second cousin. Though physically able to make love to Sylvia when she virtually forced him into it, he found it distasteful.

"When the time came for the gang to take delivery of their goods, they picked the week and asked Charles to select the best night. It seems Sylvia was staying at the downstairs flat at this time, but it was obvious to Charles that she was sleeping alternately with him and Magnus. So he took a chance and broke off sexual relations with Sylvia abruptly, gambling that when she finally understood he really meant it, she would spend more time with Magnus. Learning that Sylvia was going to a party at the manor and would probably stay all night, he told his London contact this would have to be the time and accordingly three cars converged on The Deaconry after dark, Sylvia having already left."

"That was the night," said Priscilla, "that Sylvia had a fight with Magnus."

"Right," said the inspector. "Sylvia, who was night-blind, insisted that Magnus drive her back to The Deaconry, leaving her car behind. You can imagine how Charles felt the next morning, having thought that the downstairs flat was empty all night, only to see Sylvia come out. They had loaded the drugs during the night, but she saw the men as they left in the early morning and got a good look at their faces. And of course Charles had no idea how much of their conversation or activity she might have heard. The three cars took off, leaving Charles to face Sylvia. She asked about his friends, and he said they were business acquaintances. He felt she was suspicious, but didn't know the precise nature of his business. As long as she didn't know that drugs were involved, he was all right, for he knew she had a hatred for drugs."

Priscilla said, "I know. At school her fiance died of an overdose, leaving her pregnant. Sylvia had experimented before then, but swore off and became very anti-drug."

"Well, Charles knew this, too," said Penhaligon. "He felt that although Sylvia might have suspected that his business associates were not quite legitimate, she knew nothing further, and so he was safe. Mind you, Charles had no idea of her own past activities on the other side of the law. But then he learned that one of the three drug cars had an accident outside Truro. The driver, who was the sole occupant, was killed, and the police found the drugs he was carrying. That was in the newspapers, together with a photograph of the driver, who had served a prison term. When Charles saw the newspaper, he almost panicked. Sylvia had not seen it, but Charles knew there was a possibility she might in the future. And she would certainly recognise the photograph of the driver."

"That," said Mort, "was when he decided he had to kill her."

Penhaligon said, "He made the first two attempts in London, hoping at first not to provoke an investigation at Treleggan. But Charles was a solicitor, not a professional killer, and he bungled both London attempts, as well as the third attempt with the rock slide. The fourth attempt, as we know, was successful. From his office window he saw Sylvia going out by herself. By the way, he said he had also spied on you two with binoculars from his window when you were hiking on the cliffs. But getting back to Sylvia, she was alone then, and Charles didn't know that Tony would join her briefly later. Charles told his secretary he was going out on business, but actually drove to the retirement estate, parked his car, and reached Pendorth from the opposite direction. He intercepted Sylvia, knocked her out, and threw her over the cliff. Afterwards he drove to Falmouth, attended his business dinner, and returned to pick up Elspeth at the church."

"And he almost got away with it," said Priscilla. "Apparently Sylvia thought it had been Tony trying to kill her."

"I would guess," said Penhaligon, "that Sylvia was too sophisticated to believe any well-educated person could be as ingenuous as Tony. She tried to get a detective agency to investigate him and, as a precautionary measure, started advising Magnus when she knew Tony would be with her."

"Charles fooled Sylvia," said Mort, "but he was certain to be caught sooner or later. He had too many details to cover up."

Penhaligon nodded in agreement and said, "Sylvia had a copy of that newspaper, even though she didn't read it. Giles found it in your flat and it cost him his life. That same day he had found a small bag of cocaine that was left in the upper flat. He probably thought some earlier tenant had misplaced it. Now Giles knew that Charles had secretly occupied the flat just before him, for Sylvia had told him, but he didn't associate Charles with the cocaine. It was only when he came across the newspaper in your bathroom that he was able to figure it out. He suspected foul play with Sylvia when we, the police, came to your flat earlier during the day that you arrived. Also, Sylvia had confided in two people about all three earlier attempts on her life, and the reason no one came forward to mention her suspicions was that one of the two was her murderer and the other, as he told Charles, was Giles, who was abducted that same night.

"When Giles first found the cocaine, not having much money, he greedily thought of selling it to some of the television people—he could have obtained a good amount for it. But after seeing the newspaper he realized that the drug connexion was very recent, so recent that the only other upstairs tenant at The Deaconry who could have been involved was Charles. Thus he went to the pub that night thinking he would have no trouble getting blackmail money out of Charles.

"When Charles went to the gents' at the pub, Giles followed and told him he knew about his involvement in drugs and suspected he had killed Sylvia. Charles agreed to meet Giles in the car park when the pub closed. Charles told Elspeth that he had to talk to someone about business and she should drive home alone, he would find a ride later. Actually he had to walk home from the manor via the cliffs. Giles, who was expelled from the pub along with Dinny, walked back to The

Deaconry, but didn't go inside. He got his car and went to the car park to await Charles. Charles asked him to drive him home so they could talk as they rode. On the way as Giles talked, Charles decided that rather than pay blackmail money he would kill him. He got him to stop the car, overpowered him, trussed him up, and put him in the boot, later transferring him via the tunnel to a locked room in the manor cellar. It was dangerous to keep Giles there, but by this time Charles was desperate. He left Giles's car at the manor partially hidden between two vans."

"But," said Priscilla, "Giles was home later that night because I heard him."

"No, Miss Booth. You're jumping the story, but I can tell you that it was Charles who went to the upstairs flat. Giles had told him that he had a bag of cocaine as evidence there. Charles had to recover that bag of cocaine, and he did. Then he deliberately made noises to make you think that Giles slept in his flat that night."

"But Giles wasn't killed until two nights later," she said.

"Right," said Penhaligon. "This is where Mort contributed so heavily to the solution. Once he sussed that Giles had been standing on the stool when he was hanged, he correctly deduced that the timing in the case was all-important."

Mort said, "We thought we heard Giles in the apartment early Tuesday morning. We thought he was alone at a Truro pub on Wednesday night. But the last time he had really been known to be free was when the fisherman, Dinny, saw him Monday night heading toward The Deaconry. What if he had been captured by the killer immediately after? What if his odd actions in the Truro pub had been an attempt to get help at a time when his abductor was standing beside him? What if he had been forced to stand on that stool in the cellar with his arms and legs tied, his mouth gagged, and a rope around his neck? What if the killer had tried to make the timing look different? Just examining questions like these makes you think of possible answers."

Penhaligon said, "With these questions in mind, we could start looking for someone who had an alibi for the time of Giles's death, but no alibi at other critical times. Someone who might not have had an alibi for the time when Giles disappeared Monday night. Perhaps someone who was married. When Mort posed these questions to me, I went over my interviews with every suspect and remembered that Elspeth Fitzpen seemed nervous when accounting for her movements that night. On being questioned now, she tells us that was because she knew Charles was out on some mysterious errand late that night and the next morning."

"Then at first you suspected Elspeth?" said Priscilla.

"No," said Mort. "Elspeth had an alibi when Sylvia was killed, but Charles didn't. Our list of practical suspects was confined to those who had no alibi either for the time of Sylvia's death or for our reconstructed timing on Giles's death. By the process of elimination we came to Charles. Then everything else began to fit in."

Penhaligon nodded his head in agreement and said to Priscilla, "After Charles abducted Giles, the next day he gave a lot of thought as to how he was going to get rid of him without jeopardizing himself, and he finally hit upon a scheme which, as you said, Mort, was both vicious and ingenious. He fed Giles once on Tuesday, and on Wednesday he left for a business trip to Bristol, checked into a motel there, and conducted his token business. He rented another car so it would not be recognized and drove back to Treleggan, parked at the secret tunnel entrance, got Giles and let him get cleaned, and went to Truro with him. By this time Giles was both hungry and scared for his life. By promising him that he would not kill him, Charles was able to make him do anything. They went to a pub in Truro, entering about the same time, but acting as if they were strangers to one another. Giles, as we know, tried, but failed, to get help from the barmaid. Charles ordered him to leave with his food, tied him up again, took him back to the cellar, and then let him eat."

Priscilla said, "But why did Charles take Giles to the pub in the first place?"

"Charles had apparently read too many crime novels," said the inspector, "where the police determine time of death down to the minute via analysis of stomach contents. Of course, pathologists know that such analysis by itself is virtually meaningless for a variety of reasons, including individual differences of metabolism, the effects of stress, the physical condition of the body, et cetera. He also wanted Giles to be identified as being free Wenesday night. So he thought he could take him to a pub both to get food and to let people identify him later, as the barmaid and pub owner in fact did.

"Unlike some murderers, Charles wanted the moment of death to be determined as accurately as possible; that's why he left the door open. If you hadn't discovered the body, Sergeant Booth, some of the television people would have as they came down for costumes. He especially wanted to draw attention away from Giles's actual disappearance Monday night, a time when Charles had no alibi. He was lucky at first because for other reasons we placed Giles's death within a range of two hours, and it happened to be enough to give Charles his alibi. His scheme was to have Giles die an indefinite number of hours after he had driven back to Bristol."

"And this is where the stool came in," Priscilla said.

"Having fed Giles," said Penhaligon, "he tied and gagged him again, took him into another room in the cellar where there was a sufficiently strong pipe overhead, and put a rope around his neck, throwing the other end over the pipe. Then he put Giles on the stool and stretched the rope so taut that Giles had to stand on his tiptoes on the very edge of the stool in order to prevent himself from being hanged then and there. Charles could get Giles to co-operate in return for the hope of being saved. He told Giles he would be back in a short while, and if Giles could balance himself on his toes that long, he would rescue him. Who knows what Giles thought? It must have been horrible torture both physically balancing himself on tiptoe on the edge of the stool for several hours in severe discomfort, as well as mentally knowing that if he couldn't endure, he would hang himself. Even if he tried to get a better balance on the stool, he would only have succeeded in kicking it away."

Mort said, "Can you imagine the agony? Of course Charles sped back to Bristol, returned the rental car, and went to his motel."

Penhaligon said, "Charles had a perfect alibi, even though his attempt to place the time of death was based on a false premise. He couldn't possibly have been at Penstead when Giles actually died sometime between midnight and two o'clock. In the early morning Charles drove to the manor from Bristol in his own car to see if Giles was dead. Of course he was, since he couldn't possibly have held out all those hours. Charles picked up the turned-over stool and left it standing upright in the outside corridor so it would not be connected with Giles's hanging. Then he went home to Elspeth."

"And it was Charles, of course," said Priscilla, "who tried to kill me when I went to the cellar to look for the newspaper."

"He was vacuuming the room where the drugs had been stored to have an extra margin of safety. The kitchen floor was above him, and he heard the reverberations of your walking when you were going to the door of the stairs. When he saw you in the corridor with a newspaper, he instantly knew what it was, the same paper that had worried him so much in connexion with Sylvia and the one which Giles had later told him he had seen. Obviously he had neglected to search Giles's pockets. So you found the newspaper, and Charles almost succeeded in making you his third victim."

"And he actually admitted all this?" said Priscilla.

"Yes," said Penhaligon, "he knew the evidence against him would be strong, including testimony his own wife could give that he was gone for hours the night that Giles disappeared, coming home with mud all over his shoes. When we go over Charles's finances we'll find a sufficient number of transactions that cannot be explained away other than through his obtaining money from Sylvia and his involvement with the drug ring. Of course, we'll also be checking with car rental agencies in Bristol. And for good measure, we have a Mrs. Chynoweth, the wife of the grocer, who is quite an authority on who's living where, and she can testify that Charles had occupied, at least part-time, the upstairs flat immediately before Giles. But more important now is the fact that he's told us all he knows about the drug ring, including the identity of his client who heads it. I have no doubt that Charles will plead guilty—he needs protection from the drug dealers."

*   *   *   *   *   *

"Feeling better now, darling?" asked Mort when they reached the flat. It had been a long day and he was looking forward to having a drink and relaxing with her.

"If you really want to know, Mort," she said, "I feel like hell."

CHAPTER *TWENTY-TWO*

The blood-red Ford Sierra, cruising at a respectable sixty miles an hour, changed from the A390 to the A38 at the Liskeard by-pass and headed toward Plymouth and ultimately Oxford. Mort, driving by himself, smiled grimly as he noted the light traffic on his side of the road compared to the inbound lane, which resembled an enormous freight train, automobiles crawling along bumper to bumper. It was the tourist season, and the population of Cornwall would increase by a tenfold factor.

The first movement of Tschaikowsky's *Sixth Symphony* was playing on the radio. Better than nothing, it was not something he would have chosen at this time. It was the last movement especially that he anticipated with dread, knowing how it plunged from previous heights of glory to the most utter God-forsaken despair. Echoing his own mood.

They'd had it out that Wednesday night. Priscilla had said, "It's not a matter of taking any extreme feminist position, Mort, can't you see? Though I'll have to say that you and Penhaligon certainly seemed to have a deep-seated instinct that certain things are better handled by men working alone. But more than that it's a matter of decency and trust. Were we working together or were we not? Put yourself on Fogge Island, where I was the police officer in charge—how would you have liked it if I had not given you the slightest inkling as to what was going on? And especially if my withholding information had put your life in jeopardy?"

Of course, she was right. He just hadn't been thinking. As the music jumped abruptly from lilting charm to foreshadowing of abject despair, he thought again of how the gods had treated him Cassandra-like, only in his case he had been given such tremendous analytical power, but balanced by a density that was sometimes catastrophic.

Her last words Wednesday had been, "Well, that's that. I won't bring it up again. It's behind us."

Thursday morning she rose early and had the coffee ready before he awoke. Over breakfast they made light talk. He asked her how her genealogical pursuit of a royal line was coming.

She admitted to being discouraged. "I had such high hopes when I connected into a Prowse line, for I recalled seeing some place that the Prowses could be traced back to medieval nobility. But then I remembered your book and your constant warning on how dangerous it is to rely on sameness of name alone. So I decided to give it up."

"But," he said, "Prowse is a surname that has a far better than average chance of being documented back to medieval times, even to Charlemagne. I know a man within driving distance who's an expert on the Prowses; would you like me to arrange a visit for you?"

She said yes, and he telephoned. The man was free that day and would be more than happy to talk to Priscilla. Mort decided not to go with her, and so they were separated during the day. Priscilla returned at night delighted with the encouragement she had received.

"It's documented," she said, "that some of the Devon Prowses did go to Cornwall, and we can get so close from both ends—only about two generations apart—and I can look for records in Truro first, though I might have to go to Exeter later."

They went to *The Case Is Altered* on Friday, Winifred having asked Priscilla over for a talk. The two women conferred in the upstairs office, and both were smiling as they came down.

"She was concerned about the promissory note," Priscilla told Mort. "I told her not to worry, I would never press for the money."

"Has the good Dr. Cawthorne relinquished his claim?"

"As a matter of fact he has." She gave him one of her sweet smiles. "Winifred said he told her to deal with me on the note, that as far as he was concerned it would be like trying to get blood out of a stone for him to claim it. And Winifred says that she can certainly survive and keep the pub if she doesn't have to worry about repayment at this time. I'm so glad, Mort, for *The Case* is really an institution, and it wouldn't be the same without her."

"I'm glad, too. You did the right thing."

They sat in the dining room and Winifred insisted that everything was on the house. Winifred brought the beers and Gwen carried the food to them, with Tony just a step behind her. The three of them stood smiling as Mort and Priscilla thanked them.

"I can't get over Charles Fitzpen being a murderer," said Winifred, "even killing his own cousin."

"And reviving all those old ghost stories," said Tony. "So he was the one who scared the wits out of Esme Polgony?"

Mort said, "First he encouraged rumours of the ghost at the manor to discourage anyone from wandering around; he even gave himself a bruise on his leg to convince his wife that he had had some ghostly encounter in the cellar. Then when he had to move his drug shipment from the manor to The Deaconry, he decided to revive the story of the White Lady in Haunted Lane by pushing Esme into the mud."

Gwen smiled and said, "Charles always was a strange one. I could tell you some odd things he used to do in bed." She seemed to be collecting her thoughts, and then opened her mouth to speak again.

"We really don't want to hear about things like that," said Tony, a touch of pleading in his voice.

Gwen started pouting, but she looked up at her husband, put her arm in his, and nodded agreement. They walked back to the bar area, leaving Winifred still standing at the table.

"I understand Elspeth is going to Athens to spend some time with her brother there," said Winifred.

"It will be awfully good for her," said Priscilla.

"Athens is just the kind of change she needs," said Mort.

"I suppose you two have to stay at The Deaconry another two weeks or so before you own it outright."

"I do," said Priscilla, "but Mort's leaving tomorrow for Oxford. He's terribly behind schedule on his book."

"Oh, that's too bad. You'll be by yourself then."

"Yes, but I don't mind. I have a lot of work to do on my genealogy and I want to re-read some Anthony Trollope novels and listen to music and just do some quiet thinking before I leave."

"But you're keeping the house, so you'll be back?" said Winifred.

"Oh, yes, I'm keeping the house, I like it. Tony has offered to look after it for me and handle renting out both flats to tourists."

Winifred nodded. "He'll be conscientious about it. The shop gives him a lot of contacts, so he should be able to keep it fully occupied in season."

They finished their beers and Winifred without asking took the mugs for refills, returned in a minute, and then went back to the bar.

In a short while Tony came back and began talking to them. "Oh, ah, speaking of strange ones," he said, "do you know what Elspeth told me?"

They shook their heads.

"She said she suspected that Charles might have killed Sylvia, and she discovered the blood spot by the blackberry bushes when she was out making her own investigation. She, er, told me that as much as she loved him, she couldn't take the idea that their future lives might be disrupted by his arrest for murder. If it was going to happen, she wanted to get it over now, while she was still attractive enough to get another husband. I don't think I'd like to be married to her again."

"I'd have to agree," said Mort.

As Tony strolled away, Mort turned to Priscilla and said, "I'll miss you."

"I'll miss you, too," she said. They remained silent a while.

Priscilla drank some of her beer and wiped her lips while Mort finished the last of his sandwich. She said, "You mentioned that Joanna phoned from London yesterday."

"She's looking for a new job and asked me to write her a reference."

"Oh, I do hope you will, Mort."

"Of course. She's very capable. Apparently she won't get any decent words from Magnus Mandeville and to make up for it she's trying to get all the other references she can. She ran into Robin Steele in London—he's accepted the lead in a new stage production, and he also agreed to write her a good recommendation."

"She deserves a break."

"She'll do all right," said Mort with a laugh. "She has 'survivor' written all over her."

"Yes, and Magnus, too, I'm afraid will survive. You know, the film is finished and they've all left the manor now. Magnus is already talking about doing a third series, but not at Penstead."

"I'm not as sure about his survivability as you are. Penhaligon tells me that the Inland Revenue people are interested in his tax payments, or lack of sufficient tax payments. Mr. Magnus Mandeville may have a surprise coming in the next few weeks or months."

"Good, I hope they draw and quarter him."

"That's extreme."

"He deserves it. And Cawthorne, too, though maybe he's been punished enough if you're right that he's lost a knighthood."

Mort smiled and said, "Dr. Cawthorne has probably reconciled himself by now to the fact that he will never be 'Sir Frank.'"

"But Geoffrey Penhaligon will get his promotion to chief inspector?"

"I asked him if the chief constable mentioned it, and he refused to say; he just smiled. Certainly solving an important double murder case won't do him any harm. I think he'll get it."

"I hope he does," said Priscilla.

"He said he'd keep in touch, so I suppose we'll know when it happens."

Now driving on the A38, Mort turned over in his mind all the things which could have been said, but weren't. We live in a world, he thought, full of lost opportunities.

The symphony on the radio entered the third movement and he wondered about Priscilla's chances of being promoted to lieutenant. She was well qualified and he hoped it would go her way. How he wished she were beside him now!

Had he lost her? There were things that happened in life that didn't have to happen, but once they did, life could never be exactly as it was before. The first betrayal, the first awakening of mistrust, could these things ever be forgiven?

You always kill the one you love, said Oscar Wilde. How much did Mort really love her? In his forty-eight years he had never met another like her, their mutual interests, their being in tune with each other, the tremendous importance of little things, such as an acknowledgement conveyed by a gentle squeeze of the hand, a knowing glance, the meaning behind a simple word, all these and infinitely more, as if there were such things as chemistry, magic, and predestination after all. Would it be so bad to be Mr. Lieutenant Booth in Bay City?

As they parted that morning Priscilla had said, "I have to be back in the States no later than the end of the month. You'll be busy with your book, Mort, but perhaps you can come to see me off at Heathrow."

"I'd like that."

"We can talk," she said. "And I want to do some thinking before then."

"We should talk," said Mort.

The music was now in the tragic fourth movement. Who knew what dark thoughts must have gone on in Tschaikowsky's mind as he composed it? Thoughts almost as dismal as those now going on in Mort's mind as he recalled that moment with Priscilla when the truth in her words had brought him to understand the enormity of what he had done. He felt relieved when the symphony ended and was followed by a lighter piece, Beethoven's *Für Elise*. For Priscilla, he mused.

Perhaps he'd telephone her as soon as he reached home. Yes, that was it, he would. He'd telephone and be honest, tell her he knew he'd been wrong, apologize, offer to try to make amends, see if they couldn't start again. Yes, that's what he'd do.

He crossed the River Tamar on the modern bridge and looked admiringly at the one on his right—Brunell's magnificent Victorian railroad structure—Cornwall now behind him, Devon in front. Four hours later he was back at his dwellings in Oxford.

*   *   *   *   *   *

There were a number of messages for him on his telephone answering machine. He made notes as he listened to them in sequence. He was impatient to make that call to Treleggan he had promised himself, yet somehow feared that she might be cold to him. But the last message was from Priscilla—he hadn't expected that. The blood drained from his head as he heard her voice.

"Mort, I know it's crazy, but can you come back right away? I need you, darling, I don't want to be separated from you."

"I'm on my way!" he shouted to the empty room, then paused long enough to try to telephone back and say he'd received her message. But she wasn't in, so he rang Winifred at the pub.

"It's important," he said.

"What's the message?" asked Winifred.

"The message is, 'YES!'"

END

Glossary

Anyroad: A British expression similar to "Anyhow" in American English.

Bangers: English sausages, unlike any other because they contain about12% ground rusk along with the meat and have unique seasonings.

Bloody: Considered a swear word because it was associated with oaths such as "By God's blood!" The adjective "bleeding" is used in the same sense, but is deemed stronger.

Bodleian Library: The main library at Oxford University.

Boot: The trunk of a car.

Cheesed: Fed up, angry.

CID: Criminal Investigation Division.

Cock-up: Foul-up.

Cooker: Kitchen stove.

Crisps: Potato chips. (Chips in England are French Fried potatoes.)

Devon and Cornwall CID: See both Police and CID.

Dodgy: Tricky, unsavory.

Enow: Enough.

Ghetto-blaster: A loud-volume portable radio; boombox.

Girton and Trinity: Oxford and Cambridge Universities are composed of many semi-autonomous colleges. Girton and Trinity are two of the colleges at Cambridge.

Green: A village grassy spot like a small park.

Grip, Gaffer, and Best Boy: Television jobs. The grip maneuvers the camera; the gaffer is the senior electrician, and the best boy is the assistant electrician.

Grotty: Grotesque.

Kernow: The Cornish word for Cornwall.

Knickers: Panties.

Lager louts: Drunken, often violent, yobbos.

Loo: Toilet

Lot: One, or people, as in expressions such as "He's a bad lot," or "You lot get out of here."

Metropolitan Police: See Police.

O Tempora! O mores: Latin for O Times! O Morals.

P.: Pence. There are 100 pence in the new pound.

Police: The British police system is both national and local, with the country divided into constabularies headed by a chief constable and often coterminous with a county. Some constabularies are larger than a county, such as Devon and Cornwall, consisting of two counties. These constabularies are ordinarily autonomous and answer to the county executives. However, they are ultimately under the control of the Home Office (a government department) in London, which may use its power to direct one or more constabularies at times as part of a national police force. The Metropolitan Police (the Met) is the police force for the London area and is headed by a commissioner. Scotland Yard is one of its components. The local constabularies have CID components for criminal investigation, and they may ask for help from Scotland Yard if they wish. On other occasions, the Home Office may assign Scotland Yard to take over the case of a local constabulary even against the wishes of the local chief constable. Obviously, politics are also involved between the local government and the central government in the relations between the Met and the constabularies.

Salamander: The electric coil in the grill section of a cooker.

Scarper: Escape.

Scouse: A native of, or the dialect of, Liverpool.

Scene-of-Crime Officers (Socos): Police personnel specialized in discovering evidence where a crime has taken place.

Sod: Short for sodomist. Used in Britain as a term of abuse. See Wanker.

Spotted dick: A pudding with raisins.

Superannuated: Retired.

Suss: To suspect, investigate, or discover.

Tabula rasa: Latin for clean slate.

Toff: An upper-class person.

Torch: Flashlight.

Verge: The edge, rim, or border.

Wanker: Masturbator: Also used as a term of abuse. See Sod.

Wellingtons, or wellies: Rubber boots coming up to the calf.

Yobbos: From "boy" spelled backwards. Rowdy youths. See Lager Louts.

About the Author

Gene Stratton, a much-traveled former CIA case officer, is a well-known genealogist who has had three books published: *Plymouth Colony, Applied Genealogy,* and *Killing Cousins. Killing Cousins,* a murder mystery, was the first of the Mort and Priscilla series, and he plans a number of others.